rebound

Also by Noelle August

Boomerang

<small>COMING SOON</small>

Bounce

rebound

A Boomerang Novel

Noelle August

WILLIAM MORROW

An Imprint of HarperCollins*Publishers*

REBOUND. Copyright © 2015 by Wildcard Storymakers, LLC. All rights reserved. Printed in the United States of America. No part of this book may be used or reproduced in any manner whatsoever without written permission except in the case of brief quotations embodied in critical articles and reviews. For information address HarperCollins Publishers, 195 Broadway, New York, NY 10007.

HarperCollins books may be purchased for educational, business, or sales promotional use. For information please e-mail the Special Markets Department at SPsales@harper collins.com.

FIRST EDITION

Designed by Diahann Sturge

Library of Congress Cataloging-in-Publication Data has been applied for.

ISBN 978-0-06-233108-3

15 16 17 18 19   OV/RRD   10 9 8 7 6 5 4 3 2 1

*To Veronica—for her patience, boundless talent, laughs over sushi,
and the world's greatest eggplant dip. Ever.*
—LO

To S.N.C., my Danish sister.
—VR

rebound

Chapter 1

Alison

Some nights call for a Catwoman costume.

And this is *definitely* one of those nights.

Reason number one: It's Halloween. I haven't lost my mind completely, contrary to what my parents seem to believe after my spectacular last-semester wipeout.

Reason number two: I'm on my way to a party hosted by the new girlfriend of my ex-boyfriend. I'm pretty sure that calls for an armor of sleek leather. And a whip.

I stretch out, stiff as a ski, across the backseat of my Porsche Cayenne, while Philippe—my best friend and unofficial stylist—steers the vehicle in much the same way he does everything: with the grace of a polar bear on rollerblades. It's amazing, because he's compact and lithe, and his sense of style is ridiculous. And yet, in twenty-two years, he doesn't seem to have established a firm connection between his brain and his appendages.

He lurches to a stop at a green light, and I almost tumble from the seat. Behind us, a car blasts its horn, and Philippe rockets away again, throwing me back into the plush upholstery.

"Sorry," he mutters, and his shoulders lift into a shrug.

If I could sit up in this costume—or even *breathe,* I'd never have let him behind the wheel. But a girl's got to do what a girl's got to do. Tonight, that means having Philippe sew me into a skintight leather costume, complete with a glossy mask, pert ears, and a faux mink tail, so that he can deliver me to a party where I'll get to face the living reminders of my worst mistake.

All in the name of business, I tell myself, trying to euthanize the butterflies in my stomach. Tonight's agenda: Get in, get out, and make sure nobody gets hurt, including me.

That means nothing stronger than club soda. A lesson I've learned through hard, and humiliating, experience. I just need to say some polite hellos and stay long enough to size up my soon-to-be coworkers and, most especially, Adam Blackwood, CEO of Boomerang and the person my dad plans to make the recipient of an obscene amount of money.

Philippe maneuvers the car up the winding canyon road. Wispy clouds drift overhead, framed by a hazy night sky tinged gray by the faint glow of city lights below.

"How's it going back there, Miss Daisy?" he asks.

"So funny. If you hadn't made this so tight, I could sit up there with you. I'm going to need you to cut me out of this thing."

"Well, I sewed you in," he says. "I can cut you back out again." Philippe purses his lips and glances in the rearview mirror. "And do you or do you not look amazing?"

I take a deep breath and run my hands along the costume's bodice, which is elegantly boned and cut to perfection. He's created an absolute miracle in giving me curves in this thing and in making it sexy but not trashy.

Struggling to a half sitting position, I say, "I do."

Tonight, he's helped me feel delicious and daring—as far from society girl Alison Quick as it's possible to be while in my own skin. And that, I realize, is exactly what I need to face the night ahead.

"And are you or are you not heading into a lion's den filled with ex-lovers and people you may someday have to fire?"

I laugh. "I love your imagination, but I think you need to have more than one of something to refer to it as a plural."

He tosses me a meaningful look and almost runs my car into a sage bush.

"Watch out," I say. But he's right. One ex-boyfriend. And one big mistake. I guess that makes it plural.

The GPS directs us up a steep side street, and we climb up toward a sprawling modern home that looks carved into the hillside. The backyard must have an incredible view of the city.

"I really can come in with you," Philippe says for the third time.

"But you don't have a costume," I tease.

It's tempting to bring him along as a buffer, but he's too safe. If he comes in with me, we'll be glued to each other all night, and I need to mingle with these people. Even though I'm anything but natural at this part of the game. Especially sober.

"That doesn't matter. I can just say I'm dressed as a hot-ass fashion maverick."

I laugh. "True. But I promise I'm okay. And you're just a phone call away if I need you."

As we approach the house, I see that the long driveway is crammed with cars, which means I'm facing a steep walk in high heels. Of course, these are sleek Gucci knee boots, totally worth the discomfort. Besides, I always commit, and you can't be Catwoman in sensible shoes.

Philippe stops the car, and I remind him to put it in park before getting out to help me.

He does, leaving the engine idling, then slips around to the back to give me a hand as I wriggle my way out of the car like a mackerel flopping across the deck of my dad's boat.

Finally, I manage to plant my stiletto heels on the ground. "Wow," I say. "I've never felt so graceful."

"The leather will loosen up," Philippe promises. He scans me with eyes the reddish brown of cinnamon and, biting his lower lip in concentration, makes a few adjustments, including reaching right into my bodice to manhandle my breasts.

"I beg your pardon." I glance around for other partygoers but, mercifully, we're alone. Michael Jackson's "Thriller" drifts down to us, along with murmured conversation and laughter. I feel another tingle of nerves and anticipation.

"Please," he rolls his eyes. "They're merely accessories to me."

I slap at his hands. "I object to the use of *mere* in reference to my breasts." Especially since it's true. And especially since I'm going to face Ethan's new girlfriend, Mia, who's built like a curvier Scarlett Johansson.

He runs his fingers around the mask, tugging it down just a bit. His Issey Miyake cologne wafts over me, as familiar to me as the scent of the ocean or the stables where I keep my horses—all scents I love.

"You look amazing, Ali. I promise, I wouldn't let you walk in there otherwise."

"I know." I lean down to give him a kiss on the cheek. With these stilettos I'm probably 6'2", which puts me a good six inches over Philippe. "You're the best. And I'll be fine." Now that I'm here, a part of me looks forward to the night. Not to seeing Ethan but to getting a feel for the others and making my first report to my dad later. He always says I have infallible instincts where people are concerned, though I'm not sure I've proved that to myself yet.

"I have total faith," Philippe says. "Now go have some fun."

"This is work," I remind him.

He rolls his eyes. "Fine. But 'go have work' doesn't have much of a ring to it. Besides, you're also allowed to have fun."

"I know, I know." I face up the hill and square my shoulders. "Fun it is."

Chapter 2

Adam

I take the hill up the Gallianos' street with a little heat, hugging the turn into their steep driveway and skidding to a stop in front of their house. It's eleven, and judging by the thumping music and the people milling outside who look over as my tires let out a squeal, the Halloween party has hit its stride.

A flustered parking valet jogs up to the Mini Cooper in front of me. I know that car. It belongs to my head of Human Resources, Rhett Orland. Shifting into neutral to let the engine cool, I smile as my employees pile out one by one.

Paolo emerges from the passenger side wearing a fitted tuxedo and shining wing tips. Stepping onto the driveway, he slips on a top hat and gives the cane in his hand a twirl. He makes a perfect Latino Fred Astaire.

Sadie slithers out of the backseat in a fire-red Lycra bodysuit and adjusts the gigantic blue wig on her head, the words *Thing One* in bubble letters across her chest. Pippa's next and she's *Thing Two,* naturally, since those two always do everything together. Standing side by side on the driveway, they make the absurd outfits look pretty good.

Finally, Rhett climbs from the driver's seat. For a second, I think he's naked until I see that he's wearing a loincloth.

Tarzan. Of course. Rhett is shredded and the costume lets him share that with the world. All those CrossFit hours finally paid off for the guy.

Rhett hands the valet his keys and reaches into the car for a bushel of bananas. Nice touch, I'll admit.

I lower my window as another valet jogs my way, bending his lanky body to my window.

"Is this really a Bugatti?" His eyes are wide as they sweep inside my car. "Holy shit. It is," he says, answering his own question. "Sorry. I've just never seen one of these in real life."

"Understandable. They're pretty rare."

"Look, sir," he says, even though he looks my age, early twenties. "I'm going to come right out and say this. I don't think I have the balls to parallel park this thing for you."

"No problem." I adjust my black mask and get out, leaving the keys in the ignition. "How about you keep it right here?" Slipping a hundred out of my wallet, I hand it to him.

I'm not worried about my car and, as much I'm always up for a night with friends and employees, being able to make a quick exit whenever I want is a good option to have.

"Sure, thanks!" The valet takes the bill. "Thank you!"

"Hey! Adam!" Sadie waves from the Gallianos' entryway. Her huge wig looks neon blue under the porch light. They're all there, waiting for me as I round my car and jog up the steps.

"How'd you know it was me?" I say, spreading my hands.

Pippa smiles and looks me over. "Dang, Zorro. Looking good. You should wear that to the office."

If I wasn't the president and CEO, I'd be tempted. Something about wearing the mask feels good.

"*No,*" Rhett says. He shifts the bananas to his other arm. "Please don't wear that to work, Adam."

As head of HR, he's the company's voice of reason.

"I'm with Pippa." Paolo lifts the cane, pointing at me. "We should run ads with you this way, Adam. Girls would flock. Or flock more. Now, let's party." He taps the cane on Sadie's ass. "Move your Who-ter, girl. Get it?"

"Actually, no. I don't."

"Never mind," Paolo says as we step inside. "Neither do I."

We head to the bar in the expansive living room and order drinks. I sip my Scotch and look for the hosts, my friends Joe and Pearl.

Their home is stylish, fittingly for a photographer's home, modern and sleek and packed with priceless artwork, but it looks different tonight. Less like Pearl and Joe Galliano's house, more like a Halloween rave.

People dance at the center of the room and on the patio outside. A DJ is set up on a small platform in the corner. Everywhere I look, it's a churning sea of colorful masks and costumes. Aliens. Storm-troopers. Flappers and angels. They're all here.

Cookie, my head of marketing, comes over and joins us. As a group of six now, we take over one side of the bar, and as the drinks flow, the laughs grow louder. Rhett had his upper body waxed to be Tarzan tonight and Sadie and Pippa want the details, strip by strip. Riveting stuff.

My employees are people-people, like me. Being socially comfortable is a necessary quality to be on my team. I sell personal connections—and that starts with the corporate culture. But they're also tight-knit. It's not unusual for them to congregate together before diving into the social fray, which they'll do effortlessly when they want to.

"It's so, *so* awesome," Sadie says, as the conversation shifts to Cookie's costume. "What is it again, exactly?"

Cookie scowls and sips her Midori sour. "None of your concern," she says, but her free hand does a nervous sweep over her silver gown. It has a high neckline, long sleeves, and a small train, sparkling with tiny encrusted crystals.

In a word, it's severe. In a few words, she looks like the Chrysler Building.

"She's the evil witch in that Disney movie," Paolo guesses. He crosses his foot at the ankle, striking a pose. "You know the one with the white hair?"

"Cruella de Ville?" Sadie says. "Maleficent?"

"Do either of those have spiky white hair?" Paolo shakes his head. "Geez. You don't know Thing One about Disney witches. Ha. See what I did there?"

"I know! Elsa from *Frozen*!" Sadie guesses. "That's why you did all the blue eye shadow, right, Cookie?"

When Sadie's locked into something, the girl's unstoppable.

"Cookie's not a Disney character, you guys," Pippa says. "She's the witch from the Narnia movie. Look at her shoulder pads. She's, like, the Ice Queen or whatever."

"The White Witch, you illiterate little shits," Cookie blurts, like she can't take it anymore. "But you're all wrong." She shakes her head. "Jesus. You're like human Novocain. I can actually feel my brain going numb."

"I have a question," Paolo says. "How do you *feel* numbness?"

"Should we do your annual reviews right now, children?" Cookie asks. "What do you think?"

That stops the conversation dead. Everyone takes the moment

to sip his or her drink, terrified but also fighting back laughs. Pippa, Sadie, and Paolo report directly to Cookie, but everyone's afraid of her. Even though she's just a big, soft Yeti monster. Cookie just has that kind of arctic charm. I trust her right down to her frosty heart, though.

Most people think success is built on brilliant ideas, but they're wrong. Success is built on brilliant ideas placed in the hands of great people, and I have a talent for finding those. My team can be a little eccentric, but they're dedicated and loyal, and excellent at their jobs—Cookie included.

Pippa and Sadie decide the DJ is hot and disappear to run that down. A half second later, Paolo decides the same thing and leaves as well.

I wait until Rhett's preoccupied with the bartender before I lean down to Cookie's ear. "You forgot it was a costume party, didn't you?" I ask.

Cookie looks at me, her lips pressed in a thin line. Then she nods. "Yes. But don't tell them."

I knew it. She's dressed as herself. I wink. "Your secret's safe with me."

She excuses herself, claiming she needs some fresh air, but I know she's just going to find ways to torment Paolo. I see that Rhett has donated his bananas to the bar. With him and the bartender in a deep discussion concerning daiquiri mixes, I study the room.

A petite girl in a skintight camo dress and combat boots catches my eye. Her smile sends me a clear message. She's cute but not my type. Closer, a girl dressed as Sailor Moon checks out a tall cowboy in a white Stetson. His back is turned to her, but he must sense her attention. He turns and touches his hat, giving her a cowboy salute, and her smile goes wider.

I take another sip, marveling at the connection that's happening right before my eyes. Amazing thing, attraction. Powerful. A lot of money to be made from it. Which I've done.

With Boomerang, I've captured the fun of playing the dating game in a sleek website and created a thriving online community. It's made me enough to afford the things I love. Good food and surfing vacations. A house on the sand in Malibu and a car that suits my affinity for raw speed. The best thing about Boomerang, though, is that it's a constant reminder that relationships with women should be kept strictly fun—and very temporary.

The DJ must have met Pippa and Sadie because the song "You Sexy Thing" starts playing, and the two of them come bouncing out to the dance floor.

"I love this song," Rhett says at my side, then he's singing. "I believe in miracles. Since you came along!"

He belts it out like he doesn't care. I join him for the chorus.

"Dang, Adam!" Rhett says, looking at me. "You can really sing!"

"Nah. You're just comparing me to yourself."

Rhett grins. "I'm too smart to do that. Hey, don't look now but that army girl's checking you out."

"Saw her. But I'm a lover, not a fighter."

Rhett laughs. "Right."

We both know that's not true. When I want something, like the upcoming investment deal with Quick Enterprises, I fight until I get it.

Through the patio doors, a nun, a stripper, and a handful of vampires step into the room. It feels like the beginning of a bad joke.

"Where's Raylene tonight?" I ask. Raylene and Rhett met a few months ago and they're going strong. They're a Boomerang success story—if you're of the mind that a serious, committed relationship is the end game.

Rhett shrugs. "She's meeting me here. Actually, I think I saw her outside as we were coming in. I'll go find her in a minute."

Something in his voice makes me focus on him. "Everything all right?"

It'd be a shame if it wasn't. I've never seen the guy so happy.

"Oh, yeah. We're good. We're great." He lifts his banana daiquiri to his lips and lowers it without taking a sip. "I was just wondering how things are going with you."

I know where he's heading with this, but I pretend not to. "Good. Big week coming up with Quick Enterprises at the office. We're ready. Before the year's over, that money's going to be mine. It'll be ours, Rhett."

"Yeah, no doubt. We'll get Quick on board. They'll be begging us to invest."

"Damn right."

"Right." Rhett scrapes a hand over his buzz cut. "But I was talking about you, not the company. You know, because we're coming up on the holidays and everything."

I take a sip of my whisky, buying myself a moment.

Like Cookie, Rhett's been with me since the beginning, four years ago, when I was a nineteen-year-old kid starting Boomerang out of a storage unit in Oxnard. He was twenty-eight, not my head of HR yet. Back then, he did whatever needed to get done. Creating Boomerang kept me sane after Chloe, but I was still struggling in those days. And Rhett sees everything; he always has. He learned more than he should have, which makes him the only person this side of the Mississippi who knows something about my past.

"All fine, Rhett." Then I tip my chin to the bodies grinding to the music. "Hey. Go have a good time, Tarzan. Your girl's probably waiting for you. Go trick or treat with her or something. If you get a choice, choose treat."

"Okay, Adam," he says, smiling. He knows I'm done with this conversation. "I will. But you have fun too, okay?"

When I smile back, my Zorro mask digs into my cheek. "Of course."

Rhett's eyes narrow like his lie detector just pinged, but he heads outside.

I watch him thread through the crowd toward the patio doors.

He's right. I should make an effort, but darkness is creeping in on me. I need a few minutes to let it fade.

You know, because we're coming up on the holidays and every-thing.

I shake my head.

Yeah. I know.

Across the room, I spot Mia and Ethan, my ex-interns. Mia's dressed as Marilyn Monroe, her rack spilling out of the white gown. Ethan's in a vintage Yankees uniform—Joe DiMaggio—and they're all over each other. Ethan can barely keep his hands off her, which is understandable. She looks incredible.

Seeing them together makes me happy for them. Then it makes me hungry for a woman's body.

Sex, like surfing, is always a good thing—and exactly what I need.

I slip my phone out of my pocket, scrolling to Julia's contact info. She uploaded her acting headshot as her photo, and she looks good. All shining red hair and red lips. She looks better than she does in real life, but she's a knockout either way.

She'd come over if I texted her; she always does. But something stops me. Maybe I'm getting a little bored. Or maybe it's her jealous streak—a recent complication. I'm not up for dealing with it tonight.

I like to keep things light. At fun-level. Sex level. As soon as a girl tries to claim a drawer at my place or asks for the security code on my phone, which Julia recently did, it's the beginning of the end. I'm not interested in anything deep or lasting or even . . . real.

Chloe ruined that for me. She destroyed the part of me that ever wants *real* again.

Damn, I need to get laid.

Looking around the room, I consider Army Girl again until I see that she's doing some Irish Riverdancing. While she's taking a shot.

Hilarious, but she's not for me.

I look toward the door and stop.

Stepping into the living room with a whip in one hand and a tail gathered in the other is the epitome of my every fantasy.

I don't know where to look first. There's just too much I want to focus on. Her long legs. Narrow waist. Perfect breasts. The way her hips roll as she weaves through the crowd. The girl's got everything. Everything about the way she looks is perfect.

Catwoman.

Chapter 3

Alison

I've skied double black diamond runs and been kicked in the chest by a horse, but walking up a steep hill in five-inch heels and skintight leather might take the prize for the most challenging physical experience of my life. Finally, though, I've made it and am swept in through the wide open door of the Gallianos' home.

Even though I'm masked and costumed head-to-toe, I feel strangely naked. Or, I realize, incomplete. It occurs to me that it's because my hands are empty. I've got my cell phone and a lipstick tucked into the sleek Catwoman utility belt hanging low across my hips, but I have no briefcase, no horse bridle or gym bag. And most of all, I have no hostess gift. I *never* show up without a gift. My mom taught me that.

I guess the prospect of this night had me more rattled than I let myself believe. But I can't do anything about it now unless I want to go back outside and dig into the lush pathway landscaping to present the Gallianos with their own wildflowers.

Instead, I follow a blonde in a long gown with miniature dragons perched on her shoulders into the chaos of the party. We move through a short entryway into a massive living room, with towering windows that meet a high ceiling crossed by sleek ebony beams. The furniture is luxe, a combination of midcentury and art deco, and the walls are decorated with photographs, some I recognize from art appreciation classes in college and a few I assume to be Pearl Bertram's: bold, impressionistic, and hugely riveting.

People fill the space, but I spot Ethan right away. Amazing after more than a year that I'm still so tuned into him, like I have some automatic sensor still calibrated to his frequency. He's wearing an old-fashioned baseball uniform and stands in a cluster with some other people—a muscular guy in a loincloth and two petite girls in what look like red pajamas. Well, sexy Lycra pajamas with cute blue fur cuffs at the ankles.

He's got his arm around a petite blonde, and it takes me a second to register that it's his new girlfriend, Mia, dressed as Marilyn Monroe to what I now realize is his Joe DiMaggio. Every bit of her fills out the classic white halter dress. She looks amazing in the platinum wig, too, though I can see she's having trouble containing her unruly dark hair, which she has to keep tucking back beneath the blond waves.

The music and conversation fade away as I watch them together. They're each talking to other people, but they're connected too, their bodies touching, his hand absently brushing the bare skin of her shoulder as he laughs at someone's joke.

I know I should go to them, say hello and meet the others, who may be coworkers at Boomerang. But something keeps me riveted to my spot. Suddenly, I feel shy and stuck outside what seems to be Ethan's contented little circle.

The way he stands, so aware of her, so grounded and firm, makes my throat tighten. The disastrous last few months of college rush back to me. Not only Ethan and the night I betrayed him but the crashing spiral that followed.

I breathe and push the memories away. Come on, Ali, I tell myself. This is a party. And you're Catwoman. She doesn't stand around, moping. She's sleek and powerful and gets the job done. At least that's what Philippe said when he sold me on the idea. And that's my plan for tonight.

I'm grateful for my mask. Standing here, I could be anyone. Behind all of this leather, I'm anonymous, though of course, the whip, the high heels, and the gleaming form-fitting leather keep me from being inconspicuous. That's all right. I don't mind being looked at, and I don't mind looking. What thrills me is the power to decide what I reveal of myself, and when.

A hulking gorilla sidles up to me and nudges me with a furry elbow.

"Drink?" he says from somewhere deep inside the costume and hands me a crystal glass filled with punch. It's about the size of a small fishbowl with bits of fruit floating on top like belly-up goldfish.

"Sorry," I tell him with a smile. "I don't take drinks from primates I don't know."

"Well, let me grab you one from the bar," says the gorilla. "You can watch the bartender pour."

"I'm really okay."

Across the room, Mia rises on tiptoes and pulls Ethan down for a long kiss. The people around them smile, look away politely, but they're locked in their own little world, together.

I swallow and turn my attention back to the gorilla, who's now attempting to pour the drink into his own mouth. It spills down the crevices of his rubber mask and onto the fur of his costume.

"Shit," he says. "I'm hopeless."

"Well, it's probably tough to drink with all that costume in the way."

"Tell me about it."

"How about a straw?" I suggest. Ever the problem solver.

"Awesome thinking!" he exclaims, absently scratching his chest, gorilla-style. "You sure I can't get you that drink? I mean, it's a party. Even superheroes need a night off every now and then."

Ethan laughs at something, the sound cutting through the party noise and pulling me to look again, to watch the two of them together while they laugh at one another's jokes. Touch one another.

Suddenly, a drink seems like a good idea after all.

I bid farewell to my friend the primate and head to the bar.

The bartender gives me a smile as I approach. "What will it be, Catwoman?" she asks. On the counter rests a giant silver punch bowl, festooned with cobwebs.

"What's the punch?"

"Something called Jungle Rum Blast," she says. "Try it." She dips in a ladle and gives me a heavy pour of the concoction.

I sniff. Fruity with the tang of bourbon in there, too. "What's in it?"

"It'll be quicker to tell you what's *not* in it," she replies with a grin. "Trust me; it's fantastic."

I take a sip and then a longer one. The punch tingles down my throat. It's perfect—a little tangy, a little fruity, and with a decent kick. Oh, why not? I have a designated driver. And nine lives.

Before I know it, I've downed the entire drink, which is probably two servings. The bartender hands me another, filling my cup almost to the rim, and I drift away, sipping the drink.

Warmth spreads over me, and the music and conversation envelop me in a pleasant web. I start to move through the crowd. The floor feels a bit spongy now. Or perhaps *I'm* spongy. It's tough to tell.

Once again, I decide that I really need to say hello to Ethan, to let him know I'm here and that I'm fine. We can be friends. We're friends now. It's good.

On the way over to him, I'm halted by the sight of a guy dressed all in black with a black mask like mine. Zorro, I realize. I can't see his face fully, but what I can see is chiseled and beautiful. Sharp lines, full lips curved in a half-smile.

I feel his eyes on me as I take in his powerful body in tight-fitting black trousers and a black peasant shirt laced over a broad chest. I don't know if it's the punch or the heat of his gaze, but I feel more alive, more myself, somehow. And God, I feel sexy. Philippe knew what he was doing when he talked me into this costume. But then, he always does.

I'll finish this drink, I decide, and then I'll go say hello to Zorro. No harm in mixing a little fun in with my work, is there?

I've only taken a few sips when a girl dressed as The Riddler pushes through the crowd gyrating in the middle of the room. She rushes up to me, the question marks covering her green dress swimming before my eyes. "My nemesis!" she cries.

People around us laugh. And then I'm laughing. The music throbs around us—"Blister in the Sun," one of my favorites.

I take another sip and look around the room. A guy dressed as Harry Potter grinds up against a nun. Sailor Moon, a cowboy, and a girl dressed as Eve dance in a tight little threesome, breaking apart and coming back together, occasionally making some creative—and R-rated—moves with the rubber snake Eve had coiled around her shoulder.

Vampires and ghosts and superheroes surround me. It's surreal and perfect. No one knows me, but now I feel a part of things anyway. The spirit of the room intoxicates me. It's filled with laughter and good will.

My mother's charity events never feel this way. Those are like being in a room full of scientists, lined up to scrutinize and mentally catalog your every move. This feels like a *party,* like the ones I used to go to with Ethan, the ones where I was scooped up and welcome because I was with him.

Before I know it, I've put down my drink, drawn up to full height and tapped The Riddler on her shoulder with the handle of my whip.

She turns to me, and I tell her we have a score to settle.

"Dance-off. Now!" I hear myself say. I'd forgotten how good this feels. This heavy, pleasant warmth. The unknotting of all that makes me Alison Quick, daughter and current disappointment. That girl's not here. It's only me and my mask, and here I can be anyone I want.

The Riddler laughs and does a dance step, swishing her green tulle skirt. "Oh, it's on!" she says. Grabbing the whip, she tugs me out into the middle of the room, where the crowd makes way for us.

I glance over and see Zorro still standing there, still watching.

My shoes and the constricting leather of the costume make it difficult for me to really move, but I give it my best. I circle The Riddler. She circles me. Others come to fill in the space between us, so that I find myself dancing with Little Bo Peep one minute, my friend the gorilla, the next. We're clapping and laughing, and the dancing is serious in the funniest way. Eventually, the leather does loosen up a bit more—and I can move. Really move.

Zorro pushes to the front of the crowd and watches me, a tempting half-smile on his face, He's so hot I'm surprised the floor hasn't melted beneath his feet.

I start to dance just for him, like everyone else has dropped off the face of the earth. It's been a long time since I felt this way, my whole being alive to another person. Usually, my body's about running or skiing or training my horses. Now it feels like its entire purpose is to just be there, in the middle of things, moving to the music while Zorro watches.

I give myself to the music and the movement of my body, but

over and over again, I'm drawn back to him. And every time, his eyes are on me. Every time, he greets me with that same devastating grin that cuts right to my core.

Finally, I can't take it anymore. I give in and dance his way, running my mink tail through my fingers. I smile at him, feeling light and relaxed and like no one in the world would dare deny me a thing.

"Dance with me," I say.

"Is that a question?" he asks, folding his arms across his chest. His biceps bulge beneath the flowing black fabric of his shirt, and his eyes, which seem to be a deep, penetrating gray, regard me in amusement.

"No," I reply, still swaying as the music flows through me to wrap around us both. "Come on."

He hesitates, and the moment stretches between us. What is he waiting for? Doesn't he understand how much I need to dance with him right now?

Coming up close to him, I feel the pull of his body, like gravity. I press in closer, then closer still. Smoothing a hand against the silken material of his shirt and the hard contours of his torso, I ask, "Pretty please?"

I step back, and his smile broadens. Finally, he reaches out a hand to me, and I take it.

"Okay, Catwoman," he says. "Let's dance."

Chapter 4

Adam

Catwoman and I head to the dance floor and start moving together.

It's packed around us, people jostling in the crowded space, the smell of alcohol and sweat hanging in the air. Pippa and Sadie dance nearby. Both of them have huge grins on their faces as they look from me to Catwoman, who rolls her body in front of me like she's made of liquid.

When she glances at me, I see flashes of blue—pale blue, like the sky through my bedroom window in the morning—but it's her body that has me locked in. I can't stop staring at her. The leather cat suit hugs her every curve, and she's gorgeous.

I look up, and find her eyes on mine.

"Hi, Zorro," she says. Her smile is disarmingly sweet. Surprising, considering the way she's moving.

Stepping closer, I link my hands behind her back. "Hello."

She hesitates for an instant.

"This okay?" I ask, but she's already wrapping her arms around my neck.

"Definitely," she says.

"Werewolves of London" isn't a slow song, or even a good song, but we make it work, swaying together. Smoothing my hands down her sides, I feel the shape of her. The roll and shift of her warm muscles beneath my palms is hypnotizing.

"This *song*," she says, raising her voice. People all around us are howling at the top of their lungs. She laughs—pink lips, straight white teeth. "It really sucks!"

"Criminal."

She points to her head. "My kitty ears are bleeding!"

I laugh because . . . Well, that was cute.

She's tall even without the four-inch heels on her boots. This close, it's tough not to stare right into her eyes, so I focus on guiding her hips with my hands until we're moving in perfect sync. She's slender but strong. Athletic.

Exactly what I like.

As we dance, her weight settles on my shoulders and she comes closer, her chest brushing against mine. Her costume has a deep V that shows plenty of cleavage. Flawless skin. I'm in trouble. This girl has me under her spell.

"Werewolves of London" fades into a Jay-Z song. With the howling over, the energy around us picks up, but I don't let go of Catwoman.

She stops dancing and we just stand together in the middle of the chaos of the dance floor. Her smile is gone and she's so still, it feels like she's not breathing. The smooth skin along her neck glistens with a sheen of sweat and her pulse there is jumping.

She has to know how much I want her. It's getting pretty damn obvious.

"So, I've been meaning to tell you," I say, running a hand down her spine to the soft piece of fabric tied near her tailbone. "I really like your tail."

Her smile comes back. "You do?"

I bring the black ribbon between us. "Yeah. A lot," I say, running it through my fingers. "It's the best tail I've seen all night. In months, actually."

It's the truth. I haven't seen her face without the mask, but she's still the hottest thing I've seen in a long time.

"Thanks." She leans back a little, squinting as she looks me up and down. "But what about you? I thought Zorro was supposed to have a sword."

I can't help it. I laugh. "You want to see my sword?"

Her eyes snap to mine. She doesn't say anything, but the answer is right there.

"Want to get out of here?" I ask, but her hand is already sliding into mine.

We weave through the dancing inside, then the party milling outside on the courtyard, to a flagstone path that heads away from the main house. The path splits, the left trail leading to a shadowed gazebo in a far corner of the yard. It's a decent option but a little too exposed, still in view of the courtyard. But I've been here before for dinner, so I know the property and I have a better idea.

"Where are we going?" she asks.

Her hand is cool in mine. Soft skin, firm grip. Out here, I can hear her voice better. It's feminine and refined. Delicate, like the tap of a knife on crystal.

"Somewhere private."

I reach the Gallianos' detached garage and try the door, mentally high-fiving myself when it opens. Inside it's dark, the only light coming from a few skylights and the red charging lights of power tools along the back counter.

When I close the door behind us, the noise level from the party fades, leaving only a distant pound of the base from the music. Garage smells fill my nose. Motor oil and car wax. Smells I love.

Catwoman lets go of my hand and faces me, her eyes glittering like diamonds. I wait for my vision to adjust a little more. Then I take her in from head to toe.

She's beautiful. Long and tight. Curvy in all the right places. She gets better every time I look at her.

"You want to tell me your name?" I ask, because it feels like I should.

Catwoman is quiet for a beat. She shakes her head. "No."

"Okay. Fine by me." It's more than fine, actually. It feels good not to have to explain who I am or what I do. And she's mysterious this way. Like something I've pulled right out of a dream. The masks also make this feel like it's only about right now, this moment. I get the sense she likes that too.

I step in and take her into my arms. My fingers want to dig into her hips as I bend to kiss her. She feels so good. I don't remember the last time a girl tested my control this way.

"Wait," she says. Her hands flatten on my chest and she leans away. "I just want to look at you for another second."

I nod. "Okay." I expect her to do what I just did a moment ago—when I studied her body like a present I can't wait to unwrap—but she looks into my eyes. *Deep* into them like she's staring at a stirred pond, waiting for something that's a little murky to come into focus.

Not what I expected—at all—but I make myself stay there and not look away. I need this night. I want her. So I don't move.

People say eyes are the windows to the soul. I think they're right, which is why I keep my windows locked and shuttered. Even though it's only a second with her blue eyes on mine, maybe two, panic starts to spread inside my chest, a slow, searing burn.

I'm about to look away when Catwoman rolls on her toes and brushes her lips against mine, gentle, feather-light.

My body unlocks. I pull her against me and take what I've wanted since the minute I saw her.

Her lips are soft, her tongue softer, and she tastes like berries and cinnamon. She tastes so sweet. I draw her hips against me. She makes a small sound of surprise and pleasure, feeling how she affects me. Then her fingers dig into my lower back as she pushes even closer. Raw lust sweeps over me. I need more of her—now.

I pick her up and get her against the car. I taste her jaw, just beneath her ear, her neck, then I move lower, running my tongue over the perfect swell of her breasts. I brush my thumb over the tight bud I feel through warm leather. "You feel incredible."

Her hand presses over mine, and she arches her back. "That feels so good, um . . . *Zorro*."

Then she lets out a small giggle, and I can't resist looking up. Her smile is gorgeous. I want to keep it there.

"Don Diego de la Vega, if you prefer." I grin as I pull the car door open and sweep a hand inside. "My lady."

She climbs into the Gallianos' Murano.

Inside, she scoots to the far end of the bench seat, making room for me, but I grab her around the waist and tug her to the middle.

"Come here." I kiss her as I get her legs to each side of me. Hooking my hands under her knees, I slide her close. As soon as we connect, she sucks in a breath, her fingers gripping hard into my shoulders. I hear myself let out a slow hiss as she molds to me.

"Yes," she breathes. Her hand slides down to my belt, and the last of my self-control goes up in flames.

I lift her back against the seat and capture her mouth with mine, kissing her hard, then force myself to draw back for a second.

"Hold on. We missed a key step here." I run my hands over her body again. "This needs to come off before I lose my mind." I don't feel a zipper or buttons, on her back, or her side, or her stomach. "Did this thing get *sewn* onto you?"

She laughs, and it's that same crystal-clear sound. "Actually, yes."

I peer at her. "You're serious?"

"Yes. Yours comes off, though," she says, tugging my Zorro peasant shirt off. My mask almost snags and comes off with it. I'm relieved it doesn't. We're both under a spell and our faces, our real selves, might break it.

I straighten my mask and study her costume, trying to figure out what I'm seeing in the darkness. I'm considering ripping the damn thing off her when I realize she's gone quiet and still.

Her gaze is focused on my tattoo, which is lit by a shaft of moonlight streaming in through the rear window like it's under a spotlight. I shift, searching for a patch of darkness, but she reaches up and stops me.

"This is beautiful," she says.

Shit.

Her fingers are light as they run down the length of my shoulder. Barely a touch, but I almost jerk away.

"It's nothing." It comes out sounding rough. Not like myself. But I want this girl. I don't want to get pulled into the past.

Catwoman blinks at me. "You don't like it?"

"I got it as a reminder. Of a mistake."

That line always shuts down any further questions. I lean down to kiss her, trying to get us back on track.

Catwoman's touch on my shoulder grows firmer, keeping me back. "Mistakes are everything."

"Look, can we—what?"

"Mistakes," she says. "It's how we learn. Did you learn from it? Because if you did, then you shouldn't hide it from anyone."

She must see something in my expression because she looks suddenly self-conscious.

"Sorry, I . . . I don't mean to take this in a weird, deep direction. I just think it's beautiful. And I think you should see it that way too, even if it reminds you of a mistake because that's just really . . . *real*. And, sometimes, real is good, you know?"

I sit back against the seat, my mind blown.

Who *is* this girl?

Chapter 5

Alison

He pulls away from me, and I could kick myself for coming on too strong. I don't want to derail this moment. I want it to go on and on.

I lean down to brush my lips over the beautiful, strange markings on his chiseled arm. They're a little like the Escher painting of birds that become sky that become birds, but they're falling, cascading down his arm and, I imagine, spilling down his back. I breathe in the scent of his aftershave—leather and cloves—and run my hands over his beautiful, solid body.

Give this to yourself, says the voice in my head. *What can it hurt?*

I'm not sure whose voice it is. It doesn't sound like my own. Maybe it's Catwoman's? *My* voice would tell me to slide out of the car, run down the path—preferably without breaking any bones, and call Philippe to rescue me from myself before I do something impulsive, something I might regret.

This is supposed to be about business, about proving to my parents that I'm okay now. That I'm capable of doing what needs to be done. I shouldn't be here, in the back of this car, with this gorgeous stranger. Should definitely not wrap my legs around his and pull him hard against me. Shouldn't bring my lips down to his so I can feel his sweet warm breath again, draw his tongue into my mouth, feast on his taste, which is honey and whisky and salt.

But I'm all in, already. I'm voting yes to that voice that says *no one even knows you're here, Ali. No one knows you're you.* I'm way off-task from where I started this night, but right now I don't care about Ethan or Adam Blackwood or due diligence. I've never felt this way before. Not swept up like this, tuned into another person so that I wanted him down to his pulse. Not even Ethan.

We kiss and kiss, and I melt against him. We're slippery—leather against satin—and it's so maddening. I want to feel his skin, all of its roughness and sleek, muscled planes.

He breaks away, as if surprised by something. Like something's switched on inside him. He eases me back a bit to look at me, but it's like he's actually come closer.

"What do you know about mistakes?" Zorro asks.

I'm surprised he'd bring it up again, but I answer. "Too much," I say.

I know that the choice of one moment can turn your life inside out, robbing you of everything you thought you wanted. And I know what it's like to live day after day with the knowledge that you have no one to blame but yourself.

"I know they can eat away at you until it feels like they're all you have. Like you've forgotten everything else about yourself. But this—" I trace my fingers along the bold marks on his skin—"This also means you're human, and you've lived, and maybe you're more than whatever choice led you to put this on your body."

I don't know if he's listening to me or if *I* even believe what I'm saying. I've been reckless, and I'm doing it again, but this feels different to me. It feels like a gift I'm giving to myself, one that can't possibly hurt anyone else.

Lacing my fingers behind his neck, I pull him back down to me.

"Kiss me," I tell him. It's quiet, and I feel the party throbbing in the house nearby, but I want to be distracted from that, want to just feel his lips and his hands on me again before I take myself back off into the night.

But he hovers there instead, mouth inches from mine, breath tickling my skin. His mouth curves into a smile, and he says, "Tell me something first."

"What?"

"Anything." He licks his lips, and the mask makes him look hungry and dangerous. "Something else that's . . . true."

"Something true?"

"Yes. Something real . . . Anything."

"Okay." This feels so dangerous but tempting too. This whole night is out of time, a bubble removed from the rest of my life. It's exhilarating to feel hidden and unmasked at the same time. "But only if you do it too."

"Deal."

I consider for a moment and then I tell him, "I'm not crazy about people, but I love horses."

He chuckles, deep in his throat, and even though I've never been a funny girl, I feel hungry to get a big full laugh out of him, to see his head thrown back, his face relaxed in pleasure. "Why is that?"

"I guess you know where you are with horses. They're sly sometimes, but they're always honest. And when you find the right one, it's like this amazing, powerful extension of yourself. Something that trusts you and that you trust in the most perfect way."

He's not smiling now but looking at me in that way that moves beyond my words down to some core part of me. And then he frames my face in his hands and kisses me. It's deeper this time, more giving, his mouth perfect on my own, tongue everywhere, darting, tasting.

We shouldn't be able to move together like this, tucked in the back of this Murano, but it's seamless and so hot. He's hard against me, and my hands travel down to his lower back, moving against him, wishing Philippe hadn't done such a good job of sewing me into this thing so that I could have him, *really* have him.

Zorro's mouth moves down to my throat where he dips his tongue into the hollow there. I always feel so birdlike and angular, but his lips change everything, make me feel luscious and perfect.

I want more from him too, I realize. More from this night. It can't just be his body and his hooded, intense eyes. There's something there I need to get to, something behind the mask.

"Wait," I say, though it practically cuts me in two to stop him. I slide out from under him, not at all easy to do, and he sits up on the backseat, slouching against the side window.

"I'm sorry," he says, his expression concerned. "Was I—"

"No," I tell him. "You're perfect. This is—I can't even tell you how good it feels. It's just . . . It's your turn."

"My turn?"

"Yes."

I tug him upright and throw my legs over his, straddling him, my leather pants creaking, stretched to their limits. I move close to him, closer, and feel his need for me and know that the warmth of my body where we join tells him all he needs to know about how I feel.

I have to duck toward him so I don't skim my head on the ceiling of the car, and his eyes travel down to my breasts spilling out of the perfectly tailored cups of my bodice. Then his hands brace my back and he puts his mouth there again, tongue running along the stitched leather.

"Tell me something true," I gasp. If I get only one perfect night with a stranger, this is it. And if I'm going to give him some truth of my life, I want one back from him. "Tell me something no one else knows."

"All right," he says and settles back against the seat. He's thoughtful for a long moment. The party noises drift back to us, but they feel farther away now. It's just the two of us. Just this moment.

"All right," he repeats, as though gearing himself to some confession. "One true thing."

But just as he's about to speak, a grinding mechanical sound fills the space, and the garage door starts to rise.

Chapter 6

Adam

Instinct kicks me into action. I grab my shirt and throw open the car door. Taking Catwoman's hand, I hustle us out of the garage. She's laughing as we stumble back into the side yard.

"Why does it feel like we're in high school?" she says. "Like we almost just got caught by my parents?"

"We almost got caught by Pearl, which would have been worse."

"Pearl's the photographer? The hostess?"

I let go of her hand and pull my shirt on. "Yep. And knowing her, she'd have made us pose for pictures of us making out in her Murano."

"I haven't seen much of her stuff, but what I've seen is amazing."

"Exactly how I feel about you."

Catwoman stops. I see the flash of a surprised smile just before she lets out a yelp, tripping on the flagstones.

I lunge and catch her around the waist. Then I firm my arms and lift her.

"Whoa," she says. "What are you doing?"

"It's dark and I saw your heels. Let me get you to even ground."

"Okay." She hoists herself up farther, looping her long legs around my waist. I almost trip because, Jesus. I didn't expect her to wrap around me this way. "Onward, Zorro. I saw a gazebo on the way here."

Part of me is seriously tempted to lay her out right on this path. She's pretty much in the position I want her in, minus all the leather.

When I spot the gazebo, I kiss her. And because I'm walking, because I still sort of need to see where I'm going, our kisses are quick and soft, and that makes them feel playful.

I can tell she's smiling and that makes me smile, and by the time we're actually in the gazebo and I set her down, we're laughing as we kiss, which I can't remember doing with anyone for a long, long time.

We finally separate, grinning like idiots at each other. I wish I could stay here for longer than a second, but I can't look into her eyes without feeling like I'm under siege.

"You have pretty hands," I tell her, weaving my fingers through hers. Her fingers are slender and elegant, like the rest of her.

"You have nice shoulders," she says. "I noticed earlier. Nice everything, really."

"Thanks." Glancing up, I see that she's still smiling. "I like your everything too."

I know three things about this girl now. She likes horses, she has an amazing smile, and she sees mistakes as opportunities. Three things isn't much, but she doesn't feel like a stranger anymore.

"This feels like an adventure," I say. Guess I lost my filter in the Murano. But it's not like she'll get what I mean. It's not like *I* get what I mean.

Her hand comes to the back of my neck. "Exactly," she says, like she's totally with me. Then she kisses me, a light kiss that's gentle and soft and so . . . *sweet*. It hits me harder than anything she's done so far. "Let's keep it going," she whispers against my lips. Her arms come down, and she starts twisting one of the laces of my peasant shirt around her finger. "It's still your turn. Tell me something true."

"You got it," I say, like it's easy. Like I go around speaking from the heart every day.

I draw a breath and smell her perfume. It reminds me of winter. Of brilliant snowy days and nights by a fire. Her scent is both quiet and elegant, and so much better than the climbing roses that wind up the gazebo. Unbelievable. This girl makes roses seem pedestrian.

I couldn't decide what truth to tell her earlier. I didn't want to unintentionally reveal who I am. This girl knows nothing about me or what I've accomplished. We're connecting without any interference from my money or my image. I want to keep it that way. But then I remember what she said about horses and something clicks. I know what to tell her.

"I surf because it calms me. Because after I do, I know I'll get a good night's sleep."

She tilts her head. With her cat ears, the gesture is cute. Catlike. "Do you usually lack those things? Calm? Rest?"

Nice, Blackwood. Way to set yourself up. But there's no backing out now. "At times, yes. I do." I smile, realizing how it sounds. "There's this static sometimes . . . This noise in my thoughts, and I can't settle it down. Getting out on the waves does away with it, though. It just . . ."

"Cures it?" Catwoman offers.

I shake my head because I don't think there is a cure for what I've got. Four years have passed, and I'm still not cured. "Quiets it. For a while."

I can't believe what I've just said. I've never even admitted this to my brother, and Grey knows everything.

Catwoman's eyes narrow like she's picturing it. Being on a board. Watching a wave set up. Like she's trying to imagine how that could equal quiet and calm. I like the way she looks, like she's dreaming, but it's probably been three minutes since I've kissed her. Well past time to take care of that.

As I'm leaning in, she surprises me and ducks her head. Next thing I know, she's hugging me. Just hugging me, hard, and not letting go.

"Sorry," she says. "I don't know why, but . . . I just had to do that."

And . . . I'm sold. It's her impulsiveness. Her total and complete sweetness.

Something in my chest starts to creak open, getting its first taste of sunshine in years, and I don't fight it. I let it happen.

I am *in*.

Screw the masks. I need to know who this girl is. I need to see her again. So I tell her that. I tell her I want her number. I tell her I want to see her face. "Let's keep the adventure going after tonight. What do you say?"

"Okay," she says, smiling. "Yes," she adds, nodding. "I want that too."

She reaches behind her head. My heart's climbing its way out of my chest as she unfastens the mask. Then all I can do is look.

She's more beautiful than I expected, and I expected a lot.

Graceful features. Smooth fair skin. Wide blue eyes that are intelligent, like I'd already seen, but there's something more now. Taken with all of her, with her whole face, there's something gentle in them that verges on vulnerable.

I haven't given a thought to her age but now I realize I'm surprised. Maybe my subconscious was reading her as older, upper twenties. But she's young. My age, twenty-three. Maybe even younger.

"Catwoman got your tongue?" she asks, giving me a small, crooked smile. "It's okay if you change your mind. Really. If you want to call off the adventure, I can take it."

The speech center in my brain finally comes back on line. "You're kidding me, right? Because, *you. You* are—"

Whoa, Blackwood. Settle the hell down. "Look," I say, "you should never wear a mask again. I mean it. Do the world a favor." I tip my chin to the mask, which she's started twirling around her finger. "Burn that thing. Burn it dead."

She laughs, relaxing a little, like she was actually worried I wouldn't like how she looks, which I don't get. How could she not know she's beautiful?

"Okay, Zorro." Her weight settles onto a hip. I know I'll be thinking about the way she looks right now later. "Your turn. Show me what you got."

Jesus. This girl is killing me.

"Okay. Be kind."

She laughs. "I will."

I reach for the knot securing my mask, but stop. "Before I do this, how about one more," I say, and kiss her deep and hard, hold onto this just a moment longer before everything changes. Catwoman responds, and we catch fire again, tongues stroking, pressing closer, hands exploring.

"Mask," I say, drawing away. I'm ready now. I want it done. I slip the black fabric off, dropping it on the bench beside me.

Catwoman's smile disappears. Her gaze drops to my mouth. Then to my chest, my arms and hands, and back up to my face, like she's trying to put something together.

Does she recognize me?

Do I know *her*?

No way. If I'd met this girl before, I'd remember it.

"Adam? Excuse me, Adam?" I recognize Cookie's voice, behind me. "I hate to interrupt, but there's something I need to tell you. It's important."

"Sorry," I whisper in Catwoman's ear. "Give me a minute." I force myself to turn to face Cookie. I'll deal with her first. Then figure out Catwoman's reaction.

"What's going on, Cookie?" Anger seeps into my voice, but I can't stop it. This is a private moment. Whatever she wants to tell me, I'm sure it can wait.

"You know Alison Quick?" Cookie says. "The liaison who'll be doing due diligence for Quick Enterprises?"

My brain is skidding out trying to make this turn from Catwoman to the twenty million dollars I'm raising for my company. "Yeah, Alison Quick. Graham Quick's daughter," I say, finally.

Graham is the president and owner of Quick Enterprises, the company that's going to give me the funds to take Blackwood Entertainment to the next level. I've been funding small-scale film and television projects for more than a year on the periphery, but I want to bring that part of my business front and center. I have plans to start my own production company with my best friend, Brooks Wright. The wheels are in motion. It's happening.

I'd considered going public with Boomerang to raise the money I need, but Graham Quick is a much better option. I'm not ready to do an IPO yet and Graham has deep pockets. He's smart enough to know a moneymaking opportunity when he sees one. We both win if he puts his money in my hands.

"Yep, Alison Quick!" Cookie confirms in a weirdly loud voice. "That's the one! Well, guess what, Adam? She's *here*!"

"She is?" I frown, surprised I hadn't heard about this sooner. I've been dealing with Graham Quick and his lawyers for weeks now, but his daughter is a new development. I only just discovered she was running point on the due diligence this week. Cookie met her on a video conference call on Friday, which I couldn't make, so it'll be good to do the intros tonight. "Okay. I'll track her down when I get a chance."

Cookie gives me a smile that could penetrate a tank. "Honestly, I think that's a good idea, and a little overdue." She looks from me to Catwoman. "See you at the office, Ms. Quick?"

Time freezes. The earth stops rotating. Everything just *stops*.

"You can call me Alison, Cookie," says the clear voice just behind me. "See you Monday."

"Swell," Cookie says; then she swivels on her heel and leaves.

I count to five, then I face Catwoman.

Alison Quick.

The daughter of the man who can change my future.

"This is a surprise." It's all I have right now. All I can manage. I run my hand over my forehead, rubbing away the lingering pressure of the mask. I don't know how to process this moment. I can't tell if I want to laugh or punch something. I feel like I've just had a cold shower *and* been hit in the head with a two-by-four.

I know what my image is in the business world. Hotshot, young, brash. A playboy, because I date beautiful women and drive fast cars. Doesn't matter how well I run my business, that's what the old-school guys see. They judge me. Until they get to know me, they worry, like one day I'm going to pick up a drug habit, gamble away my millions and go bankrupt, leaving the business I love high and dry.

Bullshit. Just because I'm young and I like to have fun doesn't mean I'm a moron.

Graham Quick is no different. I have sources on the inside at Quick Enterprises. I know for a fact that Graham's nervous about my reputation. So, really, the *last* thing I should do on this earth is fool around with his daughter.

Catwoman—*Alison*—crosses her arms, her posture upright and tense, like the Oscar statue.

"Sorry about all this," I say, even though she's been into it just as much as me.

"It's okay." But she doesn't look like she thinks it's okay. She looks anxious and uptight, like she wants to make a run for it. "We didn't know, Adam. It was an honest mistake."

Mistake.

That word lands like a kick to the stomach. It reminds me of the moment we had in the Murano, what I said to her. *Jesus.* Did I just tell my potential investor that I have trouble sleeping at night? *Fuck.* I want to hit Delete on the last hour.

My company is my life. It's the only positive thing I've done. To keep it healthy and growing, I need an influx of money. I want a production studio. I want a full-length film in the pipeline by this time next year. For that, I need financial backing. I need Quick Enterprises.

I also want this girl—badly—but I need this money.

Wanted this girl. Past tense. Past tense, because this ends right now.

"Right. An honest mistake," I say, echoing her statement. "I'd never have done this if I'd known who you are."

"Exactly," she says, sweeping her thick blond braid over her shoulder. "Me neither."

"It's not like we did anything significant," I say, just making words. Stupid, idiotic words.

She nods. "Right."

I don't know what else to say. Looking forward to the business lunch we have scheduled on Monday?

This is the first moment that's felt awkward between us, I realize, and I can't have that. I can't jeopardize my plans. I have to straighten things out right now.

"Listen, Alison. I'll talk to Cookie. She won't say anything. Let's just forget tonight ever happened. We'll start with a clean slate on Monday. All right?"

"Sure. That sounds good. Great." Her blue eyes are steady, but her lips wobble when she smiles. "Already forgotten."

Chapter 7

Alison

On Monday, Philippe and I sit in the first-floor coffee shop of the office building where Boomerang is headquartered. I've stalled for fifteen minutes, and with each minute I've felt more agitated, less prepared. Strangely enough, I couldn't find any tips in *Modern Entrepreneur* magazine for handling a business meeting with someone you straddled in a Catwoman costume less than forty-eight hours ago.

Philippe stops me from sorting through a stack of papers I've already sorted a hundred times.

"Look, Ali," he says, removing them gently from my hands to put them back in my briefcase, which he snaps shut with sharp emphasis. "You made out with the wrong boy, but you—"

"I shouldn't have made out with *any* boy," I say. "That's the problem. I was there to *work*."

Philippe runs a hand through his blond-tipped auburn curls and sighs. "It was a party."

"But it wasn't supposed to be a party for me. It was my *job*. I went to meet the staff and get a feel for Adam Blackwood."

Philippe chuckles and shoots me a look. "Well, you did get that feel. And you, um, met his *staff*."

I put my face in my hands. "Don't remind me."

"Stop that. You'll smudge." He pulls my hands away from my face and captures them in his own. "So, you got a little tipsy and had an adventure. Big deal."

The word "adventure" makes me picture Adam, sitting in the gazebo. Something in the way he held himself and in the sound of his voice—hesitant, relieved—when he told me his one true thing. I felt the weight of every word, and I wanted to pull more from him, let him know that I would be careful with what he gave me.

But this is business. I have to redeem myself with my parents, prove I can be trusted again. Especially with alcohol and boys. Right now, I'm down on both counts.

"I just . . . I didn't want to screw up again," I tell him. "My dad's trusting me with something huge. And I haven't given him many reasons to trust me lately."

"That's not true. You're brilliant, Ali. And hard working."

"And I almost flunked out of college. In my senior year. Who does that?"

Only Philippe knew that I'd failed a whole semester's worth of classes, burned friendships, and made such a colossal mess of things that it had taken a sizable endowment to the college to allow me to walk at graduation and make up the classes during the summer. Instead of backpacking around Europe, I got to plod through online courses. I'm still waiting for my real diploma in the mail.

I look down at my hands. Already, my French manicure is

chipped, just a fraction, at the edges. I wanted everything to be perfect today, and nothing is.

"You're so hard on yourself."

"Apparently not hard enough."

Glancing over at the bank of elevators, I catch sight of a familiar figure and realize it's Mia, rushing across the marble floor to catch the elevator doors before they sweep shut.

Oh, God. Does she know about this? Adam promised he'd keep it to himself and said he trusted his employee—that terrifying woman, Cookie—to do the same. But how do I know they're not having a huge laugh over it right now?

No. I won't have that. I'm tired of having my bad choices define me. Worse, derail me. There's no reason I can't get in there and take charge of the situation. After all, I'm the one whose father has twenty million dollars to invest. Adam Blackwood needs me more than I need him. I just have to get in there and prove that. Not let the situation rattle me.

I take a deep breath and smooth my hair back from my brow, tidying the few escaped wisps back into my chignon.

"Flawless," says Philippe.

Far from it, but I just tell him I'm glad he's with me. Nancy and Simon, the accountant and lawyer on my team, have worked for my dad for years and still treat me like the little girl who used to do horseback riding tricks for them at my father's parties. It's nice to have a real ally.

"I'm sure Graham would have preferred to hire a nice intern for you. One who knows the first thing about business."

We get up from the table and head to the elevator. Inside, I give his waist a quick squeeze. "You know more than you think."

"Ditto."

I nod. Now, I just have to own it.

Inside the bright modern offices of Boomerang, Philippe asks where we can find Adam.

Just his name makes anxiety spark inside my chest. But I don't let it show. It will be fine, I tell myself. We agreed it was just a one-time thing, a mistake. We'll move on from here.

An impeccably dressed guy rises from his desk and introduces himself as Paolo. He's Philippe's height, with bronze skin, gorgeous warm brown eyes, and a pocket square in tan and blue stripes that matches his shirt and no doubt wins him extra points with my best friend.

"I'm Alison," I say and extend a hand.

"Ah, the big kahuna. Welcome." He shakes my hand and then Philippe's. "Let me take you to our fearless leader."

We follow him, and he introduces us to a few other employees— Pippa and Sadie, who I recognize as the pajama-clad girls from the party. Then a few others who barely glance up from their work to acknowledge us. They're not rude, just intent on their work, which I take as a good sign.

I turn from a quick handshake with one of the coding team, and find myself face-to-face with Adam.

Only he's not Adam from the party. He's professional Adam, in a tailored dove-gray suit that looks sewn onto his body, the way my costume was sewn onto mine. Though it should be impossible, his clothes make him look even more impressive—and sexier—than when he dressed as Zorro.

My face warms at the sight of him, and my body responds on its own, drawing me right back into that car. I see the tattoo of falling birds winding along his muscled arm, hear the sound of his laughter, and feel, once again, the urgency of his lips on mine. That's the Adam I wanted to find here, I realize. Even though I know we can't have that again.

"Welcome to Boomerang," he says, and his smile is all white

teeth. Easy charm. "It's good to . . ." He settles on "see you," since he can't pretend we're meeting for the first time. But he doesn't add, "Again."

"Thanks," I say and hold out a hand. Part of me expects some kind of supersonic boom when we touch. But it's just a handshake—firm and dry.

We make introductions all around. When an employee distracts Adam for a moment, Philippe cuts me a look and mouths, "Oh my God. So hot." I give him the evil eye, though of course I agree.

Adam turns back to us. "I'm sorry things are a bit cramped. We're in the middle of relocating the offices and had an opportunity to lease out the space downstairs. That's making it a bit cozy here."

The word cozy makes me think of ski lodges, of snuggling under a blanket. And then I'm there, right there in that fantasy. I'm kissing his neck, smoothing my hands over his body to distract him from paperwork. We're laughing, and his eyes are on mine, and it's Adam from the car—open and warm.

God, who am I?

"No problem," I say. "Are Simon Evans and Nancy Silvestri here yet?"

"I believe so," he says. "Cookie made the arrangements for your team." He looks at Paolo. "Want to lead the way?"

"Sure, boss."

Adam, Philippe, and I follow him down another short hall to a kitchen area, next to which sits a polished partners desk with sleek chairs rolled up to it and another much smaller desk, with a set of cheap folding chairs, now occupied by Nancy and Simon.

The espresso machine burbles noisily. Stacks of supplies lean against a long center island not three feet away. And we're right out in the open, where it will be impossible to speak confidentially. Or to avoid the foot traffic of two dozen employees microwaving burritos at lunch.

Nancy and Simon look at me expectantly, their displeasure clear. They're used to being treated a certain way. If I don't take care of this, they'll report back to my father. And I'll be subject to another discussion about whether or not I have what it takes to be part of Quick Enterprises. Whether or not I have what it takes to lead.

Everything I do here is a test, and I have to pass. No. I have to excel.

"I'm sorry," I tell Adam. "But this won't work for us. Do you have a place that's a little more private? With a lot more space?"

I hate to come across as spoiled or particular, but I have to command authority here. Have to make Nancy and Simon see that I'm not just some daddy's girl put in place as an indulgence.

Adam looks at me—not into my eyes exactly, though his gaze is still intense enough to wrap around me, riveting me to the spot. "I'm sure we can accommodate you," he says in a coolly pleasant tone. "Why don't you all come with me, and we'll talk to Cookie?"

Even her name makes me cringe.

Simon and Nancy rise and gather their things.

"How about the conference room?" Paolo suggests.

Adam shakes his head. "Too much going on this month. We're putting the final touches on the team-building retreat, and I told Brooks he could set up a temporary space for the film project."

We stand there, at a cordial impasse. Behind me, my troops—Nancy, Simon, and Philippe, shore up my position. Though I can't help noticing the starry-eyed gaze Nancy levels at Adam. Not that I can blame her.

The staccato of heels clicking down the hall interrupts us, and Cookie appears.

"What's going on here?" she asks in a needle-sharp tone.

She's in a white A-line dress, with broad Tiffany-blue piped lapels. She looks like she's still in costume, like a flight attendant from a class of futuristic airships.

I can't help cutting a look at Philippe, who I know is thinking what I'm thinking. Someone needs a makeover.

"Good to see you again, Cookie."

She raises an eyebrow and gives me a limp handshake. "Yes. And you're certainly . . . *different* from the last time we met." Her mouth twists into a smirk, letting me know she doesn't think much of me, and that smirk lights a fire in me.

I want to say, *Oh, I still have my whip with me,* but I decide it's better to leave that night out of the conversation.

"Ms. Quick and her team aren't comfortable in the space we've provided," Adam says. His ramrod posture tells me he's not thrilled, either. With her, or with me, I don't know.

"We just want to be comfortable and free of distraction," I tell her. She's tall, but with my heels, I'm taller. Up close I see that her skin is almost pore-less, like glass. She may not actually be real. "I'm sure you can appreciate that."

I think of my father's words, *"Alison, when you're in a pissing contest, you gotta pee right in the eye of the big dog. Don't waste time on the whelps."*

Adam breaks in, changing the energy—like puncturing the surface tension of water.

"My office."

"What?" Cookie says. "That's—"

Exciting, I think. Terrifying. To be so close. Though I'll have my staff there too.

"Perfect," Adam says. "There's plenty of room, and I'm running around so much, we won't be . . ." His eyes shift to me. "On top of each other."

"But Adam—"

"That's so generous," I say. "If we won't be a distraction."

"Not at all," he says, giving me a challenging look. "I'm sure we'll all work well together."

I don't know if my brain will be worth a damn with him so nearby, but I can't let anyone else know that. Especially not him.

"I think so too," I tell him, and then I meet Cookie's icy glare with a wide smile. "Problem solved."

Chapter 8

Adam

"What was *that* about, Cookie? You put her in the *kitchen*?"

"Yes! It was a good place for her." Cookie drops into the chair opposite my desk. She crosses her legs and rolls her eyes. "You saw how she came in here this morning, Adam. She acts like she owns the goddamn place! She needs to know she can't steamroll us just because she represents her daddy's money."

I picture Alison moments ago, standing before her team like an army general. Cookie's exaggerating, but it's true. She showed a cool side I hadn't seen at all on Saturday night. She was totally in control, confident and assertive about her needs.

The office *kitchen* for Quick's daughter? Christ. That could have been a disaster.

"Cookie, listen. We have to play ball with her—and her team. If they perceive this as a hostile workplace, do you think they're going to want to invest?"

"We shouldn't have to kiss her ass, Adam!"

"Yes, we should! Professionally speaking!"

Nice. Way to clarify that one, Blackwood.

Cookie jumps a little, surprised by my raised voice.

I didn't sleep well last night, despite a long surf session yesterday with Grey. Nightmares of Chloe kept waking me. Added to this Alison Quick complication, my nerves are shredded this morning.

"Sorry, Cookie," I say, but she doesn't look offended. She looks like she's trying to diagnose me with her gaze.

The door swings open, and my maintenance guys come in. I'm relieved by the distraction. Darryl pushes an office chair with a small printer sitting on the seat, Ralph carries a heavy box.

"Where to, boss?" Darryl asks.

"Right there," I say, nodding to the small conference table in my office.

Cookie and I fall into a tense silence as the guys move the table closer to the wall and get an impromptu workstation set up for Alison. She'll be here with me, and her assistant, accountant, and lawyer will get cubicles outside.

"You asked me not say anything, Adam, and I won't," Cookie says after Darryl and Ralph leave. "I won't tell anyone about your romantic tryst, but I do *not* like that girl."

"What are you worried about, Cookie? That I won't be able to stay away from her? That I'll screw up the deal because a pretty girl talked to me? Trust me. I've got plenty of other options. And you saw Alison just now. She's over what happened. It's no big deal."

Actually, it surprised me *how* over it Alison seemed. A little *too* over it. Like Saturday never happened.

"She's not trustworthy," Cookie says.

Her choice of words catches my attention. "What do you know about her?"

She opens her mouth to speak, then shakes her head. "Nothing."
That's a lie.

Interesting.

Cookie always tells me the truth. Always.

"I want what's best for the company," she says quickly. "And I just don't like her."

"You've made that clear, Cookie." I push out a long breath and check the time on my phone. I have lunch with Alison in five minutes, and then I'll be taking her by the location I've leased for Blackwood Films. First, though, I need to get Cookie to settle the hell down.

She wields power in my company. She's head of marketing, but more than that, no one questions her motives. She's like a surly guard dog: you might not love her, but you trust her. You *need* her. If she doesn't like Alison, people will notice and follow her lead. I can't have that. I can't have Cookie slinging arrows at the people holding the coin purse.

"Listen, Cookie. There's nothing between Alison and me. It was a random thing. We didn't know and we were just having a little fun. She's not going to be a problem—but *you've* got to find a way to get along with her for the next few weeks. We're trying to impress the Quicks. I need them to feel great about what we're getting into. Boomerang. The production company. Everything. You haven't exactly gotten us off on the right foot with Alison."

"No, you're right. Maybe I should have *kissed* her." She looks away from me, and stares at the view of West LA through the windows. "I'm sorry," she says, the words clipped, like they hurt her. "I just like what we do here. I like working for you. I don't want anything to change, Adam."

I've only seen this earnest side of her a handful of times in four years. It's the only time Cookie actually scares me, when she's soft like this. Vulnerable. It means she's really worried.

I want to keep talking to her. I want to find out what's got her so shaken up about the Quicks, and I want to assure her everything's going to be fine, but it's time for my lunch with Alison.

I stand, taking my jacket from the back of my chair. "We're only going to change for the better. I promise you that. This money is going to bring us some amazing opportunities. Stay with me on this, Cookie. Okay?"

Her eyes don't budge from the view as she says, "Okay."

I swing by the cubicles outside to pick up Alison, who I find perched on the edge of the desk, looking more like a movie version of an executive, with her long legs and her stylish clothes. She stops talking to the accountant and lawyer on her team when I walk up.

"Adam," she says, and if I didn't know better, I'd say she starts to blush.

"Hey," I say. "You're all set up in my office."

"*Our* office," she says, smiling, and I can't tell if she says it jokingly or not.

"You two okay if I steal Alison for lunch?" I ask Nancy and Simon.

Nancy giggles. "Oh, definitely! Steal away!" she squeals, but her smile drops when Simon glares at her.

My assistant, Jamie, made reservations at a restaurant in the mall across the street, so Alison and I head there on foot. Ali's already met briefly with Rhett on some HR matters, and as we walk, she tells me she's impressed with our benefits package, health insurance options, and our pledge to support the continuing education of our employees.

It's obvious she's studied up, and the girl is smart; her intelligence shines through when she speaks. Maybe she's Quick's daughter, but as far as I can tell she's not here just because of her DNA. It's a relief. I need this deal to go right. I couldn't have worked with someone incompetent. No matter how hot she is. Hot and off limits, I remind myself.

We reach Houston's, and the hostess takes us to a booth toward the back. Surrounded by dark cherry wood and black leather, and away from the windows up front, it almost feels like night back here. Which reminds me of being in the Murano with her. How her blue eyes had almost fluttered closed when I'd pulled her against me.

We're quiet for a little while after we place our orders. Me, because I'm replaying that moment over and over again. Alison, I imagine, because I'm acting like she's not right across the table from me. Because the version of her in my mind is impossible to ignore.

We both order the sea bass special and make a successful transition to business talk. I play the part of the interested company president, ready with an answer to her every question.

Last year's numbers? Stellar.

This year's projections? Even better. Our trade show in Vegas gave us a good spike in Boomerang memberships, and even with the investment we made in the new office space, it will be a banner year.

As the food arrives, I make a watertight case for Boomerang's continued success. I find that as I talk, I can't look at Alison directly for long periods. It's a shitty consequence of Saturday night.

The stupid hang-up I have—thanks, Chloe—of letting girls look into my eyes hasn't been a problem. Nothing's personal at work, so there's no danger there. Cookie's not exactly going to gaze deeply into my eyes during our weekly marketing meetings. And when it comes to the girls I date, some notice it and don't comment. Others comment on it, and I don't answer. I've gotten by.

But Alison is different. Tougher. I told her things I've never told any girl. When she's looking at me, I can't place what it is I see in her eyes. Interest? Gentleness? Compassion? Some combination of the three that makes me want to get up and leave. Luckily, a solution presents itself before I suffer too long.

Alison wears earrings. Diamonds in the shape of the letter "A." With her hair swept up, I can see them perfectly. If I focus on those, it doesn't feel as much like she's trying to pop my soul open with a crowbar.

When we're finished with our food, we both order coffees. Double espresso for me, cappuccino dusted with cinnamon for her.

This is going to work just fine, I tell myself. With the exception of the minutes I spent fantasizing about her when we sat down, and while we ate, and the fact that I can't look into her eyes for long, we're both being perfectly businesslike.

Which is good news. And also damn disappointing.

Where's the girl who straddled me in the back of a car two nights ago?

Suddenly I feel the need to goad her. I want to know if Cat-woman's in there, beneath the pale pink blouse and the professional attitude.

"I think you're going to enjoy the initiation dates," I say.

Alison pauses, the coffee hovering at her lips.

"It's something most of my team does to learn the business," I explain. "Creating a profile and trying the service is a great way to learn the service we provide our clients first hand. It's become a sort of rite of passage for new hires. You're obviously not in that category, and there's no obligation, but I thought they might be of benefit to the due diligence. And, who knows. You might end up meeting a good guy."

As she looks at me, I can practically see her thoughts rewinding back to Saturday night. If her costume hadn't stopped me, I would have taken her in the back of a car after knowing her for less than an hour. Not exactly a good guy.

Alison takes a sip and sets her cappuccino down. "Okay." Her eyes sweep over me, probing me for something, though I'm not sure what. "Well, I'm one step ahead of you. I know about the dates. In fact, I've already gone on one of them."

"Have you?" I'm relieved that I only sound mildly surprised. "How was it?"

"He was a nice guy, but . . . we weren't a good match."

There are half a dozen different emotions in her voice, and I can't put my finger on a single one. I'm intrigued. More than intrigued. I want information—and I know where I can get it. If she went on a date, then she's in our database.

"What about you, Adam?" Alison says. "Have you done the dates?"

Amazing. Four years of owning a business and this is the first time anyone's asked me that. "No. Actually, I haven't."

She waits for me to explain. I can't avoid it. It's my business and I am trying to convince her of its appeal. Explaining why I don't use it myself only seems fair.

"I don't have any trouble getting dates."

"Neither do I." Alison's gaze on me holds steady, a silent challenge.

"Are you saying I should do the three dates?" I ask.

"From what I've heard, they're not mandatory. But they seem like a good way to learn, first hand, the service you provide your clients."

I have to smile at that. "You raise a good point, Quick. All right. I started a profile years ago. I'll fill out the rest this week."

It's the last thing I want to do. Our profile can get pretty personal, and I don't want anyone nosing around into my past. Or my present. But I can handle adding a few superficial details about myself if it scores me points with the moneyman's daughter.

"How about we take care of it right now?" Alison reaches into her purse and produces her iPad. "I'll help."

"Sure," I say. "Great."

Shit.

Chapter 9

Alison

*L*adies first," Adam says. "Let's see your profile."

My throat tightens. I could kick myself for goading him to do this now, but I couldn't resist throwing his challenge back at him. More than that, I can't resist finding out his answers to the Boomerang questions. Even though I can't *have* him, I want to *know* him.

Still, if I let him poke around in my account, he'll come across Ethan. I can't have that conversation, not on my first day at Boomerang. And not after the night Adam and I shared.

"Hold on," I tell him, stalling. "Let me pull it up for you."

He holds out a hand, grinning. "I'm pretty sure I can navigate the site myself."

"I'm sure you can . . ." I pull up my account, scroll over to Matches, and with a quick swipe, delete all traces of Ethan. I feel a pang, like I'm deleting the actual person, even though I know that's silly. "Here you go."

Handing over the iPad, I feel unaccountably nervous and exposed. Right away, I want to snatch back the tablet and make sure I like the photos I used, that my answers to the hundred or so questions are good ones.

As he scans the page, his lips quirk into an amused curve. "Great Kierkegaard quote."

I groan. "That was Philippe's way of making me look deep."

Adam glances up, his keen gray eyes locking onto me for just a second and then darting away. "I think you're plenty deep," he says. "So you don't think there are two ways to be fooled?"

I read upside down: "There are two ways to be fooled. One is to believe what isn't true; the other is to refuse to believe what is true."

The quote started out as space filler, nothing more. But now it seems loaded with a meaning that eludes me.

Shrugging, I say, "I imagine there are more than two ways to be fooled, but it's a great quote."

He grins at the image of me astride Zenith, pounding through the Santa Barbara surf after one of our last competitions. Seeing my horse, the best I ever had, makes me want to rehabilitate another one, to try to re-create our almost magical connection. I love Persephone, my current rescue, but she won't let me ride her, and I miss that feeling of being so in sync with another living thing.

I try not to squirm as Adam takes in the rest of my profile, but finally I reach for the iPad. "As you can see, Mr. Blackwood, I've already fulfilled my professional obligations and filled in a profile. Let's do you."

He arches an eyebrow. "By all means," he says, grinning. "Let's do me."

I feel myself blush. "Well, at least you let me go first," I say, thrilling a little at the feeling of walking up to some line. Flirting.

It feels safe, because I know it can't go anywhere, and dangerous, because I so wish it could.

"I like to think I'm a gentleman." Again, his gaze falls on me, giving me a little jolt, and then it moves away to focus on the iPad. He swipes around a bit and then slides the tablet over to me.

His profile's up, but he hasn't added photographs. It's just his name, the default image of a blue boomerang to denote his gender, and a dozen generic details on the page.

"Well, you certainly didn't apply the famous Adam Blackwood determination to this profile," I tell him. "Why not?"

"Like I said, I don't have trouble getting dates."

"So I've read. But still, as president of the company and the creator of the Boomerang brand, I'm surprised that you haven't filled out a full profile. Not even a photograph."

He grins. "People know what I look like."

For some reason, he's avoiding the issue, like he's avoided filling in the profile. And like he's been avoiding a direct look into my eyes. Why?

Something tells me now's not the time to probe, so I launch into the Boomerang questions. The profile already tells me he was raised in Newport, Rhode Island, to entrepreneurial parents, that he loves to surf, and that he's got one brother, Grey.

I scan through the questions until I find a juicy one, and then I take the plunge. "How many sexual partners have you had?"

Again, he gives me that amazing half-smile, and his eyes light with amusement. "Today, you mean?"

"Funny. But I think it means lifetime record."

He shrugs. "Pass."

"Pass?"

"Yes, let's go to the next question."

"Because it's so many, or because you don't kiss and tell?"

He grins. "Yes."

He answers the questions about his favorite book—a tie between *Good to Great* and all the books in The Belgariad series. Then I learn that he loves The White Stripes, French cuisine, and, of course, surfing. The most exotic place he's traveled is Tangier, and his favorite time of year is winter.

"I would have thought summer for the surfing," I say.

"I like to ski, too."

I nod. These bits and pieces are interesting, but they're leaving me hungry for more.

"Speed round," I tell him, thinking maybe I can dazzle him into giving me something substantive.

"Fire away."

"Frugal or spendy?"

He smiles. "Neither."

"Lefty or right-handed." I can't believe I haven't noticed. But then he seemed to have very proficient use of both hands during our last encounter.

"Southpaw, all the way."

"Chocolate or vanilla."

"Mint."

I smile. "Me too." I scroll through the questions, looking for something with a bit more depth. Finally, I find something. " 'Heaven is for real,' or 'that's all, folks?' "

His expression clouds. "No clue."

"Come on; what do you think? You must have some opinion, even if it's a third option."

"Why don't we save the rest of this for another time," he says, in a brittle tone. "I want to take you by the new Blackwood Entertainment complex. I think you're going to be impressed."

I miss the Adam who talked about the noise in his head, the way that surfing brought him peace. I want to talk to that person again, the one I couldn't help putting my arms around. Not this one, with the canned responses that aren't responses at all.

I save Adam's profile, still mostly empty, turn off my iPad, and slide it into my purse. "Okay," I tell him. "Blackwood Entertainment. Let's go."

We enjoy a half hour of prickly silence as he drives us to an office compound a little north of downtown. Construction vehicles line the gravel drive, and a couple of men in hard hats sit on the gate of a pickup truck, eating sandwiches.

"Hey, big man," one of them calls.

Adam gets out of the car and comes around to my side to help me out of the low passenger seat. I take his hand, and there's that warmth, that tingle. Not fireworks, like the other night. But a spark, at least, which comforts me after the chill of our exchange at the restaurant.

He holds onto me, directing me around a swirling eddy of dust, cigarette butts, and fast-food wrappers. And even though we're awkward together now, I'd gladly step into a puddle of quicksand to keep his hand in mine just a bit longer. A completely unproductive thought, I know, but a girl's allowed the contents of her own mind, isn't she?

"This place could use a clean-up," he tells the men, and there's something perfect in the way he says it. Confident. Assured of results. But respectful too. I don't know any other twenty-three-year-old with that kind of ease and authority. Sure, I can fake it— sometimes—but it seems like he sprang from the womb with a briefcase and a business plan.

"We're on it," the man says.

"Appreciate it," Adam replies, and gives a brief nod in my direction. "I've got a VIP with me today. Need to impress."

Fishing a couple of hard hats out of the bed of the truck, Adam hands one to me and says, "Come on. I want to give you the tour."

Sunlight glints on the tempered glass window as we approach the building—which is vast and made of two cubelike buildings joined by a short open breezeway. In the foreground stretches a long courtyard, with benches and a small reflecting pool in the middle. Grass stirs in the breeze, and the scent of smoke blows in from the city.

"Is this all yours?" I ask, following him along a path to a set of glass double doors.

"We're on a five-year lease," Adam says. "But I'm hoping to buy outright at that point. I think we'll easily make use of this space. Wait until you see what we have planned."

He picks up his pace, and I have to dash along behind him. It's clear he's not being rude. He's excited, and that excitement is propelling him toward his imagined future. A future that my father and I can help make happen for him.

Reaching the door, he turns and waits for me to catch up. He doesn't look at me exactly, and I find myself wanting to take his face in my hands to look right into his gray eyes, which look light in the sunshine, like the color of water rushing over rocks.

I don't want there to be tension between us. We have to work together. It has to be okay. And I know it can be.

"Hold on a second," I say, as he pulls the door open. "Aren't you forgetting something?"

"Am I?" he asks, giving me a puzzled look.

"Um . . . yeah," I say. "You're supposed to carry me over the threshold. My father arranged it."

Adam throws back his head and laughs. And just like that, the tension drops away—or at least recedes. When he looks at me again, his eyes sparkle with appreciation, and I know this is another moment I'm going to miss someday.

"I'm sorry," he says, and his voice is warmer than it's been all day. "Total oversight on my part."

He hesitates a moment, body swaying just a fraction toward mine. For a moment my heart stops, thinking he might try to scoop me into his arms the way he did at the party. But then he steps aside and gestures for me to pass in front of him. "I'll do better next time," he says.

Inside, we find a frenzy of activity. Workers haul around buckets of paint, shuffle along on drywall stilts. The space is a mess. Half the walls look like they're in the process of coming down. Dust stirs in shafts of sunlight, and tarps cover mysterious lumps around the space. Still, the bones are there—bright and modern.

"Behold the seat of the empire," Adam says, grinning. He plants the hard hat on my head and gives me an appraising look. "Fetching," he proclaims.

I can't help myself. "Who says 'fetching'?"

He shrugs. "I don't know. My mom?" Putting on his own hat, he asks, "What do you prefer?"

"I don't know," I tease. "Maybe something more in a 'dazzling' or 'perfect.'"

"I'm going to stick with 'fetching,'" he says.

"Can you use that in a sentence?"

"Yes," he says, and a mischievous grin lights up his face. "Someday your father will be *fetching* my coffee."

Now it's my turn to laugh. "That's . . . not likely."

"It never is," he says. "Until it is. I've banked on that my whole life."

I believe him. And his confidence makes me want so much more of him. "Speaking of my father," I say, "he asked me to remind you about coming sailing this Sunday. He thinks it'll be a nice opportunity to socialize."

Adam gives me a shrewd look. "To socialize or talk shop? Your father doesn't strike me as the relaxed type."

"True. But he did say socialize."

"And you'll be there too?"

I nod.

"Are you bringing someone with you—a date?"

His question makes me feel pinned, tested somehow. Obviously, if I had someone in my life, I wouldn't have been all over him in the back of a car the other night. But, it feels pathetic to say the thought never crossed my mind. I decide to split the difference. "I don't know. I might. You're . . . free to bring someone too, if you want to."

But please don't want to, I think. Though I know it shouldn't matter.

He nods. "Okay, I'll be there. Or we will. I might bring . . . someone. Julia."

I keep my face neutral and tell him that will be fine, but I'm dying to know who she is, what she means to him, whether she's just a friend to serve as a social buffer or . . . something more.

He walks me through the space, and we enter the temporary construction office, little more than a couple of tables, a few chairs, and a mini-fridge plugged into the wall.

There, Adam rolls out a blueprint for me, and with his help I get a glimpse of what the space will become. "Here's the reception area," he says, pointing with a ballpoint pen. "Leather couches, plasma screen looping our reel, and a wall of built-in display shelves to house our awards. Clients eat that kind of thing for dinner."

"That's a lot of space for awards," I say, fighting away a host of noisy questions in my mind.

Again, he grins. "We'll need it."

He takes me through the rest of the plan, and it's an ambitious one. All the most modern technology. Full-service production and post-production studios. He points out where the edit bay will be. Client lounges. Dressing rooms for the talent. A giant back deck is planned for staff to blow off steam and as a space to host the kinds of extravagant parties that put you on the map in this town. Words like "cyc wall" and "extendable light grid" come up, and though I only half-understand what he's talking about, I just listen, swept up again by the excitement in his voice.

"And this is the coolest thing," he tells me. "Most of the interior walls of the studio building will be movable and made of this special liquid crystal glass to allow them to block out light in any section, as needed. It's going to be something."

"That's amazing."

But really, I think, *he's* amazing. He's so natural in this setting. So in his element. It reminds me of Ethan out on the soccer field, charging down the field like he'd break through concrete to get possession of the ball.

And then I remember Ethan standing in the doorway of our bedroom. See the shock and hurt on his face. He had flowers for me— white tulips with just a blush of pink at their edges. I found them later in our kitchen trash.

The memory sobers me, and I feel myself draw away. I'm listening, but on the outside of the bubble of warmth created by his enthusiasm. Maybe it's for the best that there's a Julia. Not that I needed another reason to keep a distance between us, but I'm grateful to have one. I can be cordial; we can do the work we need to do together. But that has to be it. That's my purpose here. My only purpose. Anything else would be a mistake, and I absolutely refuse to make another one of those.

Chapter 10

Adam

Saturday mornings surf sessions at County Line with Grey are the best part of my week. Usually, we surf the point break, but we're not up for sharing today and it seems like everyone and his brother, or half-brother in my case, is here. So we take the beach break, which can be mushy and gutless on weaker days.

Today is not a weak day.

The rides are incredible, steep and fast, but carrying lots of power. Just how I like them. I pull myself onto my board after surfing yet another spectacular wave and check my diver's watch. Almost eleven o'clock. Grey and I have been out here since eight. It's no wonder my arms feel like lead weights.

Eighty yards out, Grey is just standing up. I watch him carve the face of a wave like he weighs nothing. I do fine out here, but these are his kinds of waves, tailor-made for a fearless nineteen-year-old shredder on a shortboard.

Grey sees me and rides my way.

"Adam! Oh no, Adam!" he yells as he draws closer, waving his hands. "Look out! I can't stop! Look *out*!"

He charges right at me. A few non-locals nearby don't know what to think, especially an older man on a longboard. They've seen him surf and know he's awesome. The best guy on the water. But Grey has a way of making you believe things even when they're clearly not true.

With fewer than a dozen feet between us, he cuts back and rides over the break. I have to duck dive under the wave, so I only see the beginning of his backflip into the water.

We surf for different reasons, Grey and I.

I come to find peace. He comes to raise hell.

We surface close together, and he's laughing. "Did you see that old guy's face? He thought I was actually going to hit you! What a moron! Like I couldn't surf circles around that old geezer!"

"Yeah, the old guy. Moron."

Grey shakes his head. "Aw, c'mon, Adam. I wasn't trying to give him a heart attack."

"Yes, you were."

"But it's not like I could *actually* do it. And I can't believe you're ditching me tomorrow," Grey says, in his classic way of changing subjects with zero warning. The kid barely graduated high school, but his mind's always churning, going a hundred miles an hour in ten directions at a time. He's brilliant, but most people can't tell. They don't see past the swearing and partying, or the tattoos. That's how Grey likes it.

"Have to," I tell him. "It's a work thing."

"Whatever. Responsibility sucks." Grey rubs his eyes, bloodshot after three hours in saltwater. We have the same father, so we look the same in a lot of ways, but he's olive-skinned and darker than me, which makes the signature gray eyes common to all Blackwood men stand out more on him.

"We need to eat," he says. "I'm so hungry, I'm about to throw up."

"Ten more minutes." I'm starving too, but I'm not ready to give this up yet. The water's turning glassy and calm, so I stretch my arms out and hang them off the end of my board.

"I'll be at the car," Grey says and paddles into the next wave.

I watch him stand up and fly toward shore. Eye color isn't the only Blackwood trait we have in common. When our minds are made up, they're made up.

A wave of tiredness hits me, a mix of sleepiness and muscle-fatigue. This is the feeling I love. I know I'll sleep well tonight. Hopefully a full night without nightmares. Without waking up at the crack of dawn with the sound of Chloe's laughter in my ears.

I try not to think about the question Alison asked. About what happens after we die. I can't think about it. Can't let Chloe seep into more of my waking life.

Out of the blue, I remember telling Alison what this means to me. The surf. How she'd closed her eyes, imagining it. I wonder if she's ever tried it.

I've caught myself thinking about her too much this week. Or watching her as she worked at the conference table in my office. Or sitting right next to her during meetings, when there were other seats available. I've been observing her. Creating my own Alison Quick profile.

She dresses to kill. Designer stuff, but she puts some flair into things, managing to look classic and modern at the same time. The only constant in her wardrobe seems to be her diamond "A" studded earrings, which works great. When we talk, I always have some-where to look.

She hums to herself when she prepares her coffee—always with cinnamon dusted on top. She talks to her horse trainer every morning and smiles the entire time. She's good with names—she had everyone in the office down by the second day—but she isn't exactly friendly with them. Even with her own team, she's courteous and cordial. It surprises me. She admitted to me that she liked horses better than people at the Gallianos' party, but all week I've seen glimpses of the girl who was spontaneous and sweet that night. And fun and sexy as hell.

I get the feeling she's holding back. Catwoman is closer to the real Alison. But why does she hide that side of herself? I catch my train of thought and mentally punch myself. I've just spent ten minutes thinking about how much I wish she wasn't on my mind. Shit.

As I paddle in, I think of the boating trip tomorrow, spending the day on Graham Quick's boat to talk shop. That's going to be special. Me, Alison—and Julia, who I had to invite after I told Alison I'd bring her along. I don't know why I said it. Maybe the way Alison looked around the new complex, drinking it in, excited. I needed to put more distance between us. Julia had struck me as a solution.

I shake my head. Great idea, Blackwood. Throw a girl who has nothing to do with anything into an enclosed space, at sea, with the people you need to impress most. But I don't have much choice. I said I was bringing a date, so I'm doing it.

When I get to my Range Rover, I see that Grey has already loaded his board on the rack, but he's nowhere to be seen.

"Damn it." I lift my board up next to his, snapping it in.

When the shit hit the fan back home a few months ago and he came to live with me, I promised myself I wouldn't become his parent. I'm not starting now. I'm his brother, not his dad.

Grey's a result of a "timeout" my parents took the year I was four. Dad hooked up with Grey's mom, Lois, and nine months later Grey was born.

Dad never made any attempt to hide Grey when he and my mother got back together. For years, I had this vague awareness that I had a half-brother out there somewhere, but Grey didn't become real to me until Lois flaked out on raising him when he was five. When he showed up at our house in Newport with a Spiderman backpack, my life changed. I'd been an only child, and suddenly I had *a brother* and I loved that. Him. Right away. But it wasn't like that with my mom. She'd never planned on a son who wasn't hers, and Grey's never been easy.

Their relationship has been tense since the beginning, but something big happened between them in August that drove Grey out of the house. Mom hasn't told me what it was, and neither has he. One day, Grey just showed up at my door and told me he was done with "your mother." Done with all the Blackwoods, except me. I let him into my house. Gave him a home, and haven't pushed him on it. I'm the last person who should judge a guy for being secretive, but I do wonder what happened.

I climb into the Rover and start the engine. In less than twenty seconds, Grey comes crashing into the passenger seat, out of breath like he just hauled ass. He has a beer in his hand and he smells like weed.

"Jesus, Grey. I left you for ten goddamn minutes." So much for not being his parent.

"I got bored. Then I met some nice people."

"Get rid of that."

He jumps out of the car, finishes the beer and tosses it into a trash can. "Hey, did I tell you Julia texted me?" he says before he's back in the car.

"No. Why did she text *you*?"

"She's done with rich business owners. She wants to try out nineteen-year-olds with *huge*—"

"What did she say, Grey?"

"She didn't want to bother you at the office or something, but she can't go to your boat outing tomorrow. She's got a callback for some role she really wants."

Awesome. This is the only time Julia's ever backed out on me— when I need her. "Were you ever going to say something?"

Grey shrugs. "When I remembered to, and I just did. Anyway, what's the big deal? You're not even into her."

"I told Alison I was bringing a date, Grey."

"Who's Alison?"

I can't believe this. I stare at the waves in the distance. I can't show up dateless. I need a buffer between Alison and me.

"Adam." Grey shoves my shoulder. "Who's Alison?"

I put the car in reverse and back out of the parking lot. "Someone from work. From the people who're going to invest."

"Ah . . . Got it." Grey laughs. "She must be a really hot investor."

If he only knew.

Chapter 11

Alison

*M*y father and I pick our way across an expanse of parched scrub, following our ranch manager and groom, Joaquin, to a squat tin shed out in what feels like the middle of nowhere. Really, we're a half hour north of Santa Clarita, in a town with a population in the double digits—just a long stretch of dirt paths leading off the highway, and ramshackle farms resting in dusty valleys.

It feels good to be in jeans and boots. To have survived the first week on the job with Adam. It didn't take long to get used to having him nearby, to stop stealing glances at him, at the way his hair curled over the pressed collar of his shirt, at the way he pushed away from his desk whenever something required real consideration, like he needed space for his thoughts.

The work is easy, at least. His records are impeccable. As Nancy says, "You could eat off them." And everything looks good. He makes sound choices, building an enterprise slowly but being brave enough to leap at the right times.

Still, there's something there, a caginess. A need to control the script. Just like at the restaurant. A couple of times I caught him looking out the window, and his expression looked so far away and sad. But when he caught my eye, the mask snapped into place, and he gave me a practiced smile that seemed worse than his sadness.

The sky is a brilliant blue with feathery clouds hanging near the horizon. The white sun bleaches the ground and angles off the shack's roof to create a blinding corona. I reach for my sunglasses, trying to tamp down the prickles of anxiety and excitement building in me. I never know what we're going to find, how damaged a horse will be, whether it will be filled with promise or too far gone to save.

"What do we know?" my father asks. For a second, I think he's asking about Adam, but I've already done my debriefing.

"Not much," I reply. "Missy from Horse Rescue just said the owner's had an ad on Craigslist for a couple of weeks. Selling two horses, a thousand dollars each."

My father frowns. "Too cheap."

I nod. "Her guess is that the owner is old and that it might be a problem of neglect rather than abuse."

"Let's hope so," Joaquin says. He lifts his baseball cap to wipe perspiration from his brow. "I don't know if we can house another angry horse. Not with Persephone still needing so much work."

"That one's unreachable," my father grumbles.

"I just don't believe that," I say. It's true the little palomino quarter horse is a hard case—but she's young, little more than a yearling. Already, she has the bearing of a champion and thoughtful amber eyes that follow my movements around the paddock. I'll reach her. "She just needs time."

"Her time's costing *me* money," my father says. "If we can't get her to do what we want, she'll have to go."

"Wow, Dad, I'm glad you don't have that philosophy about your daughters," I tease, but he's already straightening up and plastering on the wide, disarming smile he uses on people he doesn't know.

I follow his gaze to a heavyset older man who leans against a rusted cistern a few yards away. He's got a gleaming sunburn-pink scalp under thinning silver hair and wears coveralls and heavy work boots. "You Quick?"

"Depends on who's chasing me." My father's standard line.

We introduce ourselves to the man—Mr. Hance, who gives me a dispassionate once-over and says, "Suede's not much of a riding horse. No energy these days."

"How old is he?" I ask.

"Five."

That surprises me. A five-year-old horse is young, still. Energy shouldn't be an issue, which makes me think Missy was right about neglect.

"Why don't you show us," I suggest.

He leads us into the outbuilding, which has a bowed aluminum roof and no floor but rocks and scrub. Inside, a couple of flimsy partitions separate the place into makeshift stalls. There's barely any hay in here. No tack. And it's dark and full of cobwebs.

But it's the odor that gets to me most of all. The smell of animal waste and ozone, which means fear, mixed with the sickly sweet odor of infection. I'm scared of what we'll find.

"That's Suede," Hance says, pointing into the shadows.

My father puts a hand on my shoulder. "Why don't you let Joaquin in first?"

"I'm fine, Dad," I say, though of course I'm not. This part, the anxiety before the seeing, always gets to me. Still, I need my father to stop protecting me. He has to know I can handle the difficult parts. That I'm up to the challenge.

I draw a breath and move toward the stall. Joaquin, my father, and Mr. Hance follow.

Inside, a horse stands in the corner—a beautiful Appaloosa with an ebony base and a gorgeous white and black spotted patch over his rear back and flanks. Right away, I see that his ribs show, and his tail is tucked in tight to his body. He's in some pain.

I assess for a moment, trying to get a sense of the horse's level of agitation. But I want to throw myself at him and put my arms around his neck, brush his matted black mane from his face, take away whatever's hurting him.

"Suede won't cause any trouble," Hance says. "You can go on and have a look."

"Looks sick to me," my father says. I hear dismissal in his voice, and it digs at something inside me. I prepare myself for a battle, knowing I'll have to give him logic, not emotions, to make my case. "Why are you selling it?"

Him, I think.

"Just can't keep up with it anymore," Hance says. "Too much to feed. Can't run him the way he needs to be run. And to be honest, he's sickly."

I approach the horse carefully, making sure my steps are quiet, relaxing my posture and trying to slow my heart rate. Suede's shoulders bow, and his flesh jumps, but I don't see any flies or anything else pestering him.

"Look at the hooves," Joaquin says.

Gently, I lift the horse's front leg. He's shoed, but his hooves have grown over and are deeply cracked and pitted with hay and pebbles. I see what looks like the start of an abscess. That same sickly odor rises from the inflamed spot.

"Poor thing," I say.

Joaquin nods, and we spend some time examining Suede for other defects. He's got another, deeper abscess on his back right hoof, and heat rises from his flesh, making me worry that he's feverish. He's all skin and bones; but his ears are pert, his eyes gentle, and he nuzzles my flat palm, breathing out a puff of dry warmth. He needs to be rescued. By me.

I beckon to my father, and he comes over, already shaking his head.

"Not this one, Ali," he says softly. He frowns sympathetically, but the regret doesn't quite reach his eyes. "His owner lost the other one. Thinks they might have some kind of anemia, too. It's going to be too much to care for him. And you're going to be too busy with Blackwood and our investment."

"I've got Joaquin to help," I protest. "And I can take care of him in the evenings and on weekends. Let me at least try. I can pay for it out of my own money."

"Need I remind you that your money is *my* money?"

"No," I say quietly. "But this is a young horse, Dad. He just needs a little care. You'll make back your money. I'm sure of it."

"That's what you said about Persephone."

"And I'm still sure of her, too."

"Alison, you need to have your head in the game. I'm trusting your judgment where this Blackwood is concerned. And your judgment's still on probation. We're not talking about pocket change here."

I've lost track of whether we're talking about Suede or Adam, so I split the difference. "I promise you I can handle both."

"If that's the case," he says, "you'll have to bring me something meatier than the same obvious financials I can dig up for myself. I need to know about Blackwood, the man. Is he stable? What are his habits? I have Simon and Nancy to give me the dry basics. I need you to go deeper."

I'm glad the building is dark, so my father can't see me blush.

"What do you mean?"

"You need to suss out his character, not his ledger. Get personal." He rests a hand on Suede's flank, and the horse shudders. "Something scared those investors away, and it's not the way he does business."

"Adam said he turned them down because they wanted too much control."

"Well, that's his story. But there's more there. I know it." He leans against a post and scrapes mud out of his shoe with a stick. "We'll be out on the boat all day on Sunday. That means cocktails. Getting loose."

"Dad."

He sighs. "I'm not asking you to drug and seduce him, for Christ's sake. Just look for inroads. This isn't throwing around money, Alison," he says. "We have to use our heads. And protect the family interests above all. You get that, right?"

I nod. "I get it. And I'll take care of it. I promise."

"All right. We'll give this a try." He turns to Hance and says, "We'll take him and all the tack and other equipment you have for him. I'm not paying for a sick horse, but I'll give you eight hundred for the supplies, and you can throw Suede in for free." He holds out his hand. "Deal?"

The old man gives my father a vigorous handshake. "Deal."

But my father's expression as he looks over Hance's shoulder tells me that the deal's really between the two of us, and he expects me to deliver.

Chapter 12

Adam

The blender is going on Sunday morning when I step into the kitchen.

Rhett stands beside my brother, dumping protein powder into the glass pitcher by the shovel-full. He wanted ten minutes to go over some changes to this year's team-building retreat.

We've been slammed at the office, and with the Quick Investment team there, I've had even less time during the week than normal. Rhett was doing a ten-mile run this morning on Zuma Beach, so I told him to stop by afterward.

Because it's Rhett, he's already showered in the guest bath, cleaned up the kitchen and brought in yesterday's mail and set it on the counter. Brooks—my best friend, ex-roommate, and partner in Blackwood Films—is the same way, totally at home here. Always coming and going. I wonder sometimes why I have locks on the doors.

Rhett shuts the blender off when he sees me.

"Morning, Adam! I thought I'd make you guys some delicious breakfast shakes."

"Hey, Rhett. Morning." Grey is leaning on the counter beside him. He has his favorite Union Jack t-shirt on, and he's in jeans, which he doesn't wear unless he's leaving the house or just returning. "Did you just roll in?"

Grey takes down half of his smoothie in two gulps. "About half an hour ago."

He's been hitting clubs and bars since he was seventeen. He has a fake ID but, at six foot two, ripped, and inked up, he never gets carded.

"To be young and single again," Rhett says, but he's grinning and doesn't mean a word of it. I'll be shocked if he and Raylene haven't tied the knot by this time next year. He grabs glasses for me and him and brings the shakes to the table.

"What are we discussing this morning, gentlemen?" Grey says, in his version of a businessman's voice. Apparently, in his mind all businessmen have bad British accents.

"The marketing retreat in Jackson Hole," Rhett replies.

"Which I get to go to this year, correct?" Grey says.

"Wrong," Rhett and I say together.

"Bloody bollocks!"

"I think 'bloody hell' is what you're going for."

"Let me bloody hell swear the way I want to, Adam. Okay, please? And all you guys do during that retreat is ski. I'm awesome at that. I should totally go."

"Believe it or not, it's a work event," Rhett says.

"Then that's the kind of jay-oh-bee I want."

This could go on all day if I let it. "Guys, I'm on a schedule," I say, and Rhett shifts right into work gear, filling me in on the location change. Usually, we stay at a resort, but this time we'll be at a rental home. Still on the resort property, but it'll give us more privacy and better common areas. It's a great idea and I tell him so, but Rhett didn't need my approval to go forward. He just wanted to talk. The camaraderie retreat in Jackson Hole is his Christmas.

I check my watch, and Grey notices.

"Adam has a boat date with some girl," he says. "Wait. Rhett—you probably know her. Alison. Is she hot?"

I reach over and smack the back of Grey's head, which only makes him laugh.

"You're going boating with Alison Quick?" Rhett asks. He doesn't sound surprised, which means the office grapevine has been working.

"No," I say. "I'm going on a social outing with Graham Quick, his wife, and his daughter. It's relationship-building. So I can earn their trust. So I get the money we need."

Rhett frowns. "Adam . . . maybe you shouldn't go."

"You don't think I can earn their trust?"

"No. Of course it's not that. Look, I don't how to say this but . . ." Rhett casts an anxious glance at Grey. "You don't exactly *stay* with girls."

"How is that relevant to boating?"

"It's relevant to Alison Quick," he says. "And she's relevant to Graham Quick. What happens when you move on? What happens to the investment money then?"

"You're making an awful lot of assumptions, Rhett. Believe it or not, it's a work event." As I say this, I think of how many times he walked by my office and saw me and Alison talking—about Boomerang. I spent all day with her last week. But I had to. So what if it turns out I liked it?

"Come on, Adam. I know your type, and she's—"

"I'm not going to lose this deal. For anything."

"It's not that I don't want you to move on. I do, man. Just pick any other—"

"Did Cookie put you up to this?" I ask before I can stop myself. Rhett and Cookie have never pried this much into my personal life. I mean professional life.

He frowns. "Cookie? No. She didn't say anything to me. Did she come to you?"

I know I've just made him even more nervous about Alison.

"She might have mentioned something. And you're wrong, Rhett. Alison's not my type. On the surface, maybe. Other than that, she's totally different."

My words hang in the air for a few seconds.

Grey's eyebrows draw together slightly, a rare seriousness settling in his expression.

"I have to get going," I say, standing. Mia Galliano is waiting for me. Last night, I asked her to fill in when Julia canceled. Not exactly a date, like I'd told Alison, but Mia will be a great reminder that it's a work event.

"Okay." Rhett crosses his arms. "Eye on the prize, Blackwood."

"Always." I grab my keys from the hook. Grey gets up and follows me out to the garage. I climb into the Rover and lower the window.

"She's totally different?" he says, propping his arms on the car.

He wants me to elaborate, but what is there to say? I have no idea what I'm dealing with. I've just discovered a new continent. I need some time to get my bearings.

"Okay," Grey nods. He runs a hand over his forearm. He has full sleeves on both arms. On his left forearm, he has a smaller version of the tattoo on my shoulder. He got it for me. For Chloe. As a tribute.

I know he's working up the guts to say something else. I wait, hoping he'll tell me what happened between him and Mom.

"I sang last night."

"You what?"

"I sang at the club last night. It just happened by accident. I've been hanging out with these guys in a band. Their front man had to go to the hospital yesterday morning for his appendix? It ruptured or something nasty like that, so they called me. They didn't want to cancel, so I took his place. I only knew a few of their songs, and the rest were covers, but . . ." He shrugs. "I sang."

It takes me a minute to absorb this. He hasn't done anything besides surf and party since he moved out here in August, so hearing this stirs something inside me that feels a lot like relief.

I try to imagine it. My little brother with a microphone in his hands. Stage lights. A band behind him. It's surprisingly easy to *picture,* but I've never actually heard him sing. Not even in the car or around the house.

"I didn't even know you could do that."

"Neither did I until I got up on stage." He smiles. "I almost puked I was so nervous."

"But it was good?"

"Yeah. Adam, it was . . . amazing. They asked me to do it again."

I hesitate, because I know this is the million-dollar question. Whether he'll actually lock into it. Grey's not like me. I go full throttle on everything. No matter what it is, I strive to be the best. But he's choosy. Few things in this world draw out the best of him. Few things stick. "Will you?"

He pats the car twice and steps back. "You should go."

I spend half the drive to Mia's thinking of Grey as a lead singer. The second half, I spend thinking of all the ways Alison is totally different.

How is that possible? I've only known the girl a week. Granted, we got a jump on things at the Gallianos, but . . . how?

Man. It's been such a long time since a girl's been on my mind like this.

Such a long fucking time since I've felt this.

I don't want it.

Chapter 13

Alison

It's 11 a.m., and my mom's on Bloody Mary number three. Which isn't like her and which does little for her balance as Weston, one of the two people crewing the *Ali Cat,* helps her from dock to deck.

The day is warm, with a light Santa Ana wind blowing in from the northeast to chase away a wispy fog. But my mother's bundled up as though preparing to spear polar bears in the tundra. Which is funny because Vivian Quick knows how to dress—how to behave—for literally every occasion. It's like she has a Social Perfection flow-chart stored in her brain. Get her on a boat, though, and she's always a step away from a third-degree sunburn or a first-degree disaster of some kind. It's a little unnerving, given how placid and even-keeled she usually is.

"I'm going to call Catherine before we're out of cell phone range," she tells me.

"Tell her to get her ass here for a visit," Dad says. But we all know that won't happen. My sister is busy with her perfect life in Dallas. It's a miracle if I can get her to return a text.

I find myself wondering what Adam will think of my parents. I shouldn't care. It doesn't matter. But watching my mother weave off to the galley makes me feel anxious and vulnerable, like someone's peeled away a few layers of my skin to expose all my nerves.

I guess that someone is Adam. I shouldn't want him as much as I do. I shouldn't want this deal to go through so I'll have an excuse to see more of him. I should want it for the family, to prove to my father that I'm capable of taking the helm. Not because some fanciful recess of my mind wants a replay of Halloween night, when our bodies fit together like two pieces of a whole, when his body, his strong, warm hands, his smile, and the depth beneath all of it drove me to a place I'd never been before, made me feel wild and so absolutely, perfectly, *right*.

My father leaps aboard and gives Weston a slap on the back that practically sends him into the ocean. "Looking good," he pronounces after casting a sharp-eyed gaze around the deck. The sleek lines of reddish teak and white fiberglass gleam in the sunlight. Every surface glitters; every cushion and container fits perfectly in place.

As always, I feel the anticipation of movement, the power of the engines rumbling beneath my canvas boat shoes. Right away, I perch on a chair to pull them off so I can run my bare feet over the sun-warmed wooden deck. I love that feeling.

Usually, I'd be in the kitchen, helping Sandra, Weston's wife, prepare snacks or blend up pitchers of frothy daiquiris. Or I'd be in the tiny cavelike game room, pulling waterlogged paperbacks from the shelves to curl up with when I get tired of snorkeling. But today, I'm meant to be front and center to await our guests. Adam and some girl. Julia.

I get why he's bringing her. To remind us both that this is business, a social exchange between two potential partners. I thought of bringing someone too, as I said I might do, but my father nixed that, told me to keep focused on Adam, on business.

God, won't this be fun?

"Supposed to be choppy out there," my father says, plopping down next to me. "Can't wait to watch your mother handle six-foot swells. Especially if she keeps going the way she is."

"You might not want to go that way yourself," I say, glancing down at the tumbler filled with ice and bourbon in his hands.

He grins and lifts it to his lips. The ice clinks against his teeth, and the sound makes my shoulders tense.

"Don't worry. I won't get sloppy. Trust me."

That phrase: Trust me. Especially from him. I can't think about that. I want to trust. And I want to be someone who never damaged another person's trust.

I get up, needing to expel my nervous energy, and go in search of something to do while I wait. At this point, I'd swim under the boat to scrape barnacles off the hull if it meant fast-forwarding through the awkward face-to-face with Adam's date, the stilted introductions, the casting off into a day where every hour will feel like it's made of six thousand minutes.

I'm about to head down the stairs to the accommodations deck in search of sunscreen, when my father gives a sharp whistle.

"They're here," he says. "Look alive, Alison."

My stomach does a hard tumble when I follow his gaze down the long dock to see Adam coming toward us. It's not him, though, not this time. It's the girl walking beside him.

Not some mystery date but *Mia*.

He's brought Mia with him. To join us on my parents' boat, for an entire day.

Mia with her wild curls. Her famous mother. Her ease with seemingly every single thing.

I know she can't really be his date, so why is she here? And has she told him about Ethan and me? Is this some kind of weird power play?

That doesn't seem like Adam. He's not a game player. He's direct and goes for what he wants.

And then he's in front of me, wearing jeans and a slate-colored linen shirt that stirs in the ocean breeze. His smile is open and genuine, so beautiful. Deep crinkles bracket his thoughtful gray eyes as he looks up at us, into the sunlight.

"Beautiful vessel," he says to my father. His expression is so good-natured and boyish that I know this is just a coincidence, not strategy. I still don't know what she's told him. And I still don't know how I'm going to handle a day at sea with her, but my shoulders drop a fraction of an inch, and I smile at them both.

"Come on aboard," my dad says.

Adam helps Mia onto the short boarding ladder, and my father rushes forward to help her onto the boat. Vaguely, I'm aware of Adam handing off his gear to Weston, along with a bottle of champagne, which earns a distracted smile of approval from my father as his eyes are elsewhere.

"Who have we here?" he says, taking Mia's hand.

Adam steps onto the deck. "Graham, I'd like you to meet Mia Galliano."

"I can see why you'd want to bring her along." My father doesn't let go of her hands. I feel my face warm. "I wouldn't let her out of my sight either."

"Oh, no," Mia protests. Pink spreads over her olive skin. "I'm just . . . I'm an employee. Thanks for having me along, Mr. Quick."

She looks at me, and it's plain from her discomfort that there's nothing spiteful about her appearance here today.

Finally, my father lets go. "Glad to have you."

"Mia's in marketing now," Adam says. "But she's a filmmaker. She'll bring a lot of great ideas and creative energy to the new studio."

"Oh, we're not talking business already, are we?" my mother says, sweeping out into the sunlight. "Why don't we get comfy at the front of the ship?"

"The bow, Vivian," my father says and rolls his eyes toward Adam, inviting his participation.

But Adam just smiles. "I've been looking forward to meeting you, Mrs. Quick," he says, and shakes her hand. "I read that you're chairing a fundraiser over at LACMA. I'd love to get involved in some way."

"Oh, wonderful," my mother says. "We'd love your help." And her besotted expression tells me she's sold. Of course, she's easily charmed. Something my father has been banking on for years.

My mother leads the group away, leaving just Adam and me for a moment.

"You look like you belong on a boat," he says. "Or in the water. Like a mermaid."

I don't know why, but this surprises me. Maybe because it feels so personal. Or because it suggests he sees so much.

The sun feels warmer, baking me in my skin. I want to tell him he looks like he belongs everywhere, like he was born to rule the world. But of course I don't.

If we were only bodies, everything would be simple. I'd drag him off into a cabin and bolt the door, finish what we started on Halloween night.

But we're not. Our bodies had their moment. Now it's time to use my head.

I give Adam a smile. "Come on," I say. "Let's join the others."

Chapter 14

Adam

As the boat leaves the harbor and moves into open water, we settle into a covered seating area and talk about the day's agenda. The plan is to cruise to Catalina Island and drop anchor near Lover's Cove, where we'll have lunch. Weston, the captain, takes our orders right away so he can pass it along to his wife, Sandra, the chef.

This shouldn't take long since there are only five of us, but Graham seems to want to download everything he knows about barbecuing, so our meal is nothing short of perfect. Vivian Quick rolls her eyes between sips of her drink until Graham notices.

"Problem, Viv?" he asks.

"No, Graham. But I think Weston knows how to grill shrimp, don't you Weston?"

"Always willing to improve," Weston says smoothly and excuses himself.

"See, Vivian?" Graham says. "He has the right attitude."

Vivian takes another sip of her drink and doesn't reply. Instead, she turns the conversation back to the LACMA fundraiser, going over the details with me, her eyes alive with excitement for the first time since I boarded. Graham interrupts every few seconds, giving me conversational whiplash.

Mia glances at me, clearly picking up on the tension between the Quicks.

Across from me, Alison's face is cold, impassive. I can't read her thoughts, but her fingers are clenched around her glass, and her pink-tipped toes grip the deck. She's not happy about me seeing her parents like this. I want to pull her aside and tell her it's okay. I know family dysfunction well. But I remember Rhett's warning—*eye on the prize*—and force myself to focus on Graham.

With lunch ordered, he's launched into a list of all the custom upgrades he made to the *Ali Cat*.

"Sorry," I say, interrupting. "The name, *Ali Cat*?"

The boat's moving into choppier water, and we all pick up our drinks to keep them from spilling over.

"Alison and Catherine," Vivian says. "Our daughters."

I can't help but smile. "Ali, huh?"

"It's a *family* nickname," she says as a blush creeps up her neck.

"Not just family, Ali," Graham says. He seems to want to correct everything and everyone all the time. I'll need to give his controlling nature serious consideration later. I don't like being controlled. By anyone. "Philippe calls you that," he continues. "So did Ethan."

Alison's eyes drop to the drink in her hands, and her mother frowns. Something just happened, but I'm not sure what it is.

"Speaking of Ethan," Graham says, "I heard you had him as an intern this summer."

It takes me a moment to realize they're talking about Ethan Vance. But how do they know Ethan?

"I did. Quality guy. I hated to lose him to grad school, but I still see him socially. You know him?"

"Oh, yes. Great kid," Graham says. "Smart and driven. Hell of an athlete, too. He was with my Ali for a few years in college. Shame it didn't work out, but you know young love. Flash in the pan and all that."

Oh, shit. That's what this is.

Vivian sends him a warning look, but I'm more focused on Alison, who turns white, and Mia, who closes her eyes for a long second. She looks like she wants to teleport out of here—and why wouldn't she?

Ethan and Alison dated in college.

And now Ethan's with Mia.

And I brought Mia here.

Jesus.

Graham's looking at Alison in a way that seems condemning somehow, and her eyes are becoming glossy.

"I had no idea," I say, looking from her to Mia, who's starting to turn a little green.

"No idea about what?" Graham asks.

Alison answers for me. "Ethan is dating Mia now."

"Oh, dear." Vivian glances at her daughter with a look of concern.

"Nonsense," Graham says. "Bygones! Right, Ali? We're all civilized human beings. Mia took the prize this time, but another young man will come along for my girl."

Alison ignores him. "Ethan's a great guy," she says to Mia. "I mean . . . I'm sure you know that. I'm glad you two are together. And . . . happy and everything."

"Thanks, Alison," Mia says, but her expression is strained and a little panicked. Her hand flattens on her stomach. "Um, I don't mean to change the subject, but do you guys have any Dramamine? I'm feeling a little off."

"In the guest bath," Vivian says. "I'll get them." But Graham's hand reaches for her wrist, keeping her there.

"Weston!" he yells.

Mia hops up. "No, it's okay. I'll get it. I know where it is."

I excuse myself and follow her inside. Right now, Mia's priority one.

"Adam, it's okay," Mia says as we hustle to the head. "Really, it's okay. I'm fine."

I step into the small bathroom with her and shut the door behind us. She immediately bends over the sink and splashes water on her face.

"Shit. I'm sorry, Mia. Damn it. You should have said something. I'd never have brought you here if I'd known."

She peers up at me, water dripping off her face. "This deal is so important for the company, and I thought I could do it. I didn't think we were going to *discuss* Ethan. Dear God. Why is the floor moving so much? Did someone put *acid* in those drinks?"

"Hang on." I open a cabinet and find a bottle of seasickness tablets, handing her one. Mia takes two more from me. "Wait, those are really strong. One should be—"

"I feel like I'm going to die."

"We've barely been on the water fifteen minutes."

"I know, but I'm a land animal. A chair animal. Beds. Couches. I'm a comfortable stationary-place animal. But don't worry. I'll survive." Mia slumps against the door. We're still on choppy water. The yacht is still moving around a lot, the floor pitching beneath us. "I'm the one who's sorry for being a terrible date."

"No. You did nothing wrong. I just wish I hadn't dragged you here." I should go back to the Quicks, but I have a second to process all of this now.

Ethan and Alison.

That was a surprise.

I want to know more, and I also don't.

"Were they serious?" I ask, the rational part of my brain losing.

Mia pushes her hair away from her cheek and nods but doesn't say more.

I think of the condemning look Graham just sent Alison. He blames her for the end of the relationship. Does that mean Alison left Ethan? Did she betray him?

I can't picture it. I can't see Alison as a girl who'd deliberately hurt someone. She's a nurturer. She rescues horses. She hugged me when I was a complete stranger. Kindness is her default gear.

There's a story behind this. Between Alison and Ethan. And even though it's none of my business, I want to know it.

I'm about to ask Mia another question when she groans and bends over her stomach. "Ugh. *Ow.* Ahhhh. Adam, please get out. I'm going to be sick."

"It's okay. I'll stay—"

"No! *Please.* Go." She shoves me out of the bathroom. As she's closing the door, I catch a glimpse of her whirling toward the toilet.

"Adam?"

I turn to the voice, and Alison's right there.

Chapter 15

Alison

*Y*ou'd think it would give me more pleasure to see the girl who's now sleeping with my ex hunched over a toilet bowl, but I've *been* that girl too many times to feel smug now.

"I've got this," I say and nudge Adam out of the way. "Go on back up to my parents."

Mia groans from her balled-up position on the floor. "Please . . ." she gasps. "I . . . do *not* need an audience for this."

Adam hesitates, shooting me a wide-eyed, helpless look. "She's really sick."

"Go on," I tell him. "Maybe you can keep my father from wresting control of the boat away from Weston."

He smiles. "I'll do my best." But he stands there, still, looking down at me. Not into my eyes, but at my face, then down at my body. He knows about Ethan—at least that we dated. Do I look different to him now?

"Really, you can *both* go," Mia says. "Or just kill me. If you're going to stand there, you could do that much for me, at least."

"Okay, okay," Adam says. "Sorry. I'll go." To me, he adds, "Let me know if she needs anything, okay?"

I nod and turn back to Mia, who has hunched into an even smaller version of herself.

"I'm coming in," I say.

"For the love of all that's holy, *why*?"

"Someone has to hold that giant mass of hair." I riffle through a few of the cabinets until I find a stack of towels. I run one beneath the water faucet and hand it to her.

She takes it and wipes her mouth, folds it carefully and dabs it at her forehead. Moisture gathers on her temple, and her tan complexion has a greenish tinge. "You really don't have to do this."

"Please." I fill a paper cup with water and hand it to her. "I spent four years as a Kappa. You are not the first girl whose hair I've held."

Her smile is weak but appreciative. She flushes the toilet and shuts the lid. Closing her eyes, she sinks back against the wall, keeping the towel pressed to her forehead. "Why am I not surprised you were in a sorority?"

I shrug. "We actually did a lot of community projects," I tell her. "It's not all partying and boys." Not that I had much to do with the latter. I spent two of my college years with Ethan. And then it all fell apart. Or I took it apart.

The boat heaves to one side, and I fall into the narrow space. My shin barks against the small commode, and I almost step on Mia's hands, but she moves them to steady me.

"Careful," she says. "There's only room for one fatality in here."

"You might *wish* you were dead. But you're probably not going to die."

"I'm not sure that's comforting."

The boat keels again, hard enough to pop open some of the cabinet doors.

Mia puts a hand to her mouth, and her eyes go wide. "Uh-oh," she manages, but I've already read the signs. I flip up the toilet lid and push her hair away from her face just as she lurches back over the commode. She heaves, and I try to keep her hair under control while also not crowding her too much—tough to do in the modest space.

"Jesus," she moans. "This is humiliating."

She flushes and hangs over the toilet. I give her more water, and she takes a cautious sip. I want to tell her she'd be better off going up on deck to do what she needs to do. The fresh air would help, but I'm not even sure she'd make it.

"My dad said it should smooth out, but maybe I should just tell him to turn back. We can do this another day."

"No, don't do that," she mutters. "This deal . . . I don't want to screw things up."

That makes two of us. It occurs to me we have at least a couple of things in common now: Ethan and this need for things to be right.

"Let's get you into one of the cabins to lie down."

She nods, and I back out of the space to give her some room. It's so hard not to ask if she told Adam about how Ethan and I ended. So hard not to ask if Ethan's forgiven me. Really forgiven me. But now's not the time.

Rising, she bends over the tiny sink to splash water in her face. Her color looks a little bit better, but her eyes have the cool sheen of ice. She looks like she's about a minute from passing out.

Mia follows me to one of the small staterooms, and I help her onto the bed, even taking off her shoes for her. Her feet are impossibly small, and that makes me laugh for some reason.

"I know," she says. "Elf feet."

"Well, they don't curve up at the toes, at least."

She smiles and lies back against the pillows. "I'm sorry," she murmurs, and it's hard to tell if she's talking to me or to some vision dancing behind her eyelids.

"No need. We'll be fine. Just rest."

"No," she says. "About Ethan. The Boomerang date. I'm sorry if I hurt you."

"It's totally okay," I tell her. "You couldn't have known."

She nods. "No, but I'm still sorry." Her eyes close. "Anyway . . . Adam . . ."

I wait for her to finish the sentence. "Adam what?" I say, because I can't help myself. But the cabin fills with the light rhythm of her breathing. She's asleep.

I get a plastic pitcher and fill it with water, then pour some into a glass to leave on the nightstand by her side, along with another Dramamine because there's no way she kept the first one down.

After I've switched off the lights and shut the door gently, I go back up to the forward salon.

Adam's in there, standing by the window. He's untucked his shirt, and his pants are rolled up at the ankle, exposing bands of tan skin. He looks like a surf kid, his skin sun-brightened, sandy blond hair wavy from the sea air. And his lean swimmer's body, with its broad shoulders, taut muscles. He's devastating.

Something inside me catches, like I've been hooked, like there's an invisible filament spanning the space between us, and he's drawing me to him. He's not even looking at me, but I feel the pull.

I walk up to him, and he turns and smiles.

"Where are my folks?"

"Your mom's crashing on a chaise upstairs. And I'm afraid I lost the battle with Captain Graham."

I roll my eyes. "Great." I'm waiting for some other shoe to drop. For him to ask about Ethan, for me to have to decide what to tell him, what to keep to myself.

Instead, he surprises me. "Hey," he says. "Want to go for a dive?"

That might be the best thing I've ever heard in my life. I'm so hungry to shed this ridiculous day, to get into the ocean, into the cool, magical world beneath the waves. Without my parents and my past.

With Adam.

"I'd love to," I say.

Chapter 16

Adam

Instead of Lover's End, Weston modifies our course and takes us around Catalina, where we drop anchor at West End. The water on this side of the island is smoother and with Mia as sick as she is, it was the obvious choice. Alison and I take turns changing into our swimsuits in the room next to Mia's and meet back on the rear deck.

"My dad likes Lover's End better, but this is my favorite place to dive out here," she says as she pulls her hair into a ponytail. She's got her wetsuit half on, the arms hanging limp at her waist, and a black tank up top. She looks like she's done this a thousand times. "The best visibility and the kelp forests are incredible."

"What kind of marine life?" I ask. The news about Ethan's still on my mind. I want to know more.

"Oh, you'll see everything here," she says, her blue eyes lighting up. "I've seen moray eels, leopard sharks. Yellow tail. Lots of

Garibaldi. I haven't seen any horn sharks lately, though. You have to catch them at dusk, or on night dives, but who knows? Maybe we'll get lucky. And it's always pretty private. The currents can be strong, so you only get advanced divers."

She pulls her tank top off, no warning whatsoever, and I'm looking at her in a black bikini. She's beautiful, so gorgeous. Toned arms. Long, slender neck. My eyes drift lower, and suddenly I'm trying not to stare at the way she fills out her bikini. Trying and failing. I make myself think of sharks, moray eels, kelp forests, so I don't go full mast right here.

"Are you okay with that?" she asks. "Advanced-level diving?"

"I'm an advanced-level diver, so yes. And I'm good with everything that's going on right now."

Ali pauses in the middle of slipping one of her arms into her wetsuit. Her gaze narrows in question.

I want to answer that question.

Yes, Alison. You're beautiful.

"Horn sharks, huh?" I say instead. I turn and focus on pulling my own wetsuit out of my dive kit. Gulls circle above us, and I see a thin tail of barbecue smoke rising from the opposite end of the boat.

"Yep," she says behind me. "I've always liked them. They're so clumsy in the water and slow—and super sensitive to light intensity and water temperature—but they're still successful predators. Amazing. All those strikes against them but they still manage to make it work."

What's amazing is that I'm practically getting wood just looking at her, and she's talking about a fish.

"Fan of the underdog, are you?" I shake out my suit and step into it. "I guess we really weren't meant to be."

Ali laughs. Her gaze feels like sunshine on my back, but I don't turn around. I pull my wetsuit up to my waist, adjusting myself so I'm comfortable. The cool Neoprene layer feels familiar and my body responds, my heart thumping hard, anticipation rushing through my veins. The prospect of the ocean always does this to me. This has nothing to do with the girl behind me.

"Adam?"

Ali's voice is close. Turning, I almost bump into her.

Her wetsuit is all the way on, which is good. And terrible.

"What's up?" I ask.

She smells like suntan oil and peaches. This close, I see that her cheeks are turning slightly pink from the sun. With her hair pulled back, no makeup, and the wetsuit covering her completely, she looks better than she has all week at the office. Better than she did in the Catwoman costume. There's something powerful about her now. The way her slender legs are planted firmly on the swaying boat, like she's not trying at all. She's at home on the water. This from an admitted equestrian. I can only imagine what she's like with her horses.

"Sorry, but . . ." She smiles and points at her back. "My zipper's jammed." She turns around and pulls her ponytail up. "Can you help me out?"

"Sure. You want this on, right? Just want to be sure."

I can't see her face, but I know she's smiling. "Yes. On please."

I allow myself a moment to enjoy the way she looks right in front of me. Then I take the zipper leash, letting my knuckles drift over her back, just above the knot of her bikini.

If I weren't completely focused on her, I'd have missed the way she curls slightly toward me.

Focus, Blackwood. Zip the wetsuit up.

"Tell me something," I say, tugging on the jammed material. "Do you have some problem with zippers?" I ask, remembering her cat suit.

She laughs. "It was Philippe's doing on Halloween night. He says zippers are the scars of fashion."

With both of us barefoot, she's a few inches shorter than me, and I like it. How she feels a little smaller. The urge to wrap her in my arms is strong. To peel the suit off her and kiss her shoulder. We're alone back here with the sunlight and the seagulls. I could lay her out on the chaise lounge and spend the rest of the day exploring her. I could sink myself—

Graham's voice carries down from a deck somewhere above us. He's laughing. It's a loud sound, a downright *guffaw*. I know he's on the phone because he hasn't sounded that happy once with his wife or his daughter. Shitty. Shitty family dynamics. But Graham's laugh gets me back on track.

I finally get the jam sorted out and zip her up. "All set."

"Thanks." Ali's smiling as she faces me, but it fades as her eyes travel to my tattoo. I wonder what she's thinking. If she's remembering our time in the Gallianos' garage. How we'd been all over each other. Just completely crazed to taste and touch as much of one another as we could.

When her blue eyes come back to mine, I see curiosity in them and sweetness. Her attention on me is complete but somehow soft. It's an expression that's uniquely hers and it's a temptation. It makes me want to let her in and tell her everything. The whole fucking sob story of my life. Of me and Chloe.

I look at her earrings. "You going to wear those in the water?"

"Yep. I never take them off." She tips her head toward our tanks. "So, Blackwood. Are we doing this?"

"We're doing this. Quick. Or slow. Whichever speed you prefer."

Ali smiles, her eyes narrowing. "You've been waiting to say that."

"Resisting. But I'm glad it's out of the way now."

Weston comes down as Ali and I are checking our tanks and clearing our regulators.

"Perfect day," he says. "Not every day is this clear and calm. It's going to be the dive of a lifetime."

Ali and I exchange a smile, anticipating the adventure. The freedom. As soon as we're in and our masks come down, I know that for the next hour, I won't think about Boomerang, or about getting the money I need to launch Blackwood Films.

Diving is like surfing for me, except without the rush. Underwater I'm breath and energy, nothing more. My mind empties. Time stops. But I know this won't be like my usual dives. Even before Weston's comment, I knew that.

We descend to forty feet and head toward the kelp forest, Ali leading. She's true to her name, quick through the water. I push to stay with her, more aware of the dangers of diving than ever. When we reach the kelp, I'm practically her shadow, but it's easy to get tangled in the long vines. Easy to lose sight of someone or get caught in a strong current, and I'm not taking any risks with her safety. It only takes a few minutes for my worries to fade away though.

She's a good diver, calm and smooth, but it's the moment she looks at me and bugs out her eyes, imitating a grouper nestled in the kelp, that makes me laugh and finally chills me out. From then on, we move without the need for words, showing each other starfish. Staring in awe at the twenty leopard sharks that fly past us. Pointing at the bright orange Garibaldi, weaving through the long strands of kelp.

We follow a ridge that parallels the island, visitors in an underwater world, but I'm on a mission. I keep an eye out along the murky edge of the cliff, where the sandy bottom is darker and shadowed from sunlight.

Finally I see one. I catch up to Ali and bring her back to the spot.

There, drifting along the bottom, is a horn shark. It's about a foot long, tan with dark brown spots. It looks uncomfortable with all the attention it's suddenly getting, but it stays put.

Ali looks at me, her eyes smiling. *Thank you,* her eyes say.

It feels so good to please her. I've done a lot of things for girls in the past. This, I won't forget.

We hover there a while, watching the clunky, somewhat pathetic predator until it decides to swim away.

Ali looks at me again and I don't look away. It's safe, with masks and an ocean between us. Without the permanence of words. So I let myself relax. I let myself see and be seen. What I feel or want or think is all the same right now.

I like you, Ali.

I don't want to, but I do.

Chapter 17

Alison

When Catherine and I used to dive as kids, I couldn't wait to glide away from her in the water, to move off to my own undersea kingdom, where I could be Ariel from *The Little Mermaid*. I'd pretend to be born to this world of shifting light and shadow, of pulsing life that invited me to secret places. The world above seemed so noisy to me—so full of chattering conversation and rules I didn't like. But here, I could spend hours watching schools of manta rays spread like dark kites near the surface above me. I could trail my fingers through the kelp, stare off at the far-off corona of sunshine and tell myself that if I stayed down here long enough, I'd grow a tail the way Ariel grew legs on land.

Now, as Adam and I swim around one another, I feel that same pull. Only it's different now. It's not about escaping to some world of my own. It's about having a world to share, someplace away from my parents and the family business. A bubble where just the two of us exist, two bodies circling one another. Contained and secret, like the backseat of the Murano on Halloween night. Only with fish.

We move together, and I'm conscious of the power of his muscled thighs encased in Neoprene, of his strong arms, pulling him along like the water offers no resistance at all. He smiles from around his regulator and points behind me. I do a lazy turn and come face-to-face with a sea turtle.

Drawing back to give it space, I bump against Adam. He steadies me, and even with the layers between our skin, his touch galvanizes me. We follow the turtle for a while, watching as it passes over undulating anemone and crabs scurrying along the ocean floor. At one point we're on either side of the creature, close enough to count the spots on its reptilian face, and Adam gives me a look that's so excited, so alive, that my breath catches in my chest, and I wonder if I've run out of oxygen.

Finally, we let the turtle move on without us. Adam points up toward the surface and, reluctantly, I nod.

We climb toward the sunlight, bodies close, and break through. We take off our masks and regulators and grin at each other. A few yards away, the *Ali Cat* bobs on the water, which is calm now.

"That was great," Adam says. His wet hair looks shades darker now, creating a deeper contrast with his glistening tan skin. A bead of moisture rests on the indentation above his lip, and I want to touch my tongue to it. I want to touch him, period, so I paddle back a few inches to give us both space.

"Now I'm starving," he adds.

I laugh. I'm hungry too. For so many things. But among the available choices, lunch seems safest.

"Come on. Let's see what we can find."

We climb aboard the *Ali Cat* and strip off our scuba gear. Adam's bathing suit slips down low on his hips, so that I can see the smooth contours of his lower abdomen, the hint of white flesh there, untouched by the sun. Our eyes meet for just a moment, and then Adam's drift away once again. We leave our scuba suits on the deck, like skins we've outgrown.

I jump into the shower just long enough to wash the salt from my hair, then dry off and reapply sunscreen. By the time I find another bathing suit, locate my dress, and climb up to the galley, I find Adam with Mia and my father at the narrow banquette. Plates of food and a couple of icy pitchers sit in front of them.

Adam has a couple of sandwiches on his plate plus a heaping serving of sliced mango. He sees me and gestures to the seat beside him. On the table, he's laid out a plate with the same food. It's exactly what I want right now.

"Best cure for what ails you . . ." my father says to Mia, but whatever he's offering, she demurs.

"I'm . . . still a little shaky, but thank you." Her color looks better and her green eyes more lively, but the smile she offers is still a shaky one.

"What's a cure?" I ask.

"Bloody Mary," he says. "Electrolytes."

I laugh. "Dad. She might want to try Gatorade or something instead."

He waves a hand at me and turns his full boat grin on her. "Come on! Girl like this has a stronger constitution. Don't you, dear?"

"I'm flattered you think so, sir, but I think water and crackers are probably about my speed right now."

Dad tsks. "You're no fun."

Sitting here, watching my dad's flirting, Mia's discomfort, drags me back to every awkward sorority dinner hosted by my parents, back to my sister's wedding, where my dad seemed to corner every pretty girl on the dance floor. Most people think he's wonderful, charming, and he can be. But he also doesn't know where to stop. That sometimes you can't have it all. I learned that the hard way.

Images bloom in my mind: our family cabin in Colorado, snow angling down in an opaque blanket. Two sets of boots in front of the fireplace. An empty bottle of Grande Cuvée sweating in an ice bucket. And a jewelry box on the table. Tiffany. Though I never found out what was inside. Or saw the woman who wore it.

I'd come early for our family ski trip, wanting to surprise my parents by stocking the kitchen. Instead, I got the surprise.

"It doesn't mean anything, Alison," my father said. "We don't want to hurt your mother. Not with something like this. What matters is family. Loyalty. That's what's real. The rest is bullshit. It's nothing."

I don't know what's real or not. I just know that my definitions feel shaky. Love. Family. I don't know what I can count on—least of all myself. So that means focusing on the things I can manage.

"Speaking of fun," Mia says. "Is Alison doing the dates?"

My father leans forward, eyes keen with curiosity. "What dates?"

Adam's posture stiffens, and he casts a look my way. The sun carves in from the portholes to shadow his eyes. I wish I could see them.

Mia peels a piece of bread from the top of her sandwich and takes a cautious nibble. "Oh, it's this thing we do for research. Whenever anyone starts working at Boomerang, they have to go out on a few practice dates. To get a feel for the company." She shoots me an apologetic look. "But I guess . . . you already did that. In a way."

I can see she's sorry she brought it up, so I try to let her off the hook. "Yes, I've tried the site. I think I have a handle on it."

At lunch, Adam and I never resolved the issue of the dates themselves. It wouldn't bother me to do them; it would be business, just like Adam bringing Mia along today. But talking about it now seems wrong, like it will erase the magic of my time in the water with Adam.

My father puts down his drink, and his gaze sweeps between Adam and me. He gives me a subtle wink and offers, "How many of these dates do your employees do, Adam?"

"Generally three. Though most employees go on to do more. We have a good product, as you know. Great algorithms mean great matches."

"But just for fun, eh? For people on the rebound." He doesn't have to say, "Like Alison." The words hang in the air, unspoken. "Or do you make real love matches too?"

Adam nods. "Of course. The site is for people who want to connect without a lot of expectations or drama. But we're happy when it brings people together in a real way, too."

His choice of words strike me. *In a real way.* Which means the way he is, the parade of girls through his life, that's not real? Were *we* real that night in the Murano?

"What do you say, Ali?" my father asks. "Need to get back on the horse, right? And it's research."

"It's not my first order of business, Dad," I tell him.

"C'mon, it will be good for you," he insists. "And if you're too busy, why don't you just consider today date number two? Mia and I can give you some more alone time."

Adam and I exchange embarrassed looks. I wish I could sink through the bottom of the boat and swim to shore. He's pushing me at Adam, and I don't like it. It tells me he doesn't think I can do the job on my own. And it tells Adam . . . what? That I'm pathetic and need help finding a date?

Images wind through my mind: Adam treading water in the ocean next to me, water pooling on his skin. Ethan in the doorway, tulips drooping toward the floor. My father, hurrying out of the bedroom in Colorado, his shirt unbuttoned, after I'd dropped a bag full of groceries on the floor.

Suddenly, all of it feels like such treacherous terrain, like it's unsafe to love or trust in any direction. Like it's unsafe to love or trust *me*. I have to focus on the work. *Only* on the work.

"That's a great idea," I say, lightly. "So, that's two down and just one date to go. Adam and I will make a plan Monday."

"Atta girl," my father says, approvingly.

I know he thinks I intend to plan something else *with* Adam, and I'll let him think so. But *I* know I need to run as far away from that as I can. Far away from any possibility of being hurt or hurting someone else, of wrecking what my father is trying so hard to build. Far away from Adam's secrets and my own, back to some safe space, like our world under the water. Only this time, I need to swim out on my own.

Chapter 18

Adam

*A*lison's already sitting at the small conference table in my office when I arrive on Monday.

"Morning," she says, pushing to her feet. She's in a cranberry red skirt, a black silk shirt and cat's-eye reading glasses that remind me of Halloween. "We're meeting with Brooks Wright at ten, correct?"

Her tone is so crisp and businesslike that I stop inside the door. Something changed after our dive yesterday. I felt it as our boat trip ended, and I feel it now, in the cool look she gives me. Something got into her head—about *me*. I want to know what it is.

I want to know why she was suddenly so chipper about going on her last Boomerang date. I want to know what happened between her and Ethan. But I'm not supposed to be thinking about a girl. I'm supposed to be securing the Quick funds.

I take a seat at my desk and fire up my laptop.

"That's correct," I say, following her cue. "He's the producer I told you about—my buddy from Princeton who's been at Lionsgate for a few years. I asked him to get some materials together to give you an idea of what we're planning on doing with our first feature. He's bringing some storyboards and a few test audition tapes. A couple of other things."

Brooks was my housemate up until September after Grey moved in. My place has four bedrooms, but my brother manages to occupy three. For two years before Grey, Brooks and I lived together and spent a huge amount of our time dreaming and planning out our production company. We're totally in step. As soon as we can start writing checks, we're going to kick massive amounts of filmmaking ass.

Today is about showing that to Ali. I know she has a vision. I see it in small ways, like how she dresses, how she doesn't rush when she's considering new ideas, but I wanted this meeting so it would give her concrete information that she can take back to her father. Graham's got the keys to the safe. I need that safe unlocked.

Ali checks her watch. "That's in fifteen minutes. Do you need me for anything before then? I thought I'd work in Philippe's cube for a bit. Give you a chance to settle in for the week."

I don't need anything from her—nothing I can have, anyway. But I feel like I'm being dismissed even though she's the one leaving my office, and I don't like it.

"Actually, there's an HR meeting right now you should sit in on."

Lie. Rhett texted from the café downstairs, offering to pick up coffees. My "HR meeting" is the delivery of a double-espresso, a latte dusted with cinnamon, and two Danishes. I'm not sure how I feel about the order I put in for Alison now, but whatever. It's done.

"Oh," she says. "Okay." She sits back down, pressing a key on her laptop to wake it back up. "I'll just power through a few emails until then."

I look at my email, thinking I'll do the same. Then I consider wadding up a sheet of paper and throwing it at her, just to get her attention. Fortunately, Rhett arrives with a coffee carrier before I do.

"What's up, boss man? Hey, Alison." He sets the drinks down on the conference table. "How'd the boat trip go?"

I take the seat next to Alison. Her face is emotionless. Carefully composed.

"Great," I say. "I had a great time." What else do I say? Vivian had a few too many? Graham was pushy as hell? Mia spent most of it cuddling with the toilet? I had one of the best afternoons I can remember until the very end? "The Quicks were generous hosts."

"We were happy to have you, Adam," Alison says, with as much feeling as a DMV clerk.

Anger shoots through me, and I stare at her. This is bullshit. I spent all goddamn night reliving it in perfect detail. Then embellishing it. I *know* she had as much fun as I did. Why are we both pretending otherwise?

A flush of red creeps up Ali's neck, but there's no other sign of the girl who imitated grouper for me yesterday.

Rhett looks between us, like he's seeing everything.

"For you," Rhett says, handing over Ali's latte.

"For me? But I didn't—"

"Adam likes to treat visiting executives when he can," Rhett says.

A nice warning jab by Orland.

Ali's eyes cut to me, then back to Rhett. "Thank you," she says, and I think she sounds a little contrite.

With the coffees delivered, Rhett turns for the door.

"Rhett," I say, quickly. "Didn't you want to talk about the retreat? I was just telling Ali . . . son. You were going to give us a quick update on it."

I'm lying because of this girl and I hate lying. I do too much of it already. Chloe filled up the Lie Reserves for the rest of my life.

"Update?" Rhett says, freezing. He gave me the update yesterday, over breakfast smoothies at my house. His eyes narrow for an instant, then he realizes he needs to cover for me. "Oh, right." He pulls out a chair beside me and drops into it. "You know the basics, right? About the retreat?"

Ali frowns. "No. I don't." I can tell she's disappointed in herself. Since she's been here in the office, it's been less like she's learning about my company and more like she's simply verifying what she already knows. Somehow our annual retreat slipped past her, and she doesn't seem thrilled about it.

"We do a team-building forum every year in Jackson Hole, Wyoming, the days right before Thanksgiving," Rhett explains. "We call it Camaraderie Camp because it's all in the name of fostering closeness among the team." His leg starts bouncing up and down as he gets more excited. "We ski some runs. Chill out in hot tubs. Do some trust exercises. It's a really fun few days, and it always gives the morale a boost—not that we really need it, but who's going to say no to better morale, right?"

"Absolutely. It sounds like a great event," Ali agrees.

"It is. It's the best," Rhett says.

"Will you join us?"

My question sucks the air out of the room.

First, because my voice came out sounding strangely hushed and private, almost like I whispered the question to Alison alone. And second, because neither Alison nor Rhett was expecting it.

"Oh," Alison says. She turns her coffee cup in a circle on the glass conference table. "It's good of you to offer."

Not sure what to make of that. I focus on Rhett, sending him a pointed look. He's worried about me inviting Alison for personal reasons and he's dead-on. It's exactly what I'm doing. I want her there, and it has little to do with the investment. But he has to back me up.

Slowly, he starts to nod. "Yeah. It's a good idea. It would give you a chance to get to know people around here better."

Good enough.

Alison seems to consider it. "Okay. I'll come."

"Great," Rhett says. "We just need to book travel for you and your team."

"Well, I don't think Nancy and Simon would want to come along. It'll just be Philippe. And me."

"I'll get on it."

My attention moves to the commotion in the hallway. Through the glass walls, I see Pippa and Sadie laughing. Today they've stepped up their work outfits to heels and body-hugging dresses, which happens every time I schedule a meeting with Brooks. He's out there with a motorcycle helmet tucked under one arm, telling them something that can't possibly be as hilarious as it appears to be.

I have no idea how he got the presentation materials here, but I'm not worried. I know he handled it. Brooks might always look like he just rolled out of a bar at 2 a.m., but he's brilliant, competent, and as motivated as I am to get this film studio online.

Philippe and Paolo show up, and they look just as excited about Brooks as the girls do. For a few seconds, it's like a mime show outside. Everyone talking animatedly, hands flapping around.

"Looks like marketing has the floor," Rhett says, standing. He glances at me, giving me back the pointed look I sent him a moment ago. "Oh, Alison, I almost forgot. I just saw Cookie in the elevator. She told me to tell you that your dating pool has been refreshed. I think she spent a lot of time over the weekend finding good matches for you, in case you were going to get around to them."

Touché. Rhett—and Cookie—are fighting back.

"All you have to do is log in and pick your date," he continues. "I really hope you meet someone nice and have a great time with it.

Even though I know you're really here to get a handle on Adam's business."

Rhett cringes, realizing what he just said. It's an apocalyptic slip for the guy. Just a tragic choice of words, and I pray to every god there is that I won't start laughing.

Ali meets my eyes. Her smile is genuine and open.

She's enjoying this as much as I am.

"Thanks, Rhett," she says. "I'm sure it'll be fun."

Chapter 19

Alison

*O*ut in the hallway, Philippe and Paolo engage in animated discussion about the latest episode of *Fargo*. I watch for a moment, awed by how well Philippe fits in with everyone, how smoothly he ingratiates himself. That we brought in leftover swag bags from one of my mother's recent events for the Boomerang staff to pick through this morning only sweetens the pot.

Paolo straightens Philippe's collar while they speak, which makes me wonder if there's a possible connection there. They seem cut from the same cloth—adorable, fashion-forward and, from what I've seen of Paolo so far, they have similar keen but fun-loving dispositions. Philippe is single and pretty much open to anything with anyone. I make a note to get the scoop on Paolo.

Even though Boomerang has a strict no-dating policy within the

office, I decide that "visiting executives"—to use Rhett's phrase—
don't count. All of which brings me right back to Adam, to our night
together, and to the fact that I have to get close enough to dig for
information from him while keeping enough distance between us to
protect my heart.

I'm twenty-two, and already I feel like the real world's too much
to handle.

Philippe catches my eye and gestures for me to come join him.
Excited chatter rises around us, like an ice cream truck's due to
come down the hall any moment.

In the conference room, I slide in close to Philippe, who gives me
a sharp elbow nudge, meant to serve as a greeting.

"How's it going in there with Mr. Mysterioso?"

"Just fine."

He quirks an eyebrow but says nothing. I reach for the pitcher in
front of us and pour us both glasses of water.

"How's it going over there?" I whisper, nodding in Paolo's direction.

Philippe shrugs. "Taken, I think. But I've got my hands full with
you, anyway."

"Yes. I know how high-maintenance I am."

He's kidding, but his comment stings a little. I'm conscious that
he's had to take care of me this last year. That he's the one who
stayed after I drove off all my other friends. He picked me up when
I needed it, and I needed it a lot.

Rhett, Mia, Adam, and a couple of others take seats. Mia smiles
at me, and I ask how she's feeling.

"Much better on dry land," she says.

Brooks—Adam's producer friend—comes into the room, and all
attention shifts to him, like he's a magnet to our metal shavings.
He's husky, with a broad forehead, thick brown hair, and five o'clock
shadow that looks like it begins coming in around noon. He also has

thoughtful brown eyes, and a dazzling smile that puts half the room in his pocket before he's uttered a word.

Adam stands before a wide-screen monitor set into the wall. "All right, gang," he says, and in an instant it's like Brooks has disappeared. Everyone's focus shifts right to him, and he seems so easy with it. No, he seems entitled to it.

For about the twentieth time today, I find myself admiring the tailored lines of his clothes, the way they encase his elegant, powerful body. Like they're a container for his boundless energy and confidence. It's like he's more alive than most of us, somehow, and the clothes are there to give us a fighting chance of functioning in his presence. But that perception could be mine alone.

He continues. "I wanted you all in here so you can take part in what's going to be a historic event—the launch of Blackwood Entertainment as a full-scale film and television studio, starting with this teaser for the first feature we plan to make."

Adam explains that in the future, casting will be done by casting directors, the same way they are for commercials they've made for the website. But today, he tells us, he wants his team around him.

"Besides, it's fun!" Pippa says, and everyone laughs.

Adam grins. "Definitely. And you know I want that to always be the case. We work hard, and we play hard, right?"

Cheers and applause come from everyone at the table.

"*Yeah,* we do," Rhett exclaims with his usual exuberance.

"We're building Boomerang into something really special," Adam says. "I know we can do the same with this. The website has taught us how hungry people are for experiences, for entertainment. Even"—his eyes drift in my direction, and I hold my breath—"connection."

"And stories connect us," Mia murmurs, as though she's taken the thought right from Adam's mind. I feel a pang of envy that they're so in sync and that they share this, share a passion.

"Exactly." Adam nods. "I want to add something fun and worthy and smart to the world of film. Lots of things. I think we can do that and make a bucket of money at the same time."

"Amen," Paolo says.

"Hear, hear, boss," Rhett booms. "We're going to take over the world."

Hoots and whistles follow, and then Brooks connects a hard drive to his laptop and, after a moment, a good-looking guy appears on the flat screen. He's got earrings in both ears, a chiseled brooding face, and a full sleeve of sepia tattoos, spilling out of a sleeveless t-shirt.

"Oh, yum," Pippa breathes.

"Slate for me," says a voice off-screen that I recognize as Brooks's.

The guy gives the camera an incredulous look. "Why the fuck would I *slave* for you?"

"*Slate,* you dumbass. Say your name."

"Oh, well, Christ, why didn't you say that?" He looks into the camera, and it's all smolder and self-assurance. "Grey Blackwood," he says, then fans out his hands in a showgirl gesture and gives the camera a cheesy grin. "*Super star!*"

Mia turns to Adam. "Is that your—"

Adam rubs the back of his neck and grimaces. "Yep, my younger brother, ladies and gentlemen."

"He sure has star quality," Paolo says.

"Yeah," says Brooks. "If you're making a prison documentary."

"Are you kidding?" Sadie says. "I'm sorry, Adam, but your brother is a *hottie* with a capital 'hot.'"

"Is he auditioning?" Mia asks.

"No," Brooks says. "He was just helping me get the light right and reading with some of the actors. Moving on." He taps at the computer, and we move through the next person. A nervous blond girl fumbles even her name, and the rest of her audition is of the same caliber.

"Poor thing," says Mia.

"Well, it's not like someone dragged her out of bed in the middle of the night to audition," Paolo says. "Her name should be the easy part."

"Next," says Adam.

I've been on-screen a couple of times—interviewed at various galas and other events. I never thought much of how I looked other than that the camera seemed to flatten me out somehow, rob me of life and dimension. But it's amazing to see how different the auditions are, how not just the personalities come across but the *life* behind those personalities.

A beautiful African-American girl comes onto the screen.

"Who is *that*?" murmurs Philippe. Like I said, open to anything.

"Hi, there," the girl says into the camera. Her ease and presence are undeniable. The camera sharpens the high planes of her cheekbones, makes her black eyes look even more exotic and luminous. "I'm Beth Pierce."

"She's one of my best friends," Mia tells the room. "So, um . . . totally let that sway your opinion."

But Mia doesn't have to say that. From the minute Beth starts her line-reading, she's head and shoulders above the others.

"Wow, Mia, she's really good," says Paolo.

Mia's eyes shine with pride. "I know. She's a star."

"I agree," says Adam. "What do you think, Brooks?"

"Definitely top three," the producer replies, and to Mia he adds, "But don't tell her that yet."

She nods, but I can see her excitement's not likely to be contained.

Sitting here with the others, present for what might be the launch of someone's dream, I feel a sharp rush of gratitude. I get what makes Adam so fired up about this. I get what it's like to be in on the first stages of something great. In this moment, with all of these people, I want so desperately for Adam to have everything he wants. I just hope, more than ever, that I don't discover anything that gets in the way of that dream.

Chapter 20

Adam

*O*n Fridays, Grey and I usually get the weekend started with a few beers on my back deck as we watch the sun set over the Pacific.

Most of the homes on my street are the vacation residences of people who never take vacations, so the beach is almost always quiet. There's only one person out there now. Linda, my next-door neighbor and an Illinois state lottery winner, picks her way along the sand as she tosses a tennis ball to Lucky, her Labrador retriever.

After the long hours and hustle of a workweek, the quiet's a nice contrast, but it won't last long. Tonight is poker here at the house.

"Drink up," Grey says, handing me a High Tide IPA. "Ethan just texted me. They're coming up on Zuma."

My conscience prickles. I know I shouldn't let Grey drink, but a part of me knows he needs every opportunity he can get to blow off steam. This thing with Mom hurt him bad. I know it's tearing him up inside. A night of beers and cards is a temporary Band-Aid, but it's about as much as he's open to right now. And it's better than him being out all night at clubs.

Besides, who am I to judge? We're both hiding from something in our past. We just cope differently. Grey kicks and thrashes. He rebels and self-sabotages. His struggle is unrestrained. It lacks discipline. That's not me. I lock shit down and build. I achieve. The harder it is for me on the Chloe-front, the more money I make.

We watch Lucky launch into the waves over and over, retrieving the tennis ball. Grey puts away two beers before I finish my first. It's when he cracks open a third one in less than ten minutes that I have to say something.

"Something up, Grey?"

His eyes flick to me, then back to the ocean. I wonder if it's the singing. He hasn't mentioned it since last Sunday morning in the kitchen.

"Your mother called me today," he says.

For fifteen years, she was his mother, too. At least in practice. This "your mother" thing happened when he left home.

"Did you talk to her?" I ask.

"Why would I want to do that, Adam? So she can feed me more bullshit about how much she loves me?" He shakes his head and takes another long sip. "No way."

"She's trying, Grey. If she called, then she's trying."

"Out of *guilt*. For *Dad*."

I don't reply, because guilt can be a powerful motivator. On the right person, guilt gets things done. I've built an entire company on it.

I feel Grey look at me, like he's following my thoughts and is about to mention Chloe, but thankfully the doorbell rings.

Rhett, Ethan, and Ethan's buddy Jason come in. Brooks arrives right on their heels. We do the introduction thing for Jason's sake.

He's the only new recruit to the game, since Paolo cycled out in favor of samba night.

We grab drinks, Rhett puts out snacks, and eventually we sit down. I deal, and we play a few hands, the money moving around the table.

My favorite part of playing, besides winning, is observing how they each play according to their personalities. Ethan is straight out there, strategic but not a big one for bluffing. Jason's a little more canny, analyzing the other players' moves, making calculated bets. Rhett thinks every hand is the best hand. Brooks has an endless supply of funny stories about actors and location shoots, but he's a multitasker. He can entertain and stay competitive. And Grey plays like his head's on fire, jumping up from the table every couple of deals, acting like he's bluffing when he's got a straight flush, just generally being a train wreck and taking everyone else with him.

With Ethan right across the table, the mystery of him and Alison is alive and kicking in my mind. What happened? Graham wouldn't have given Alison that look if they'd just grown apart. I remember Ali talking about mistakes on Halloween night and wonder if she meant Ethan.

I force myself to make what's now become a familiar mental adjustment—steering my thoughts away from Alison—but I can't pass up the opportunity to learn more about my future investor and partner.

"What can you tell me about Graham Quick?" I ask Ethan.

Jason almost chokes on his beer. "Shit. There's a question."

"Meaning?" I look at Ethan.

He shrugs. "Graham defies description in a lot of ways."

That's nowhere near enough for me. "But you knew him fairly well. You dated his daughter for how long?"

Ethan shifts uncomfortably, sending Jason a look. "About two years."

"Hey." Grey spreads his hands. "We're playing poker here."

I'm not trying to be a jerk. It's just that this man wants to own a large share of my company in exchange for a large amount of capital, and his daughter's installed in my ranks. I've done all I can on paper, but I can't miss this chance at a deeper view.

"No, it's okay." Ethan shuffles the cards, his face a little grim. "I mean, you've seen for yourself," he says. "Graham's got a big personality. Kind of a steamroller. Lots of jokes and smiles, glad-handing, big tipper. When he likes you, he's all in—trips, expensive restaurants, tickets to games. I haven't been on the other end, but I imagine it's ugly."

Which is what I'd already figured.

"What else?"

Ethan picks up his cards. "After Alison and I ended, he kept in touch for a while. Email. Phone calls. He sent me Lakers tickets for my birthday. Box seats."

Interesting that he said "ended."

"You said he liked you, right? You'd become a part of his family."

He nods. "I thought that too. And then I thought maybe he was trying to get me back for his daughter. To make her happy."

So Ethan left. And she didn't want him to. This development only creates more questions for me.

I look at my hand, carve off two cards and toss them to him. "But you don't think so?"

"I'm sure that was part of it," he says, handing me two back. "But it felt too determined. And kind of impersonal. Like he needed me to fill the son-shaped slot in his life. It felt like I could have been anyone." Ethan nods to himself. "Yeah. Something like that. I mean, he got to know all about me. Brought me on skiing trips and bought me a custom set of golf clubs. He'd always show up with something. Sports bios. Stuff he knew I'd like. So, it was personal to that degree. It just felt—"

"Engineered?" I offer. But I think "manipulative." And empty.

I move my cards around, arranging them in a full house and keeping my face neutral.

This is the man I'm entering into a business arrangement with, and that worries me. Worse, he's Alison's father. As the night wears on, I find that worries me even more.

When I wake up, the sky is just starting to lighten from black to purple.

Saturdays are harder because I don't have a company to rush off to in Century City. They're calmer and I have more time to think, and thinking usually takes me to Chloe.

She hated early mornings. Anything before nine was an ungodly hour to her.

It's been a few days since she's been on my mind this clearly. Maybe even a week. That makes me bury my face into my pillow and press my eyes shut until they ache.

I don't want to stop remembering her, but it's the guilt, it's the fucking guilt that somehow I avoided the pain and it felt good. The guilt of knowing that it wasn't work or surf that gave me the relief. It was another girl.

Even with the work complications aside, even if she wanted me, if I could get to her, if I could somehow hold onto the girl who jumped into my arms at the Gallianos', Alison and I can never happen. I don't have room for her in my head, or in my life. I don't have the heart to fuck up again and lose the girl I love.

Just . . . no.

I roll onto my back. Then I glance at the sketch that started in Chloe's notebook and ended up on my skin.

I remember the day she drew it.

She was lying on her stomach under a tree by the art studios on campus, the white page slowly filling with birds and clouds under her sure artist's hand, her battered combat boots just peeking out of her long dress. At 5'2" and petite, everything was long on her. Everything she wore had frayed edges—and usually ink or paint stains—like her hands almost always did too.

In my button-down shirts, with my computer science major, she was completely exotic to me. My opposite in every way. My compliment. We were just freshmen at Princeton. Barely there a few months. I was already in love with her.

I remember noticing that day how her long auburn hair looked red when the sunlight hit it. At night, by candlelight, it looked almost black. I remember thinking she was like that. Fire and darkness, rolled into a beautiful girl who had my heart.

Chloe had set down her pencil. She'd looked at me and laughed.

So her, I'd thought. To laugh when most people would only smile.

Something on your mind? she'd asked.

And I remember being too embarrassed to tell her how much I felt right then, under a tree on campus. Just watching her. So I nodded to her sketchbook.

"Why birds all the time, Chloe? They're kind of beaky and their scaly legs are freaky. They're freaky and beaky."

"No way, Adam. Birds are perfect creatures! But not all of them. Just the flying ones. Ostriches? Chickens? Dumb. A waste of feathers. Birds are supposed to fly. *They're supposed to soar up the clouds—not be stuck on land. Why be something if you can't actually* be *that something?"*

"I love you, Chloe. But sometimes you make no sense."

"I love you, Adam. But sometimes when you pretend I make no sense, yet you clearly think I make the most sense ever but you're too proud to admit it? Then I really *love you."*

My throat gets raw, and my chest feels like it's stretching, about to rip open. I look outside and watch the waves through my window blur and then clear as I lock it back down. Shut everything back.

Will I ever be free of this? She's not even here anymore. Why doesn't it stop?

The lockdown isn't working. My skin feels like it's going to break open. I feel like I'm going to break open.

My mind seems to want to torture me, because I remember that it's Saturday. Alison has her Boomerang date tonight.

And that puts me over the edge.

I jump out of bed. "Grey!" I yell. I pull on swim trunks, yank sweats over them, and tug a beanie onto my head. By the time I grab my keys off my dresser, Grey's standing at my bedroom door, pinching the bridge of his nose.

"Fuck, it's early. What time is it?"

"Early. Six."

He lets out a long breath. "I think I'm still drunk." After poker, Brooks and Grey went out to the bar at Malibu Inn. Grey's bloodshot eyes finally focus on me. "How you doing, bro?"

"How do you think I'm doing?"

He frowns at the anger in my voice. I rarely let my temper go.

"Get your board loaded up." I want the water. I want his company. I want to shake off the image of Chloe drawing in her sketchbook, and of Alison, staring at my shoulder like she wants to know. Like she'd listen and understand.

Grey doesn't move. "You know there's no magic wave, right?"

"What the hell are you talking about?"

He shrugs. "You act like going out there and surfing is going to fix it. Like this film company's going to be the thing that saves you. Same thing you did with Boomerang. Same thing you're doing with me. Nothing's going to save you, Adam. Not until you face your shit. When are you doing to do that? When are you going to face your shit?"

"Good advice from someone who's wasting his life sitting around. You call partying every night facing your shit, Grey? Avoiding Mom's calls? You're like a three-year-old having a tantrum. You're making her—and Dad—miserable."

He's quiet for a moment, eyes blazing. "At least I don't go around pretending everything's fine. You're a coward."

I almost punch him. "Fuck you, Grey." I push past him and head to the garage. I open my door and get up on the footboard, pulling my surfboard onto the rack on my Range Rover. The door opens and Grey comes out. He heads to the other side of my car and climbs up on the passenger side, snapping my board in place. Then he loads his short board up.

At Nicholas Canyon, we pull our wetsuits on, jog over the sand and throw ourselves into the water without saying a word. It isn't until we're floating side by side on the sea, the sun glittering in the water all around us, that Grey speaks.

"Sorry, Adam," he says.

"Yeah . . . me too."

Chapter 21

Alison

I cue Persephone into a trot, hoping to move her into a canter, though that might be a bit much for today. This is only the second time she's let me put a saddle on her and take her into the training ring in the backyard, so we're both a little skittish. But I can tell by the way she keeps her tail high and her ears angled back toward me that she's excited and alert to my signals.

"How's it coming with Suede?" my father calls from his chaise on the back deck. Just like him to jump to a problem instead of appreciating the small triumph in front of him.

Persephone tosses her head, white mane flying, like she's personally affronted that he'd mention another horse in front of her. I can feel the tension in her haunches, the stuttering rhythm to her gait. She'd love nothing better than to dump me into dirt, but I can't let that happen. For her sake.

"He's coming along, Dad," I call. It's true. It just might not be *quite* as true as I'd like.

"Joaquin says he's having a hell of a time healing those abscesses. You know, I can't pour money into that horse forever."

"We just got him," I remind my dad. "It won't be forever."

"No," my father says. "It won't."

It feels like everything makes him impatient lately. Every evening, he grills me about Adam, about the other employees, about the new complex and the equipment being installed there. I don't know what he's looking for, but I tell him everything I know. And every night he seems disappointed, like I'm not delivering on some promise I don't remember having made.

Gathering up a little slack on the reins, I try to show Persephone who's in control, but she's not having it. I force her forward a few paces, but she stops suddenly, hindquarters dropping, and I know she's about to rear.

"You've got spirit, P, I'll give you that." I pull my left rein to my hip. Persephone's head follows, and she has no choice but to turn in a circle. She goes around three times, head jerking in protest, before she gets that I'm the one in charge. I hate playing the bully, but it's the language we speak. And keeping her in line means keeping her here. Cared for and loved, with plentiful food, the best care, and acres of soft grass as her playground.

We play a bit more tug-of-war, but finally she settles down and moves into a smooth trot. It's hard not to throw my arms around her powerful neck and give her a hug, but that's not affection in horse terms. Instead, I pat her back and give the crest of her mane a gentle pinch, mirroring the way horses groom each other. I smile because there's apology in the soulful, long-lashed eye that stares up at me.

"See, Dad?" I say, looking up at the deck.

But he's already gone.

After my shower, I sit in front of my vanity in my towel and finally let myself think about the night ahead of me. My date. I smile a little to myself because I'm gaming the system, as my dad would say. I skipped all of Cookie's choices and went right for the hottest-looking guy from the "men looking for men" section. Of course, it took a little cajoling, and a promise of a future date with Philippe, who was only too happy to provide a picture.

At least I'll be relaxed tonight, for what feels like the first time in ages. And I'll have done all three dates.

My mother knocks and then enters, dressed as she almost always is on a Saturday night—for an evening out. This time, she's wearing a simple black sheath and a double strand of freshwater pearls, which tells me it's nothing too formal.

"How's Persephone doing, darling?" she asks. The endearment means she hasn't started into the cocktails yet. Where some people—like me—get lubricated and loose, she gets more and more brittle the more she drinks. Sharper-tongued and pinched. Maybe her reserves come down when she's drunk, and her unhappiness comes to the surface.

"Really great," I say. I take my shoes off the tufted bench across from me and gesture for her to sit. "She just needs a little work."

"And Suede?"

Funny that both parents have had the same questions for me today. Usually, they seem miles apart in every way.

"He's good. We're still having trouble with his hooves, but his teeth are good, and he's gaining weight. I think we'll be able to save him."

"That's wonderful," she says, and I know she means it.

Staring into the mirror, I see the reflection of the two of us. She could be my older sister, thanks to good genes and some injectables. Her blond hair is lighter than mine—almost platinum, and her lower jaw is fuller, the only part of her to really show her age.

But she's still so beautiful. Still has this amazing bearing—like a queen.

"Where are you off to tonight?" I ask.

"An art auction in support of the Children's Hospital," she says. "We already have early bids totaling a half-million dollars. I'm quite proud of some of the wallets I pried open this time around."

"That's wonderful, Mom."

In this way, we're all alike, we Quicks. When we want something, we're dogged.

"I'm frankly surprised I got your father to come along," she says, smoothing a nonexistent wrinkle from her skirt. "He hates Venice Beach, especially anything on Abbot-Kinney. He thinks he'll be infected by hippies."

I laugh. "He's not that bad, mom."

She frowns, and it's like a tiny spell's been broken. I don't know what she's looking for from me. Just sitting here with her makes me feel guilty and angry at them both. If they're so unhappy, why stay together? I know that family is everything, but is family only about the papers you sign and the promises you make?

"Anyway," I say, trying to move us into different territory. "I don't think Venice Beach is overrun by hippies."

"I'm sure not," she murmurs. Then she gives me a smile that makes her eyes look even sadder. "You have such beautiful hair, Alison. Why don't you wear it down tonight?"

I'm surprised. Usually, she wants me to tidy it up into a chignon or at least a ponytail. But I guess that's when we're going to more formal events—not a fake date with a guy who's going to be looking around at every other guy in the room.

"It just takes so much work," I tell her. "And I never know how I want to style it."

"What are you going to wear?"

I gesture to the bed where Philippe has laid out a silvery-blue dress with an asymmetrical neckline and a chunky leather belt. Over that, he's left me a choice of a thigh-length leather duster or a camel cashmere throw.

"Depends on how much of a bad ass you want to be," he told me and laid the leather duster closer to the dress with a wink.

"That's a beautiful color for you," my mother says. "Brings out your eyes." She rises and comes to stand behind me. Lifting my still-wet hair, she brushes it over one shoulder, smoothing it with her hands. "Why don't you curl it just a bit, and wear it over one shoulder, like this? The one left bare by the dress. I've seen girls doing it."

I nod, and we both stare at my reflection for a second.

I feel a childlike impulse to ask her to brush my hair for me. But as I open my mouth, she says, "Well, I'll leave you alone," and I keep the words trapped inside me.

Instead, I nod, and for a moment we both stare at my reflection in the mirror.

"You're a lovely girl," she says, and bends down to kiss my head. "Have some fun tonight," she adds. "It doesn't have to be all work, every minute."

"I'll have fun. I promise."

"Good," she replies. And I want to tell her to do the same, that she should find something that makes her happy—even if it's not my dad.

She leaves, shutting the door silently behind her. I stare back at the mirror and pick up my hair dryer. I think I'll style my hair like she told me—keeping it in loose waves over one shoulder. Who knows? Maybe I'll like it.

Chapter 22

Adam

When I get to The Ivy just after eight o'clock, I see Brooks, Julia, and Carla already seated at a table on the outside patio.

I'm here to meet them. My best friend, Brooks. My ex and occasional sex buddy, Julia. Her cousin, Carla. But as the hostess leads me to the table, my eyes scan for Alison. The Boomerang dates are always the subject of office gossip. Just took a little judicious eavesdropping—something I don't usually bother with—to find out she'd be here.

I see her right away. She's sitting at a table just past mine, laughing, her long curls shifting over her exposed shoulder, her hand resting on the stem of a martini glass.

I've almost reached my table, but I stop and allow myself a moment to look at her. She looks amazing in a blue dress, her skin smooth and flawless. The patio is dim, lit by string lights and candles, but she has a brightness that's undeniable. I'm drawn to her like she's the sun. Like she has some gravitational pull over me.

I want her. I can't kid myself anymore. I want her like I haven't wanted anyone since Chloe. But I can't go after her without blowing up my plans for Blackwood Films.

I still wanted to see her tonight, though.

Even if she is on a date with another guy.

Her date smiles at her from across the table. A slender guy in a sharp navy jacket with a trim five-o'clock shadow, he's a dead ringer for Jake Gyllenhaal. Alison laughs again, tilting her head to the side. She looks relaxed, like she's having fun, and like she might even like Jake.

"Adam!" Julia stands and moves right in for a kiss on the lips. "Hi, gorgie-gorge!"

"Hi, Jules," I say, and wonder if it would be rude to draw the back of my hand over my mouth. I feel a slick coating of her lipstick on me—which is red like her hair. Not Chloe red. Julia's hair is almost fire-truck red. I have the odd feeling that she's just branded me.

"Sit, sit!" she says, pulling me into the chair next to her.

The table is small and Julia's arm stays linked through mine even though I'm tense, definitely not loving it. Julia doesn't seem to notice.

Brooks and Carla—Julia's cousin, an olive-skinned girl with a sleek black bob—break off what seems like an intense conversation to greet me.

"Ordered you a bottle of your favorite," Brooks says, tipping his head to the open Roar Pinot Noir on the table.

"Good man." Wine is the perfect choice. Maybe it'll take the edge off. Or maybe it'll get annoyed that I have to drink it with my left hand.

A waiter sweeps by, pouring me a glass, and I manage to get in the right frame of mind to make casual conversation, even though what I really want to do is throw Julia off and tell Jake Gyllenhaal to head home.

"What are you working on these days, Brooksie?" Julia asks, taking a healthy sip of her drink. She thinks it's hysterical to give people ridiculous nicknames.

Brooks and Julia know some of the same people, both being in the business, but Brooks's stock is higher. He's been working with the top producers and directors in the business for years at Lionsgate, while Julia's still trying to land a speaking role in a feature.

He casually mentions a few projects he's wrapping up before he comes over to Blackwood Films full-time. A few heads turn at nearby tables and Julia's eyes light up, but Brooks is done talking work. He drops his arm on the back of Carla's chair. "Adam, listen to this. Carla was just telling me she's been a dog groomer, a singing bartender, a preschool teacher, a PhD candidate in—what was it?"

I'm not surprised he's changing the subject. Unlike most film guys I know, Brooks doesn't like getting his ass kissed. You actually have to impress the guy to win him over. And he's interested in everything, which explains the chemistry I see sparking between him and Carla, who fights off a smile like she's embarrassed at his attention but also loving it.

"Nineteenth-century German philosophers." She smiles. "You know. Super sexy stuff."

"Now she's a war journalist," Brooks says. "She just got back from Afghanistan. And, dude. She's our age. We're losers, Blackwood. We gotta step up our game." He leans back in his chair. "Can you believe she's done all that?"

I take a sip of my wine. "No," I say. "I Kant."

Carla and Brooks laugh but Julia lifts her menu. "I'm starving, you guys. I did two hours of Bikram today. It almost killed me."

Brooks lifts his eyebrows. "Death by yoga." He turns to Carla. "Bet you didn't see that in the Graveyard of Empires."

"I can't say that I did."

Our waiter arrives to tell us the specials. I listen, but I'm distracted by Julia, who hasn't let go of me yet. She's started to knead my forearm and I'm not sure what the purpose of that is. It feels like she's prepping to draw blood.

I want to pull away, but Julia has a temper and I don't want to cause a scene. Maybe I'm here to see Ali, but Julia's here to see me. We've done this sort of thing a few times. A casual night. Dinner. Then back to my place. I understand her expectations.

While the waiter gives us a full detail of the grilled salmon, I glance at Ali's table and catch her looking at me. Her eyebrows are drawn down a little in confusion, or maybe in irritation. My guess is she's not happy about seeing me here.

Does she think I'm cramping her style? It's looking like a love connection between her and ole' Jake—who now holds one of her hands in his, pretending to carefully examine her bracelet. Like he cares. Like any guy fucking cares about a bracelet. Besides, it's her earrings that are meaningful to her.

"Hey," Brooks says, leaning my way and lowering his voice. "Isn't that Alison Quick?"

"Yeah," I say. "It is." I remove my hand from Julia's grip and stand. "Excuse me a minute."

Julia blinks up at me with wide eyes. "What's up, Scoobalicious?"

"Just saw someone from work. I'm going to go say hello."

And maybe punch a guy I don't even know.

Chapter 23

Alison

*M*y "date" Paul glances over my shoulder, and his eyes widen. "Oh, my biscuits and gravy," he says in his honeyed Mississippi drawl. "Is that Adam Blackwood coming our way?"

I know it must be, so I take a long fortifying sip of my second ginger martini and turn. And there he is, approaching our table with an expression of feigned nonchalance that's as transparent as air. Well, non-LA air.

"Try to pretend you want to have sex with me," I whisper to Paul. "Or at least like you *don't* want to have sex with him."

"I'll give it my best, darlin'," he whispers back, as his eyes rake across Adam. "But that's a tall order."

Adam's wearing dark jeans and a midnight blue sweater that looks soft and touchable. And does amazing things for his broad shoulders and long, elegant torso.

As he comes closer, the amber light from the nearby space heaters shadows and brightens his face, making him look brooding one second and opaque the next. He smiles, and his whole face softens. I feel the usual prickle of attraction, a fluttering in my belly like I'm about to deliver a speech before a massive audience. Or take off my clothes before a much smaller one.

We say our hellos, and I introduce him to Paul, who, to his credit, affects a look of only mild interest and gives Adam a curt handshake. Then he settles his arm along the back of my chair in a possessive manner that makes me smile.

Adam sees, and his own lips turn down a bit. "You two look like you're having fun," he says. "So I won't keep you. I just wanted to stop by for a second and say hi."

I take another long sip of my drink, grateful for its sedating effects. "I'm surprised to see you, actually." I look over at his table and spot Brooks, who's sitting next to a gorgeous brunette with a sleek asymmetrical bob. Beside her slouches a redhead, with one of those long, large-featured faces just made for film and a hostile look in her eyes.

Adam nods. "I know. I just wanted to make sure everything was . . . going okay."

I'm brought back to my first Boomerang date—my disastrous reunion with Ethan. Now that all seems so far away—like something that happened years, rather than months, ago.

Paul's arm moves to my shoulder, and he squeezes me close to him. He's definitely earning that date with Philippe.

"Don't worry," he says. "I promise she won't end up in the trunk of my car."

I'm mid-sip, and that makes me choke down the spiced liquid. It sears my throat, and the laughing makes me light-headed, makes the table float for just a moment. I do love this feeling of drifting in my own skin, warm and buoyant.

A waiter approaches, and I tap the rim of my glass, signaling for another. Then I drain the rest of my martini.

"That's right," I say. "I'm more of a strapped-to-the-roof kind of girl."

Paul laughs like that's the funniest thing he's ever heard. But Adam's lips sharpen into a thin line, and his posture stiffens.

"Maybe you should go a little easy, Alison."

"I'm fine," I tell him. And I'm better than fine. I think of Persephone, trotting along the beach, and the word "unfettered" comes to mind. "Maybe you should go back to *your* date. She looks like she wants to poke your eyes out with a swizzle stick."

"She'll be fine," Adam says. "I'm not worried about *Julia*."

"Well, maybe you should be," I tell him. "Seriously, Adam, she looks like she's about to have an aneurysm." I drop my hand onto Paul's knee, not because I'm trying to play at an attraction between us but because my mind keeps telling me to reach out and touch Adam, to at least brush my fingers across the soft sheen of his fitted sweater. "Anyway, we're fine here, aren't we?"

Brooks rises from the other table and heads across the patio toward us. He's pulled back his hair into a sleek ponytail, but he still looks rugged and rough-edged, so different from Adam's polish and grace.

He greets me with a big grin, shakes Paul's hand and then claps Adam on the shoulder. "I'm heading to the can," he proclaims. "You better get back to the table before there's a meltdown."

Adam's jaw flexes minutely, but that's the only indication he gives of his annoyance. "All right, man. Thanks."

Brooks passes through the open doors into the restaurant, and Adam looks back down at me, his gray eyes light and dark at once. Warm and cold like the night. Like the way I feel.

Then he shifts his attention to Paul. "Put her in a taxi, all right?" It's definitely not a question.

Paul nods. "I'll make sure she gets home in one piece."

Adam hesitates, like he wants to say more. And I wait, because I want him to say more, too, though I'm not sure what I want to hear.

"Okay, great," he says. "Goodnight."

I watch him return to the table and engage in some kind of whispered exchange with Julia, who gestures like she's conducting an orchestra and spits what seems like a nonstop string of words at him. I'm glad I can't hear them though I'm burning with curiosity, too.

"Someone is in *trouble,*" Paul sing-songs.

"Most definitely."

The waiter delivers another round, and Paul and I clink glasses. Some far-off part of me weighs in with disapproval—both at the drinking and at the way I treated Adam. But it's easy to shrink that part to the tiniest dot. Another sip makes it disappear completely.

Paul and I finish our meal, sharing plates of chicken enchiladas and lobster macaroni and cheese, which taste like absolute heaven to me now. We chat a little bit about our work, and Paul talks my ear off about his job as an environmental activist. His passion gives me a giddy feeling, it's so infectious.

When it's my turn, I find I can't talk about my father's investment company or Boomerang or Adam. So, instead, I talk about Suede, about finding just the right caretaker for her and about Persephone and our first successful ride along the beach.

"Oh my God," Paul breathes. "I'm terrified of horses."

"You shouldn't be," I tell him. "Next to an LA County Commissioner, a horse is a kitten."

"True."

Our conversation turns to Philippe, and of course I make him sound like the absolute best thing since Kate Spade clutches, which he is. I promise a date soon, in payment for this evening.

"No need to repay me," he says, and leans in to give me a sweet kiss on the cheek. "I've had an awesome time."

He insists on paying the bill, and we weave our way toward the street, passing Adam's table. I feel his eyes on me as Paul hooks his arm around my waist, shoring me up. A cab is a great idea.

Paul and I stand on the street for what feels like hours, watching cars crisscross the busy road—but no taxi.

"Why don't you go on?" I tell him. "I'll grab my cell phone from my car and call someone for a ride."

"Are you sure?"

"Yes, I promise, I'll be fine."

He nods and gives me another kiss on the cheek and a long hug. It feels amazing to be touched by someone, and I find myself holding on for a second. But I'm also so aware of how close all my feelings are to the edge, of how unseemly it would be to peel aside a gay man's jacket and burrow in like a mole.

We part ways, and I wander down Alden toward my car. The ground tilts a bit, and I stop for a second, pressing a hand to my eyes to try to stave off my dizzy feeling.

"You have great taste," says a voice right beside me.

I turn to find Adam standing on the curb, hands thrust into his pockets, smiling at me.

"What?"

He motions to the sleek, smoke-colored sports car a foot or so away. "That's mine."

I straighten up, taking in the car's aerodynamic lines. It is exactly the car that Adam should have—powerful, sexy, and in a color that matches his eyes.

"I thought you were getting a cab."

"I am," I tell him. "I thought you were placating your date."

"That ship has sailed, sorry to say." But he doesn't look sorry at all.

"Where'd everyone else go?"

"I sent them with Brooks. They're fine. Let me drive you."

Not one part of me feels like launching even a token protest, so I just say, "That would be great, thanks."

The car alarm chirps, and he leans down and opens the passenger door.

I fold onto the seat. The inside of the car smells like leather and like Adam's cologne. Again, the scent of him hollows my stomach. I want to curl into it, but I buckle my seat belt and focus on keeping my hands to myself, instead.

We discover we're both in Malibu, which seems impossible and perfect at the same time. I imagine Adam walking along the surf at sunset, water drenching the hem of his pants, breeze blowing his shirt against his lean frame.

God, he better get me home.

We wind along the side streets, zipping around traffic. Adam lives on the beach north of Point Dume, while I'm up on the canyon side, with all the ranch properties. We compare notes on our favorite restaurants and the best coffee spots. I hear us talking, and we sound so normal. But I don't feel normal. I feel drugged, swimming in the feeling of just being close to him.

I sense something gathering inside Adam, a tension in his forearms, his face. His focus hones as the road starts to clear. When there's nothing but winding open asphalt ahead of us, he looks at me. "You ready?"

The next thing I know, my back thuds against the seat.

Zero to sixty in less than three seconds feels like taking off in a rocket.

The car cuts left and right as we weave along the coast at a speed that I didn't think was possible, the ocean blurring on my left, the canyon walls on my right. It's a thrill, a thousand times more exhilarating than any rollercoaster ride. I squeal with the pleasure of it and then laugh because I've never been the squealing type.

I glance at Adam. He's so zoned in, so lost in what he's doing.

Watching him, I feel like I'm seeing something deeply revealing, almost intimate, and the sight lights every part of me.

He decelerates after a few more seconds and looks at me. "Highway Patrol always sets up around the next bend," he says. The intensity leaves his eyes, and he smiles. "So what did you think?"

"I think I've never had so much fun in a car."

He raises an eyebrow. "Really?" he asks, grinning. "Never?"

My face heats as I remember.

I *have* had more fun in a car. *A lot* more fun.

I don't answer, because there's no need. I know we're both thinking about it, both remembering our bodies together, the perfection of our hands and lips on each other. I smile to myself, because even though we can't have that again, we can have this—this wild, exhilarating ride.

Chapter 24

Adam

As we fly through a yellow light passing Malibu Inn, I downshift and glance at Ali. I find her watching me with an expression like she's dreaming with her eyes open.

"What's on your mind, Ms. Quick?"

"You love this, don't you?"

It takes me a moment to realize she's talking about driving the Bugatti—not about being with her.

I nod. "Cars are something my dad and I always did together. He runs a few restaurants and bars back East. He was always busy. I didn't see him at all during the week or on Saturdays, but Sundays we spent together. We went on drives or to car shows. We took care of his car collection."

She's still watching me, like she wants to hear more. I let myself keep going.

"When I was thirteen, he bought a Shelby Cobra kit, and we spent that entire year building the car from scratch on Sundays. It turned out perfect. Well, almost."

"Oh, no. What happened?"

"My younger brother, Grey. He was around eight at the time and he didn't have the attention span to help out. I don't think he has that attention span now, at almost nineteen, but anyway. Dad and I had just finished the car. The paint was barely dry when Grey flew into the garage on his skateboard and wiped out. The board popped out from beneath him and smacked the Cobra's driver-side door. The jury's still out on whether he did it intentionally. He never copped to it."

Ali laughs. "Poor kid."

"Poor Adam. I busted my ass for a year on that car." I shake my head, remembering. "I was so pissed at him."

"What about your dad? Wasn't he angry?"

"Oh, he went red. But he never punished Grey. See, our dad was always telling us it's good to leave evidence of your impact on the world. It's why he's into restaurants and real estate . . . 'Get out there, make your mark,' he'd say to us. 'It means you're living.' Well, Grey quoted those words right back to him. He stood there and told our dad he'd left evidence of his impact on the world on that Cobra. He got off scot-free. The car's still in our garage back home. Still has the dent, too."

Ali giggles. "Your brother sounds like a handful."

"You have no idea." I realize I've been talking her ear off. "What about you? Tell me about the horses you love so much. Do you do dressage—that kind of thing?" That's about as knowledgeable as I can sound on the subject of horses.

"When I was younger, I did." She turns in the seat a little, to face me better. "Show-jumping. Competitions, horse shows. All of that."

"You don't anymore?"

"No," she says. "We had to put down my horse, Zenith, a few years ago. I loved him. I've never found another horse I trusted like that. Who trusted me. Now I just ride. And rehab them. I've grown to love that just as much."

"What does rehabilitating involve?"

She tells me about how it varies, case by case. Some have poor health, or injuries that require nurturing that's primarily physical. Others need treatment that focuses on their behavior, or rebuilding trust. She tells me she's only been rehabbing horses for about a year, but she sounds sure of what she's saying and passionate about it.

"The ones who've lost the ability to trust are the hardest," she says, "but those are my favorite to rescue. They're the most rewarding."

Some invisible force pulls my eyes to her; I couldn't stop it if my life depended on it. The canyon walls rise higher, and shadows bleed across the dashboard. All I can see is her shining white-blond hair and the sparkle of the charm bracelet on her wrist. I want to reach for her hand.

"Will you show me?" I ask instead.

"You want to see my horses?"

"Yes." But the truth is I want to see *her* with her horses.

I have to focus on the road again as we reach the turnoff to her home. The engine rumbles deeper as I decelerate, a reluctant, displeased growl that's a good reflection of my mood. This drive went too fast. My time with her is almost over. What an idiot. I should've driven fifteen miles an hour all the way here.

"How about tonight?" Ali says. "If you wanted to . . . How about right now?"

"Sure," I say. "Now works."

We reach her house, and Ali gives me the gate code. Heavy wrought-iron gates swing open, and I drive into the property.

I rarely come up to this part of Malibu, with its sprawling

ranches. Suddenly, it feels like we come from different sides of the track, even though my house is only a mile away and on the beach side of the highway. My place is house, sand, ocean. Simple. This, I see as I pull inside, is an estate.

A long crushed-oyster-shell driveway leads to a main house, which sits up on a slope. Even from a distance, I can tell it's massive—a Mediterranean villa, all stone columns and topiary hedges. To my left, I see the white fencing of a horse enclosure. To the right, well-lit paths weave through landscaped gardens.

Wealth doesn't intimidate me. I grew up rich and got a lot richer on my own. I like finer things. More than that I like the ability to execute on just about any desire I have. It's not the extravagance on display here that unsettles me. I can't really place what it is. But I feel a sudden protective urge to whisk Alison away from this place.

She directs me to a tidy white building with a red tile roof. She's practically out of my car before I put it in park, but she waits for me to join her.

"I know it's hard to believe," she says, "but I usually don't ride in dresses."

"That's not what my sources say, but okay. I believe you."

She laughs and slips off her heels, slinging them over her shoulder. "Hope you're okay with a little hay and horse smell."

"I'm okay with making hay. Does that count?"

"Blackwood, are you flirting with me?"

"Sorry, Quick. I'm here strictly for the horses."

"Then you won't be disappointed." She drops her heels by a shrub and unlatches double doors. They're heavy, and I'm mesmerized by the sight of her, barefoot, in an elegant dress, using all the strength of her slender body to slide the doors open. She steps inside, hits the lights, and twirls around, flourishing a hand. "Behold! The glory of a real-life stable."

Everything, I think as I follow her inside. Everything she does when she's playful this way is perfect.

Inside, there are four stalls on either side of a central dirt corridor dusted with strands of hay. Leather gear hangs from hooks along the walls, and the smell of horse and hay is potent. I glance at Ali, who's pulling on some boots by the door that are way too big for her.

"That's Persephone," she says, smiling. "She's my girl." A horse peeks out of the first stall on the right. She's a stunning animal, big blue eyes, a powerful neck, and a golden coat that shines in the light.

"She's . . . extraordinary," I say, stepping closer.

I don't think I've ever looked at a horse the way I am now, through Ali's eyes. Knowing what she told me on Halloween night about how much she trusts them. Knowing how much they mean to her.

Persephone looks from me to Ali, ears flipping back and forth. She's curious, but she looks intelligent and somehow regal.

"Thank you," Ali says, patting her neck. "I think so too."

She takes me to another stall, where a horse is hidden in shadows at the far end. "That's Suede. We're just at the beginning of a long road, but I know it'll be worth it. I just picked him up a week ago."

"I know," I say.

Ali looks at me. "You do?"

"I've heard you on the phone. In our office."

"Oh," she says. "Sorry. I try not to take personal calls—"

"It's okay. Don't apologize. I like hearing you talk about horses. It's sexy. All that talk about teaching softness by being soft," I repeat her own words back to her. "Knowing just how much hard is required."

Ali smiles. "Soft just means responsive."

"Still hot."

"In horse talk, a hot horse is one that has plenty of energy to burn."

I open my hands. "I rest my case."

She laughs and clomps over in her sexy dress and huge boots to a wood locker in the corner, rummaging inside. "Here, Suede," she says, coming back to my side with two carrots.

Slowly, the horse moves forward, and I see an animal that's in much worse shape than Persephone. Suede's eyes are glazed, he's less muscular, and his coat doesn't have the same luster.

"He's a little nervous," Ali says, "but give him a second. Here. Give him your bare hand first so he can smell you. Then you can feed him."

Ali hands me the carrots, then makes a kissing sound. "Come here, gorgeous boy."

I step closer to her. "How's this?"

Ali rolls her eyes at me then turns back to the stall. "It's okay, Suede. You can trust him."

Finally, Suede comes close enough. He doesn't peek his head out of the stall like Persephone, though, so I reach carefully inside.

"Hey, there," I say, holding my hand out. Suede's horse lips flutter around on my palm for a few seconds. "No pressure, buddy, but it's really important we get along. I need to stay on your owner's good side." Suede smells the carrot, his head bobbing toward it, so I give it to him. "There you go. Good for the eyesight, carrots. But don't eat too many or you'll turn orange."

I feel Ali smiling beside me and find that I'm smiling too.

"He likes you."

"Well, he's my favorite horse. I think he senses that." My eyes go to her bare shoulder. She has goose bumps.

Before I can think about it, I reach out and run my hand along her arm. Her skin is smooth, softer than anything I've ever felt.

Alison goes perfectly still. I keep going, drawing my hand over her shoulder and burying my fingers into her hair. "Are you cold?"

Her lips part as she inhales. "No, I'm . . . I'm fine." She shakes her head a little, then she lets out her breath, long and slow. Her blue eyes stare into mine, open and gentle. I'm so here with her. I want anything she'll give me, but it's more than that. I'm going to lose my mind if I can't have her.

"Tell me you want this," I say.

She's been drinking. I can't forget that. She's sobered up since the restaurant some, but there's no denying it.

Her hand brushes along my chest and stills on my neck. "I want this."

That's all I need. I crush my lips to hers, and it's fast—and hot. I can't take it slow. Our tongues are darting, doing an urgent dance as I pick her up and lift her against the wall. She wraps her arms around my neck and I yank her dress up to get her legs around me. Her heavy boots clunk to the ground, one, then the other. Then her ankles lock behind me, and she pulls me in tight. I let out a groan at the feeling, her pressed to me, open for me.

Alison feels me and moans low, kissing my jaw and my neck. I shift, freeing up one hand, and try to draw the sleeve of her dress down, but it won't budge.

"Ali. I want to see you." I don't have to explain. Both of my hands are occupied, holding her up.

She straightens and tugs at a zipper along her ribs. Her blue dress loosens and slips to her waist.

Chapter 25

Alison

I can't think of anything else but Adam.

I don't want anything else, either.

He looks down at my body, and I drink in his expression, offering myself to him, letting myself be seen in a way I never have before. I've been a lights-off girl, an under-the-covers girl. Now, I can't imagine why.

"Your skin, Ali . . ." says Adam. "You glow." His hands still cupped beneath me, he hefts me closer, bending over me, his tongue tracing along the lace of my bra, dipping into the hollow of my throat, sucking and nipping and tasting me. "God, you even taste good," he groans.

"That's not fair," I tell him. Again, it's like I'm someone else with him. Someone with no shame, no guilt, who can speak her desires plainly. I don't know what kept me from being that girl before, but I'm glad she's shown up now, when I need her most. "I want to taste you. I want your tongue in my mouth again."

He makes a sound like a tortured sigh and presses his lips to mine, driving his tongue between my teeth. My legs lock tighter around him, and I pull him against my body. I'm wrapped in the soft heat of his mouth, his darting tongue, and in the hardness he presses against me, so close, only the sheerest bit of fabric keeping us apart.

I'm no longer drunk, but now I tumble into an intoxicated, elated state so powerful I literally feel like I might faint. I hold onto him, molding my body against his, feeling how much he wants me—it's all here for me, his hands, his sweet, artful tongue, the feel of him pressed against my core, sending a deep, carving pulse through my entire body.

I reach down between our bodies for his belt. He groans, and the sound shatters me. God, I want him. Somewhere. Now.

"Adam, I need—"

Something pokes me hard in the back, and Adam and I stagger together, breaking contact.

We turn to see Suede's long elegant muzzle right up close to us. He knickers softly.

"What's wrong, boy?" Adam asks, lowering me to the ground.

Heavy footsteps crunch on the drive, and in lightning quick succession, Adam pulls up my dress and zips it, then buckles his own belt and takes a subtle step away from me, his expression reforming into one of nonchalance.

My father appears in the stable doorway. He's in jeans and has an ill-fitting sweater tossed on over his pajama top, making him look old and disheveled.

"There you are!" he exclaims, as though he's searched the ends of the earth for me.

My heart pounds so hard that it's on the edge of painful. I try to make myself sound normal. "Yes," I say. "I was just introducing Adam to Persephone and Suede."

"I see that." My father's gaze sweeps over Adam, and there's a new brittleness to his expression. I can't read whether it's disapproval or something else.

"I gave Alison a ride home," Adam says smoothly. He doesn't add why, and I know he never would.

My father steps closer, and the space seems to shrink with his presence. His face is ruddy, eyes glassy. I guess I'm not the only one who's been drinking. Suddenly, I feel like everything about me is pre-designed. Like I'm just part of this great machine, which for generations has been spitting out discontented perfectionists with a fondness for booze.

I pat Suede's neck and whisper, "Thank you," in his ear. At least he's got my back. Adam too, I know.

"And how was your date, Alison?" my father asks. "And how is it that he didn't drive you home?"

"It's a long story, dad," I tell him. "Why don't you go back inside, and I'll come tell you all about it in a second. I want to walk Adam out to his car, okay? I know we both have big days tomorrow."

"Big week," Adam confirms.

"That's right." My father nods. "Your team-building trip."

Adam nods. "Yes, lots to do before we head out."

"Well, I won't keep you," my father tells him. Once again, his eyes move between us, but I keep my expression neutral. Masked.

"Thank you," Adam replies. "When we get back, I'd like to sit down with you, go over final details. I think you'll have everything you need for a decision by then." His eyes shift to me.

"We'll have much to discuss, I'm sure," my father says.

I settle Persephone and Suede in for the night, and Adam draws the big double doors closed behind the three of us. We head toward the drive together, and I expect my father to part ways at the path up to the house, but he remains with us, claiming he wants to take a closer look at Adam's car.

It's quiet now. Only our footsteps and the light murmur of the surf fill the air. I think about how often I've wished to go backward since I've met Adam, back to the breathtaking moments we've shared. Maybe they're better than normal life because they're forbidden. Or maybe they're better because it's just the two of us, sharing some raw part of ourselves we tend to keep hidden from view.

I don't know what it is, except that those moments feel high-definition to me, every touch and breath sharper than life.

We reach his car, and after giving my father a quick tour of the interior, Adam slides inside and pulls the seat belt across his shoulder. "I'll see you tomorrow," he says, and his eyes say so much more that I want to dive into the seat beside him and have him carry me off into the night.

But I just smile and say, "tomorrow."

Inside, my father fixes himself a bourbon and ice then sits in our formal dining room, looking strange and shrunken at the head of a table that can be set for twenty.

"Nightcap?"

"No thanks," I say.

"Well, sit with me, anyway."

I pull out a chair and sink into it. Suddenly, I'm exhausted. I just want to crawl up to bed and relive every moment with Adam, and then wake up to a new day where I get to see him again.

"Already had yours?"

"Yes," I say, because there's no point lying about it. "I had a few. That's why Adam drove me home."

"Did you make any inroads with Blackwood?"

The air seems loaded with double meanings, and I feel a sudden tension, like I'm about to walk into a trap. "Not so much," I say, trying to keep my voice calm. "He doesn't open up about much." And as I say it, I realize how true it is. For both of us. Our bodies are way more honest with each other than our words seem to be.

"No, I imagine he wouldn't."

"What do you mean?"

"Well, let's just say I found out something interesting today. Or at least the first part of something interesting. I'm not sure what to do with it, but I think that's where you come in. If I can trust you to stay the course."

"Of course you can."

"I don't mind you getting close to him. In fact, I applaud the strategy. But you can't lose your head. You have to stay in control. On top. You understand?"

I don't know what to say to any of that. Everything that's happened between Adam and me is the furthest thing in the world from a strategy. Or control. But if I explain that to my father, he'll question my loyalty.

"Okay, Dad," I say. "Yes, I understand. What did you find out?"

My father takes a long swallow of his drink. He sets the mug down with a thud and says, "Adam Blackwood's been married."

The words crash around in my head for a second but don't line up in a way that makes sense. "What?"

"Married. He was married. When he was just a kid. But there's something more there. I know it." His eyes glimmer in a way that bothers me.

I can't understand why this is important. Or how I'm supposed to feel about it. I know it must mean something—but I can't imagine what. Only that Adam loved someone deeply enough to marry her, to feel sure he'd spend the rest of his life with her.

"When?" I ask. "To who?"

"A girl named Chloe Randall. She died." He shakes his head. "Twenty years old."

"How?"

He shrugs. "I don't know. That's where you come in."

"But, I mean, when was this?"

"About three years ago. They were only married for a few months. Information is locked down tighter than Fort Knox, and I need to know why. I think we're onto something here."

"But how does any of this really matter?" I ask. "I mean . . . whatever the reasons, why do we even have to know?"

"Because I'm giving this guy twenty million dollars. And he's keeping secrets. Expensive secrets. However this girl died, it should be public knowledge, but there's nothing. Not a newspaper article or police report. At least none that we can find—yet. He covered it up for some reason, and that doesn't look good."

"Then how did you find out?"

He waves a hand. "Don't worry about that. I need to know what this is about though. You've got four days with him now. Work on him."

I feel queasy, imagining that. Imagining trying to "work" Adam for answers. But my dad's right. I don't want to admit it, but that's a lot of money. Family money. And Adam's hiding something. From the world, not just us. For three years, he's built his life on a secret and seemed to go about it so coolly, with such ease. It makes me feel like I can't trust anything at all.

"All right, Dad," I say and get up from the table. "I'll get answers. I promise."

Chapter 26

Adam

I'm sweating in my ski jacket as I reach the cornice I spotted from the chair lift. Sliding my skis and poles off my shoulder, I stake them into the snow.

Casper Bowl, my favorite run here in Jackson, dips and turns below me, coated with more than a foot of pristine powder from yesterday's storm. It's more work to hike to the runs that aren't accessible by ski lift, but blazing a trail over a white blanket that hasn't been touched by anyone is my style. The trek is more than worth it.

After I catch my breath, I snap into my skis. Then I adjust my goggles, firm my grip on my poles, and push.

The initial five-foot drop gives me the acceleration I wanted, and I'm off, slicing back and forth, just the mountain and me. Usually there's no room for thought once I'm carving down a mountain, but this time is different. Ali is in my thoughts. She has been all week, and flying on a pair of skis doesn't change that.

I see her face just before I kissed her in the stable—an image that's been sustaining me for days—for the week that's passed since that night. A meeting with some potential co-producers cropped up and took Brooks and me to New York. Promising leads, but I spent too many days without Alison.

That ends today.

And it can't happen again.

Graham, Ali, and I will have to work things out. Ali is twenty-two—old enough to make her own choices about her personal life. Graham will have to recognize that and see it as separate from the investment deal. There's no reason—no good one—why I can't have her and her father's money.

I can't believe this. I'm crazy about a girl again. What's harder to believe is that I'm *hiding* that I'm crazy about a girl again—but that's going to change immediately. I'll talk to Ali, then deal with Graham.

I punish myself on the slopes, burning off the energy that's been pent up inside me all week, leaping off a shoulder of snow like there's no danger of breaking my neck. Eight inches of fresh powder should cushion me, but the impact jars every bone in my body. The pain feels good. Real and sharp. The blinding white snow, blue skies, and a blazing yellow sun even better, but I'm struggling to get a rhythm. I sink deeper into my legs, picking up speed to see if I can lock in.

Something shifts as I move into the shadow of the mountain, and I suddenly feel Chloe racing with me, her breath in my ear, the sting of her loss cramping my fingers, making my movements jerky and stiff. The wind lashes at my face, penetrating my goggles, and my eyes water, blurring the trail.

She's so clear to me. I feel her with me, curled in my lap in an Adirondack on the deck back home, her breath warm against my ear, her fingers playing with the hair at the nape of my neck, tickling me. I hated it and she did it anyway, and I loved that she did it anyway. She whispered our dreams to me at night, whispered everything we'd become like we were a bedtime story. A loft in Manhattan. Her, an artist. Me, starting a business. She had a plan we'd do that until she turned twenty-five, then we'd move to Paris.

But we never became anything. She never turned twenty-five. She turned into a memory. A constant reminder of my mistake and . . . and, *fuck*. I can't screw up like that again, not with Alison.

Some asshole in yellow ski pants bombs past me. He catches an edge and goes down hard, windmilling and blasting me in the face with a slurry of snow. I'm blind, my legs shuddering until I jam in hard and practically snap both of my knees trying to stop. A wave of rage crashes through me. I want to charge back up the mountain and wrap my hands around the guy's throat, choke him. But I don't. Anyway, those stupid yellow pants are their own punishment.

Breathing in deep, I feel ice form in my veins. The sky's brilliance calms me. I dig my poles into the snow, start again. I feel rusty, my body still out of sync with my intent. I think about the people waiting back at the lodge for me. Rhett and Cookie. Mia, Sadie, and Pippa. Paolo. People whose lives depend on my getting my shit together. I dig into the powder, pushing until the snow is a blur, my poles tucked up tight against my body, a rocket shooting toward an endless horizon. I cut through a narrow crevice, along the more dangerous path. Every cell in my body warns me I'm in danger of failing, that if I crash, it's going to be brutal.

I don't care. I know I can't outpace the memories. I'm alive and Chloe isn't, and I'll never forgive myself, or forget her. But every day is mine to determine now and I want to move forward.

There's a chance with Alison. I'm going for her—for us—and I won't screw it up. Not this time. Not with her.

The end of the run smoothes into a straight downward shot that finally makes me feel like I know what I'm doing. I sail over the last hundred yards, and although the run gives me plenty of even ground at the end, I come up hard near a stand of firs by a path to the lodge. I unclamp my skis, hoist them over my shoulder and step into the Four Seasons, setting my skis on a rack.

It feels too hot in the resort, but I know it's just my body being used to the outside cold and still cooling down from skiing. Ahead of me, there's an enormous two-sided fireplace with high-backed benches upholstered in slate and pearl leather. I head to the bar, thinking I'll have a quick drink before heading to the cabin where my staff awaits. I just need a minute to clear away the fog.

The bartender is gorgeous—flaming red hair, pale freckled cleavage—and she locks into me with blatant interest, licking her peach lipstick as she smiles.

"What'll it be?" she asks, her question filled with invitations.

Normally, I'd accept that invitation, but now there's no temptation. I order a Manhattan. When it arrives, I take a few sips. Then I check my watch and find myself smiling. Ali should be here by now.

"Hey, Adam!" Rhett says, sidling up to the bar. He takes the bar stool to my left. Cookie sits to my right. "How was it out there, man?"

"Oh, cut the crap," Cookie says. She pauses to order two more martinis. "Make them strong and quick," she says to the bartender. "Give me some nuts, too."

The bartender's eyes dart to me, smiling, before she moves to mix the drinks.

Cookie folds her arms. "Okay. What the hell is going on with Alison?"

I laugh. "What is this? An Alison intervention?"

"That's exactly what this is, and we're serious."

"As a heart attack," Rhett adds.

I take a sip of my drink. I haven't been in the office for a week, but Rhett and Cookie have caught onto me anyway. While I was in New York, I checked up with both of them a few times to make sure Alison had everything she needed. Even from across the country, they've picked up on where my head is. Or to be more specific, my heart.

"Nice of you guys. But don't waste your energy. I'm going to see her if I want to, and . . . I do."

"You're not thinking straight," Cookie says. "I don't trust her. I've never trusted her."

"So you've said."

"It's not just Alison," Rhett adds. "It's Graham Quick. I've been thinking about what Ethan said at poker. I'm worried, Adam."

"Worried about Graham?" I look from him to Cookie. "You mean you're worried about the deal?"

"Yes," they both say.

"I've been asking around," Rhett says. "Getting some other opinions on Quick. I haven't been able to get *anything*. The three guys I talked to who had worked directly under him wouldn't bad-mouth him. But get this. They wouldn't say anything *good* about him, either. They just kept making these really canned, neutral remarks about how they'd learned a lot from Graham. They're scared of him, Adam. It's the only explanation."

"Exactly," Cookie says. "The only thing they learned was how to be scared shitless of Graham's wrath."

"I'll keep digging," Rhett says. "I've got a few other contacts who—"

I hold up my hand, stopping him. "Look, Rhett. Cookie. Do your research. Do what you feel you need to do." I stand and peel a hundred dollar bill out of my wallet, dropping it on the bar. "But let me ask you this. Do you think I built my company by being scared?"

They have no answer, and I knew they wouldn't.

I leave them to grab my gear and head over to the lodge.

It wasn't fear, I think, as I step back out into the snow. It was grief. Grief was the fuel that built Boomerang.

Chapter 27

Alison

*P*erfect.

Philippe and I hover in the doorway of one of the lodge's bedrooms, Gucci bags strewn at my feet, and take stock of the sleeping arrangements. Two bunk beds, three already littered with luggage that looks like it fell from a gypsy caravan, and one low-slung lumpy bottom bunk, apparently for me.

I should have known from the smirk Cookie gave me on the plane that something unpleasant lay in store. This, I'm sure, is her way of reminding me that my money can only buy so much. Or her way of keeping me from Adam, who she guards with the ferocity of a bullmastiff. Not that it's been a problem this week. With Adam away in New York, I never got closer than the occasional Skype conference.

My phone chimes in my purse, and I dig it out—hoping it'll be Adam letting me know he's here. But it's just a text from my father.

Dad: Text when you arrive, and let's make a plan of attack.

Sighing, I text back.

Ali: I'm here. Let me do things my way. Trust me.

I slip my phone into my purse and zip it closed, like I can zip away my anxiety and my father's pestering.

"Cozy," Philippe says. Thank God he's here too—my touchstone.

"I guess you're sleeping with the boys." I heft my bags and bring them over to the available bunk, where I bounce on the flat mattress a couple of times to get a feel for it. At least, my dad is still letting me bring Philippe along as my assistant, though he's spent a lot more time chatting up Paolo lately than he has in assisting me.

He arches one perfectly tended eyebrow. "Any chance we can sneak off to the Four Seasons?"

I shake my head, though I'd happily trade team-building for room service and a gold-filled sunset over Rendezvous Mountain.

To be fair, it's only the sleeping accommodations that are sparse. The central area of the lodge includes an elegant modern kitchen and a sunken living room with burnished wood rafters, a stone fireplace, plush leather sectionals covered in faux fur blankets, and floor-to-ceiling windows that look out at the mountains and miles of already well-carved ski trails.

"Of course, Cookie has a hot tub suite all to herself," Philippe says. He waggles his eyebrows at me and says, "I bet Adam does too. Maybe you can trade up."

Instantly, I imagine Adam in a hot tub, water pooling against his lean, muscled body. Then the two of us, slick bodies twined together.

I tamp down those thoughts and remind myself he's not who I think he is, or he's not *all* that I think he is, and I'm afraid to drag those shadowy parts of his past into the light.

Only, I promised my father I'd do just that.

"I wonder who your roomies are," Philippe remarks.

As if summoned, Pippa and Sadie come giggling into the room, pushing by Philippe to launch themselves at the bunk bed opposite me.

"Hey, *Roomie*!" Sadie says, flopping onto the bed and using her tapestry carpet bag as a pillow. Her long black hair fans out in all directions and spills off the edge of the bed like a waterfall of ink. "What do you think of the accommodations?"

"They're fine," I say. And they really are. I've mucked out horse stalls, picked pebbles out of hooves, and scraped barnacles off the *Ali Cat*. I'll be fine. Just uneasy. And uneasy won't kill me.

"Aren't the mountains glorious?" Pippa asks, sitting on the lower bunk with her legs drawn up and her arms around her knees. She's wearing a long skirt over long johns, and the effect is adorable. She looks like a little girl, all huge blue eyes and delicate limbs, but she's got a savant's talent at visual arts and those eyes take in everything.

"They really are," I say. "My family has a place in Aspen, and it's beautiful there, but Jackson Hole is amazing."

"Are you a big skier?" Sadie asks.

I nod. "Yes, I love it." Next to horseback riding, it's my favorite outdoor thrill. I love the feeling of flying over the snow, everything white and glittering and soaring past.

The thought of *indoor* thrills brings Adam to mind again, and I busy myself with my bags for a moment, trying to hide the blush I feel rise to my cheeks. It's so strange to feel rooted in two places at once. Part of me is in the stable, locked together with Adam, and part of me stands at a distance from all of that, measuring, trying to establish for myself what's real and what's not.

Philippe says, "Not me. Going downhill, fast, on ice, while strapped into metal blades is *not* my idea of a good time. But I'll keep the lodge cozy for you all."

"I'll definitely keep you company," says a voice behind him, and Mia slips beside him into the room. She's wearing fitted jeans and purple suede boots with a chunky high heel—totally impractical for the snow but somehow so suited to her. "I'd just be a hazard to myself and everyone else if I got on skis."

She climbs up the bunk to the top. "Sorry if my stuff kind of exploded around the room."

"It's all right."

"Where's Adam?" Philippe asks, supplying the question he knows I'm dying to ask.

"He got here early," says Sadie. "I think he went for a ski, but he should be here soon."

I wish I could go out and join him on the slopes. I'm sure he conquers a mountain the same way he conquers everything else—like nothing else is possible.

"He'd never miss *Jasmine,*" Pippa says.

"Who's Jasmine?" asks Mia.

"Newbies!" Sadie says. "She's the camaraderie expert."

"What's a camaraderie expert?" I ask.

"Do you know Luna Lovegood from *Harry Potter*?"

I nod.

"Imagine that but, like, old," says Pippa. "Like fifty."

"Wow," Mia says, her tone amused. "Ancient. But what does she *do* exactly?"

"She conducts the team-building sessions," Sadie replies. "And dude, she's tough. It's like if a pixie and Arnold Schwarzenegger got married."

Pippa giggles. "Oh my God, it is *just* like that! Except if they had a baby."

"What?" Sadie asks.

"If they had a baby. If they just got married, it would still just be a pixie and Arnold Schwarzenegger."

"Right. If they had a baby. And that baby was in charge of making you climb trees and fall on top of each other."

"Falling on top of each other is a team-building exercise?"

"Well, like a trust exercise. Like stage-diving, only into a group of your coworkers."

The thought horrifies me.

"Shit," Mia cries. "My purse!"

A torrent of objects spills down in front of me: a cosmetic case, wallet, various papers, birth control pills, and her phone, which strikes me on the knee and bounces on the floor in front of me.

I bend to retrieve it and see that of course the wallpaper image is of her and Ethan, dressed in their Halloween costumes. They're standing in front of a window with a blazing sunset creating a tangerine halo around them, highlighting Mia's blond Marilyn wig, her smooth olive skin. Ethan's behind her, wrapping his arms around her waist. His mouth is close to her ear, and I imagine he's whispering something to her—something to make her laugh, to make her whole face brighten with joy.

They're beautiful together, and the sight creates an ache in me. For Adam. For that night. For endless hours in that car and garage doors that never open.

Everything's a flurry of activity as we help Mia reassemble her possessions. Then we're quiet for a moment.

My phone rings in my purse again, but I ignore it.

"Hey," I say to Mia and the others. "Let's go make a fire in the living room and have a drink or something."

I want to be there when Adam comes in, I decide. I just need to *see* him. My father laid out my mission, and it's one I plan to carry out if I can, but more than that, my own need drives me. I *have* to know him. I have to know his secret, yes, but more than that I have to know *him*. Know his heart. Know what beats there beneath his bravado and his beautiful smile.

"A drink sounds like a brilliant idea," says Philippe.

"I make a mean Irish coffee," Mia offers.

I look at her and smile. "Let's go," I say.

Chapter 28

Adam

Between a quick shower and emails I couldn't ignore from Brooks on potential screenwriters for Blackwood Entertainment's first feature, followed by a call from Grey trying to convince me to let him drive the Bugatti while I'm out of town, it's seven before I head downstairs for our traditional retreat kick-off dinner.

I hear Jasmine Star, our camaraderie specialist, before I see her.

"We're going to be working a lot on our vibrational frequencies this week, lovelies!" she says in a singsong lilt. "Each one of you is a sacred entity, made up of millions of molecules that are connected energetically. What is your energy, Marvelous Mia? And yours, Perfect Paolo? What about you, Caring Cookie?"

As I round the corner, she points a ringed finger at me, and her hazel eyes light up. "What is *yours,* my darling Adam?"

I move right to her. "Hi, Jazz."

She frames my face and looks at me. "Hello, sweetheart."

"Younger every year, Jazzy," I say, smiling. She's one of those older women who—to use her term—has very youthful vibrational energy. Her face is plump and wrinkled, but she still manages to seem girlish and playful.

The smell of incense and natural soap floats up from her jeweled top. Jasmine zeroed in on my eye-contact thing within five minutes of when I met her a few years ago. She keeps trying. But I have the same trick I use on Alison. Jazz wears about seventy-two million necklaces. Beads and feathers and, I swear, bones, hang around her neck.

"You wonderful flirt," she says affectionately, then she smacks her lips against mine—something she does to everyone. "Get an apron on. We've already gotten started!"

Alison's standing behind an expansive kitchen island, between Philippe and Mia. She's wearing an apron with the words *Mmm, good!* across the front, and I couldn't agree more. Her hair is up and there's a dusting of flour on her chin and along her neck. In front of her, I see a number of bowls and spoons, measuring cups, and glasses of wine.

She looks amazing—I've been waiting for this moment for over a week—but seeing her in the kitchen makes me smile. She looks nowhere near as comfortable as she does in scuba gear or with a horse lead in her hands.

"Where do you want me?" I'm speaking to Jazz, but Ali looks down at her hands, and I see her blush. Philippe—who's in a *Hot Cook* apron—gives her an elbow nudge.

"Well, dinner's almost done," Jasmine says. Rhett and Mia stand over a huge pot, having a small argument about how much salt to add to the boiling water. Rhett looks up, catching my eye. There's still a trace of the worry I saw on his face earlier at the bar, but he seems to be relaxing. Paolo, Sadie, and Pippa are chopping salad ingredients, and Cookie, in an *Eat Meat* apron, is finishing up setting the table. "Why don't you open some wine?"

"Sure," I say, and get us set up with white and red on both sides of the table.

I keep looking at Ali. I'm glad she seems to be having fun with the team, but I'm starting to realize that finding some time alone with her these next few days might not be easy to pull off. But I need that. I need to touch her. I need to talk to her. I need to explain to her that we can see each other. We'll talk to her father. I'll do it with her, if she wants. But Graham has to come around.

The food is set out on the table, family style, but Jasmine stops us before we take our seats and makes us stand around the table, holding hands.

She does this every year so I'm ready, and I've put myself right next to Ali.

It feels like a victory, just getting to hold her hand. And when I glance at her, her face softened by the candlelight, I see something warm in her blue eyes. Heat blazes through me, and I entertain a quick fantasy of making a break for my room and locking the door for the next few days.

"Now, everyone close your eyes," Jazz says. "It's safer for most of us to be honest this way." That feels like it's meant for me, but everyone follows along. "Good. Now I want us to take a moment and check in with our intentions for the next few days," she continues. "Say them out loud in your thoughts. Think of sending those thoughts to the people around you. Energy loves energy. Do it now. Send forth your energetic wishes."

I want to make you quiver. I want you naked and clinging to me and saying my name.

I glance at Rhett and hope I sent my energetic wish in the right direction.

"Good. Okay, everyone open your eyes, but please don't sit down yet." Jazz picks up a glass jar in front of her. Everyone's hands come down, but I linger, holding as long as I can to Ali's.

"Usually, we don't get started until morning," Jazz says, "but I thought we'd do something different this year. I'm going to put you in trust partner pairs right now, and we're going to jump right in with an exercise. Sound good?"

Everyone looks terrified except Rhett, who nods excitedly. "Awesome, yes!" he says. "Let's rock it."

"Very good." Jasmine smiles, and reaches into the glass jar, removing two strips of paper. "Our first pair is Rhett," she says, opening one strip. "And Pippa," she adds, opening the other. "You two will be trust partners for the duration of the retreat. That means you'll be working closely together, even during group events. You're a team. Start thinking about that. Please take a seat next to each other, but don't speak to one another. I'll explain why in a moment."

Interesting. The silence thing is new.

Pippa and Rhett sit down and Jazz moves on, selecting the next trust teams.

Sadie and Paolo high-five when they get each other, which makes the extreme stillness that follows the announcement of the Cookie/ Philippe team even more pronounced.

Then Mia gets Jazz, which is surprising, but we have an odd number. I feel a little bad for her, but mostly I'm fucking flying because Ali and I are together.

"Trust partner," I say, pulling her chair out for her.

"Ah, ah," Jazz says. "Remember, no talking—and that's because we're going to do our very first trust exercise right now." She sits to a jingle of bells and beads. "It's very simple, actually. You will be speaking for each other for the rest of the night. So, you may whisper anything you wish to say to your trust partner, and that person will be conveying your thoughts on your behalf. It's an exercise that will show you the power of speech. Words are gifts, and gifts must be chosen with care. You are representing the interests of someone other than yourselves. It's going to be fabulous, lovelies. Trust is just waiting for you to—"

Jasmine stops speaking as Paolo leans over to Sadie and whispers.

"Paolo is starving," Sadie says. "He wants to know if he can eat while you explain the rest of the exercise."

Jasmine smiles. She leans over and pushes Mia's curls out of the way, whispering.

Mia's lips twist a little as she listens. "Jasmine says, go ahead and eat."

The exercise is entertaining for a while.

Sadie whispers to Paolo, then Paolo says, "Sadie wants to know if she'll get any time at the spa because she's a huge diva that way."

Sadie whispers again, and Paolo delivers another message from her: "She just told me I'm an even bigger diva."

Then Philippe speaks for Cookie: "Cookie thinks you're both imbeciles."

It goes on like this, controlled chaos, as we dig into ravioli and salad.

Ali hasn't whispered anything in my ear yet, and I haven't said anything to her. I'm more than satisfied, for now, just to sit next to her and enjoy my marketing team's antics. I'll be spending a lot of time with her over the coming days—exactly what I wanted.

When the conversation's at a dull roar and the rules about who's speaking for who have relaxed a little, I lean toward Alison. Her winter smell surrounds me, a clean elegant scent that takes me back to Halloween night, and it's all I can do not to brush my lips against the soft skin in front of her ear.

"You look incredible, Ali," I say. There's been a lot of whispering at this table tonight, so no one notices us. We're invisible, right here in front of everyone. No one even sees the small shiver Ali gives at the sound of my voice, or the way she leans closer to me. "I can't take my eyes off you. I can't stop thinking about you."

I settle back into my chair. Sparkling blue eyes regard me for a moment before she leans by my ear. "Is that just for me, trust partner, or would you like me to share that with the group?"

I don't bother whispering this time. "Tell anyone you want," I say to her as the conversation swirls around us. "It's happening, Ali. *We* are. Trust me."

Chapter 29

Alison

The air is crisp and carries that fresh mountain smell, like linen and pine, as our team tramps across a snow-packed hillside. It's too early—just past dawn—for the two full-scale snowball fights that have already broken out among the others, though Philippe's wild pitch, which knocked Cookie's ear muffs right off her head, almost makes it worth it.

I'm bleary, wooden-limbed, and it feels like there's not enough coffee in the world to prepare me for the day ahead. I couldn't sleep all night, thinking about Adam whispering to me at the table, his breath warm in my ear, just the nearness of him turning my body warm and liquid.

I can't stop thinking about you, he said. And even though I deflected that, I can't stop thinking about him, either. I can't stop thinking about his brilliance and ambition, his gorgeous tapered fingers wrapped around a wine glass, his appraising gray eyes taking everything in, the faint shadowing of lines at the corner of his lids that speak of days out in the sun, in the bracing salt air.

His face gives so much, I think, as I watch him chat easily with Philippe beside me. His body even more so. But then there's that shadow, too, that wall I can never breach, the place where deep inside he's locked away pieces of himself, locked away his own history.

On that front, my father's campaign to drive me insane has reached new heights. Eight texts before I went to bed last night. I tried to placate him, to tell him that Adam and I had been paired for the weekend, that I'd have plenty of opportunity to find out what he wanted to know. But he just kept firing at me.

The group reaches a plateau where Jasmine Star stands in front of a broad wooden platform about shoulder height. Next to it rises an elaborate climbing wall with the caps of rough-hewn logs jutting from it and lengths of bungee cord shuffling together in the wind. On the ground, a Day-Glo fuchsia line brightens the white terrain.

Jasmine claps her hands excitedly at our approach. She's bundled in a patterned alpaca coat that looks like she fashioned it from one of the lodge blankets.

"Good morning, lovelies!" she calls. "And here's my magnificent partner!" she cries, homing right in on Mia, who seems even more clumsy and slow this morning than I feel. "Look at all that hair! You're like a Botticelli!"

"It's just really hard for me to find a hat to go over it," Mia says.

"Well, it would be a shame to cover it," Jasmine exclaims then dashes a few steps toward us to give Mia a morning kiss—on the lips. "Minty!" she exclaims.

Mia angles a "just shoot me" look at Paolo, who laughs and gamely leans in for his kiss from Jasmine.

Then it's a flurry of kisses and pats in sometimes questionable places. Her hands are cool against my skin as she pulls my face toward hers. I can see every pore, see the manic delight in her hazel eyes, and the spray of capillaries on her ruddy cheeks. "Good morning, you beautiful creature of light," she says to me. "Who are you going to trust today?"

Even the word sends a dart of panic into my solar plexus. "Um, my team? I'm . . . I'm going to learn to trust my team."

She shakes her head. "No, my special darling. You're going to learn to trust *yourself*! Isn't it marvelous?"

It's not a question, really, though she still punctuates it with another kombucha-scented kiss on the lips. "Today, you're going to learn to trust each other, yes. But you're learning to trust *yourselves,* most of all. Trust that you can push yourself harder than you believe. Trust that when you fall—" she nods at the raised platform— "you're truly worth catching!"

My cell phone buzzes in my pocket, and I lift it out and clear off the condensation on the screen with my gloved finger.

Dad: Any progress?

Part of me wants to ignore him, to smash the phone under the heel of my boot and forget all about Adam's past, about my "mission." But I know he'll persist, and giving him an answer now is the best way to keep from having to deal with a text every hour on the hour.

Ali: Just getting started. But I told you, I've got it. Will fill you in tonight.

Now leave me alone, please, I want to add, but I don't. Here's hoping I've bought myself a few hours of peace, at least.

I thumb the switch to silent and thrust the phone back in my pocket.

"Everything all right?" Adam asks, kicking up little clouds of snow as he closes the space behind us.

I nod. "Yep, just had to let my dad know I got in okay."

"Too bad he's not here," Adam says with a hard-to-read grin. "He could use some trust exercises himself."

I hear my dad say, *"Trust me, Ali. We have to keep this between us. It'll break your mother's heart, and for no reason. I don't want to destroy our family. You have to understand that. Things like this . . . they mean nothing."*

Trust me.

Family is everything.

"I'm glad you took my advice," my dad says, and with a flourish, he hands me a small box. It's Christmas. Catherine, my parents, and I sit in the cozy family room, warm cinnamon-sprinkled hot chocolate in our hands, tinny holiday music playing over the expensive speakers. My parents give each other cordial smiles, and I open the box. Two earrings—large A's for Alison—studded with diamonds. "Just for you," he tells me. "Because you mean so much to me. You all do."

Now, I run a finger over one of the earrings, feel the softly pebbled texture of the diamonds, now cold in the November Wyoming air.

"All right," Jasmine exclaims, bouncing on the toes of her boots like a little kid. "Our first exercise is called 'Walk the Line!' Doesn't that sound like fun?"

She pairs us with our team-building buddies and ushers us over to the end of the fuchsia line in the show.

"All right, she says. "Stand side by side, facing me. Cookie, you put your left foot on the line. Philippe, put your right foot on it, right up against Cookie's. Get cozy!

"*Don't* get cozy," Cookie snaps, but I can see from the mischievous sparkle in Philippe's eye that she doesn't intimidate him.

"Now the trick, my sweetest pets, is to simply walk the line— from here to the end."

Cookie starts to stride forward, but Jasmine reaches out and tugs her roughly back by the collar, almost lifting Cookie right off her feet.

If I hadn't seen it for myself, I'd never have believed it. The pixie Arnold Schwarzenegger is everything Sadie and Pippa promised.

"Now, now, my hasty one, let me finish."

Cookie sighs and rolls her eyes but returns to stand near Philippe, her ankle aligned with his.

"The trick is for the two of you to walk the line *together,* to keep connected, your feet in contact with each other at all times. But you're not allowed to touch one another otherwise. And you're not allowed to speak. You must go deep within your partner's energy and intuit his or her movements, fall into a rhythm that speaks to both of your hearts. You see?"

From the mystified faces around the clearing it's obvious we're all lost, but Cookie and Philippe gamely try again. And again. Jasmine stops them every time they fall out of sync, which is often.

"Cookie, my darling, you have to *give* something to our dear Philippe. Slow down. Allow yourself to consider his rhythm. You can't bully your way through something like this."

Mia and Sadie giggle at Cookie's frustration, and at someone having the guts to call her a bully to her face. Finally, they're able to walk the entire length of the fuchsia line, and Philippe celebrates by wrapping Cookie in a bear hug and rocking her back and forth until she finally, reluctantly, puts her arms around him.

"Oh, how honored I am to have seen that!" Jasmine cries. "Truly, so special to see your souls at work together."

She lines the rest of us up and coaches us through the activity. It takes Rhett and Sadie about twenty tries to align their grossly mismatched strides—like watching a bear and a hummingbird attempt a salsa. While barely touching.

Everyone else bumbles through the activity with greater or lesser success. Then it's my turn with Adam. We line up, the sides of our feet touching in the center of the fuchsia line. I feel the warmth and solidity of him, and even without looking, I can feel that his eyes are on me.

We start to move, and with no conversation, no touching, and no trouble at all, our strides fall in together. Our feet stay pressed together as we move, a single fluid unit, across the line.

The others cheer us on, but Jasmine stands frozen, her hands pressed to her lips like she's witnessing a legitimate miracle.

"Oh, my, that was the most stunning thing I've ever seen! You two are perfectly in sync. I predict great things from your partnership."

All of which brings my father, Adam's secrets, my obligations, crashing right back down again.

Next, Jasmine tells us we're going to do an old-fashioned trust exercise.

"You'll climb up to the platform there, and all of these beautiful souls around you will gather to give you a safe place to land. But you'll line up with your buddies, all right? I want you to get in a row before the platform. Hold hands, and really latch onto each other. Imagine that there's a steel rod running between you that's unbreakable. And know that you're responsible for the safety of another living being. That we're all trusting each other with our hearts and our lives. Understand?"

This all feels a little dramatic for what's essentially a five-foot drop. But when she asks for volunteers, I find my arm is the first to shoot up. I have to know what it's like. To fall into the arms of people I barely know. To open myself up to their strength. To trust.

My whole body trembles with excitement—and with cold—as I climb up the log ladder to the platform.

"Oh, my dear, kudos to your bravery!" Jasmine says, and the others applaud for me.

Mia comes to stand near Jasmine. She looks up at me, her wild cloud of dark hair whipping around in the wind. "We've got you," she says and smiles. Then she and Jasmine clasp hands.

Next to them Rhett and Sadie. Then Paolo and Pippa. Then Cookie and Philippe. All clasp hands, making a kind of human rope bridge for me, with Adam standing at the end.

"You've got this, Quick," Adam says, making me want to believe.

I turn, smiling, even though no one can see me.

Then I stretch my arms out over my head and let myself fall.

Chapter 30

Adam

On the afternoon of our first official day at Camaraderie Camp, Ali and I pile out of the Four Seasons's vans with the rest of the crew and shuffle into the snowmobile park. Rhett and Jasmine have already arranged for everything, and I know where I'm going from past years, so I lead Ali around the small double-wide that is the park's office and head to the snowmobile course around the back.

I move to the helmet rack and hand one to her, taking another one for myself. We pull them snug over our ski beanies.

"Looking *Mmm good,* Quick," I say, remembering her apron from the other night. I offer a hand down the slushy slope to the course below.

"Thanks, Blackwood," she says, grabbing onto my arm.

We keep touching each other now, thanks to all the camaraderie work. We've only been at this for eight hours or so, but it's already become natural. My hands are almost always on her, zipping up her coat for her or resting on the small of her back. Trust work—the art of supporting your partner in ways big and small, as we've been told endlessly by Jasmine—completely rocks. Jazz is getting a huge tip from me this year.

The snowmobile is my favorite event of the retreat, and I'm more pumped for it than usual because of my partner this year. At some point yesterday, between trust falls and scavenger hunts through the lodge, I started having a legitimate blast with Ali.

She's competitive, maybe even more than I am, and her eagerness, the way she's enjoying herself, her whole attitude, is addicting. Totally addicting to be around.

"Hold up, guys," a snowmobile guy says, blocking us at the bottom of the path. "Hey, I'm Gooter." He steals a glance at Ali beside me—who looks amazing with her cheeks pink from the cold and her hair in a long braid that hangs to the side—and I watch his Adam's apple bob up and down. "Sorry, but, I just need to show you how to work the snowmobile and tell you how to run the course."

"That's all right," I say. "I've done this a few times. Just point me in the direction of the fastest vehicle."

Gooter appreciates a speed junkie when he meets one. He smiles. "Cool, bro. That one's got the best pick-up. Get her running for a minute to warm her up, and she'll fly for you."

I snag it, and Ali swings her leg over, mounting behind me and scooting close. The feeling of her thighs tight against mine is one I have to take a few moments to enjoy.

"I didn't even ask you if you want to drive," I say.

She wraps her arms around me. "You drive. I'll grab flags."

I fire up the engine and get us out on the starting line then explain the rules to Ali.

The object of the game, I know from past years, is to ride the course while keeping an eye out for yellow flags along the way. Each team has to collect four flags to qualify, and then it's pretty much a race to the finish line.

"What do you think?" I ask, as the other teams assemble around us. "Who do we have to look out for?"

She's quiet, and I feel her studying the others. Rhett and Sadie, who are ten kinds of awkward together. Paolo and Pippa, who've created some kind of leg kick and cheer. Mia and Jasmine—who, in snow gear, looks surprisingly like she was born riding snowmobiles across Alaska. And Philippe who stalls again, and again, and again, until finally Cookie yanks him back into the passenger position and takes over.

"No one," Ali says. "We've got this in the bag."

I'm suddenly grinning from ear to ear. "Damn right, Quick," I say, wanting to hang onto this feeling, that we're invincible. Together, that's exactly what we are.

When everyone's set, Gooter walks out to the starting line lifting what appears to be a pink dog toy in the air. "Are. You. Ready?" he yells.

"Wow! This race feels so official," Mia says gamely.

Pippa and Paolo do a cheer, their legs kicking left and right.

"Hell yes!" Cookie yells, revving her engine.

"Hold on tight," I say to Ali.

"I am," she says, firming her arms around my chest. "Don't hold back."

Jesus. What I wouldn't do to have her this close in private. Saying these things in private. With less clothes. Maybe sitting in front of me, where I could—

"On your marks! Get set!" Gooter lowers the dog toy. "Go!"

We shoot away from the starting line and I put us right into the lead, going full throttle down a steep drop. Ali and I come up off the seat as we catch air, and when we land, the impact is jarring. I feel her arms clamp around me, and the snowmobile finally gets traction again.

"You all right?" I yell.

"Yes! Keep going!"

I can't open up the throttle any more, so I concentrate on finding the best track.

"Flag!" Ali points. "Right there!"

I see it, and make a sharp turn. When I stop, I bury the bottom half of the flag in the spray the snowmobile kicks out.

"Shit. Sorry," I say, but Ali's already hopped off, taken four steps to the flag, and pulled it out of the ground.

"It's okay. Go!" she says, hopping back on.

I look behind us. Pippa and Paolo, and Cookie and Philippe are just coming down the steep decline Ali and I flew over.

"Go, go, go!" Ali yells, and my chest fills with the sound of her voice this way. So competitive and sure.

We tear back onto the track and find another flag. I get us close, Ali snags it. We blaze on. We're strategic. Efficient. Ruthless. And we don't make any false moves. By the time we come up to the fourth flag, I don't even see anyone behind us, but we're still gunning for the finish line, the two of us racing some imaginary competitor.

Ali jumps back on the snowmobile, the fourth flag tucked in her arm, but I don't go anywhere. Not yet.

"Adam, go! What are you doing?"

I turn so I can see her face. We're alone, but I can hear the hoots and hollers of the others approaching. "I'm kissing you."

The urge is so strong I won't be able to do anything—move, think, breathe—until I answer it.

I bring my mouth to her soft lips. A brush was all I thought I wanted. We're both out of breath and we're in the middle of a race. But a passing taste isn't enough. It never is with her.

My tongue sweeps in and strokes hers, and she's warm and sweet, and so willing, so responsive, I almost forget what we're doing until our helmets clack together.

I kiss her nose, which is a little red from the cold, as I back away. "What do you say, Quick?"

She smiles at me. "I say let's finish this."

And we do.

We're sipping hot chocolate with Gooter before the next team even crosses the finish line.

Chapter 31

Alison

I know when I see the blindfolds that I'm in trouble. Well, I think, mentally replaying Adam's kiss during yesterday's snowmobile race, *more* trouble.

We've gathered on the expanse of lawn right beyond our lodge's back deck, which has been littered with colorful mini pylons in what seems like a randomly arranged pattern but that no doubt reflects the perfect symmetry of a hummingbird's flight or the pattern the brain makes when it falls in love.

Jasmine seems to have a transparent bag filled with blindfolds, along with several lengths of bright yellow rope coiled in her hands.

"Oh, look everyone," says Paolo. "It's *Fifty Shades of Grey*, mountain edition."

"At least buy me some flowers first," mutters Mia.

Philippe snorts.

The early morning wind carries a cutting chill, the temperature easily twenty degrees colder than yesterday. I shiver and zip the collar of my coat up as high as it will go. Adam stands next to me, and I feel the tension of him wanting to put his arm around me. The same tension I feel, wanting to snuggle close but knowing it's the wrong thing to do. Maybe just here and now. Or maybe anywhere, anytime. I still don't know.

"Supposed to be a big cold front coming in," Rhett tells me. Wearing only a heavy sweatshirt, he jogs in place and blows on his hands as we await further instructions. "Maybe an ice storm." To Adam, he adds, "Gotta keep an eye on that."

Adam nods. "I'm checking the alerts. We'll probably know more in an hour or two."

Jasmine gives a sharp ear-piercing whistle, and all eyes turn to her.

"I know it's become a bit bracing out this morning, my lovelies, but we'll get you warmed up in no time with a little game I call 'Blind Pilot.' "

"Umm, blind pilots crash," says Sadie.

"Not if they have expert navigators," Jasmine replies. She explains that each team is to select one mask and one rope. The pilot and navigator will be tethered together, and the pilot will wear the mask. "You'll find three blue cones among all of the orange ones on your course. Your job as navigator, my precious angels, is to guide your pilots to each of the blue cones by giving them directions and gently guiding them with the rope. Each time you reach a blue cone, you've come to a Trust Layover."

Adam shakes his head and shoots me a grin. "Well, I like the blindfold part, at least."

Jasmine continues her instructions. "At each layover, your navigator's allowed to ask you any question, and your job is to answer truthfully. Unburden your heart so it has more room to be filled with love and life. And trust that your truth is precious to your partner, and that truth will be cared for and protected."

I can't help looking at Adam again, wanting to know if I can believe that, if I can give him my secrets. If he can give me his.

It strikes me that this exercise is tailor-made to my father's purposes, but that using it that way is the lowest thing I can imagine. I can't do it. I won't. And that realization unburdens me, makes me feel light and a little giddy. The way I felt when he kissed me on the back of the snowmobile. The way he makes me feel, period.

"Come on, Blackwood," I say. "Let's get a blindfold on you."

"Not if I get one on you first," he says and darts off toward Jasmine.

"Oh no, you don't," I say, and race behind him. But trying to run through calf-high snow is pretty much a futile pursuit, so it ends up looking like two people in the clumsiest slow motion ever.

We're laughing when we reach Jasmine, and Adam manages to snag a blindfold just a second before my fingers reach for it.

"Oh, I adore this enthusiasm!" Jasmine says. "You're such lovelies!"

"Come on, lovely," Adam says, and twirls the blindfold in the air. "Let's get this on you."

We walk down a gentle slope, and I direct him toward one of the little obstacle courses that spreads out in a patch of sunlight. A green cone marks the starting point, and I hold out my hand for the blindfold.

He gives me a skeptical look. "Are you kidding, Quick? There's no way I'm letting you put this on yourself." Moving closer, he reaches up and smoothes my hair back behind my ears. "You have the softest hair," he tells me. Then he places the silken fabric over my face. "Hold that," he instructs. And I hold it against my eyes, hating to block out the sight of him.

I feel the weight of his arms on my shoulders as he reaches

around me to tie the blindfold, giving it a sharp tug to secure it. His body brushes against me, and the hard length of him grazes my hip.

"Sorry," he whispers in my ear. "I guess masks excite me."

I tremble, not from the cold but from the growl in his voice, the feel of him against me. The memory of our last time in masks.

"A good navigator wouldn't try to distract his pilot," I tell him. Of course, a good pilot probably wouldn't want to throw her navigator into a snow mound and jump on top.

Adam fumbles around with something for a moment, and then I feel the length of cord circling my waist, being tugged taut. "Shit," he says. "Blindfolds and rope. I'm in big trouble here, Quick."

I laugh. "I'm surprised you can be around horses at all then," I say. "All kinds of sexy tackle."

"Don't say the words 'sexy tackle' to me. I'm having a hard enough time."

"Yes, I noticed how hard a time you're having."

He laughs and then I feel him move away from me. "Okay, let's do this," he says. "Take about a half step to your right and then walk about two short paces." He gives the rope a gentle tug to my right to align me, and I step forward.

"Perfect." He gives me further directions, tugging just a bit here and there as needed, but mainly guiding me with his voice. Even blindfolded, I feel perfectly secure, attuned to him. And there's a freedom to being locked in this world without vision. Everything becomes his voice, the gentle pull of the rope, my careful steps in the snow. All the chatter in my head falls away, and we're just a perfect, choreographed dance—flawless together.

"Okay, stop right there," Adam says. "We've reached a blue cone."

My feet plant, and I wait, thrilled and afraid of the question he'll ask.

"Tell me what happened with you and Ethan."

My throat tightens. I don't know what I expected, but I didn't expect this. I'm surprised he doesn't already know. Mia works for him. He plays poker with Ethan. I'm touched that neither of them told him, and their kindness makes me bold.

"I cheated on him." In my mind, the words freeze into ice and hover in the air between us. I don't offer anything else. I see it all so differently now, and no other words seem necessary—especially not excuses.

I wish I could see Adam's face now, see how he's looking at me. We're quiet for a moment, the chatter and laughter of the others echoing around us.

Then he just says, "Okay. Move about four inches to the left."

He guides me through the course until we reach another blue cone. Coming to stand close to me, he asks, "Why?" His voice is gentle and probing but without an ounce of accusation.

I sigh. "It's such a long story," I tell him. "We'll freeze."

"Imagine my arms are around you," he says, and his breath stirs against my cheek. "I'll keep you warm. Just tell me."

And so I do. I start with all of the things I see now that I didn't see then. I tell him about that weekend I found my father with another woman, how I ran away, spent the night at the airport, got back to college, and couldn't tell Ethan anything. Because I felt I needed to be loyal to my father and because Ethan seemed to admire him so much. I kept it a secret, and that secret made everything different between us. It made *me* different.

"I started partying more," I tell Adam. "And just . . . I stopped caring. I stopped believing in whatever Ethan and I had. And to be honest, I knew I wasn't in love with Ethan. And he wasn't in love with me. Not really. We had a lot of nice moments together, and I was excited by his success, I think, because I felt all of this pressure to be successful myself. I don't know. I just know that I let it all get out of hand. Because I didn't know what to think or feel. I just numbed myself to everything. I cut myself off from him and then I resented that he couldn't share my pain. It was so wrong of me. But I couldn't pull out of it. I just kept making terrible choices. Telling myself I didn't care. That none of it mattered."

"And the guy you cheated with?"

"One of those terrible choices." Tears sting my eyes, and I reach under the blindfold to wipe them away. I could remove it entirely, of course, but there's a comfort in it, in not being able to see Adam while I tell him my story. "I was so lonely. It felt like I didn't have my family anymore. Not in the same way. I pushed Ethan away and blamed him for being so busy with soccer and studies and his friends. The guy was my research partner, and we were with each other constantly. I just wanted to feel like . . ."

"Like what?" Adam asks, and his tone is so earnest and so understanding that more tears come.

"I wanted to feel like I mattered, I guess. Or like . . . I don't know . . . I wanted to know if it was true, what my father said. That it *didn't* matter. That it could happen and not mean anything."

"But it meant something?"

I nod. "I let myself go with it because I was buzzed, and I wanted to escape myself. But I pretty much hated it—which wasn't the guy's fault. He was . . . nice enough. He stopped when I got upset, but we were still in bed together when . . . when Ethan found us."

I start crying again, my whole body seized by the memory and the pain—and, in some small part, by a sharp sympathy for the person I was just a few months ago.

"I'm happy Ethan's found someone. They seem so . . . in love. But I'll never forget that look on his face. I spent six months trying to forget that look, drinking and acting like none of it mattered. It killed my studies. I mean, *I* killed them. I lost almost every friend I had. My parents had to bail me out of the whole thing. It was just a disaster. *I* was a disaster."

"But you're not anymore," he says quietly.

I shake my head, shivering. "No. I'm not."

"Come on," he says, and gives the rope another gentle tug. "Just a few steps straight on, and we'll be done."

I follow his directions and come to stand in front of him. "Last question," I say. The air temperature has dropped again, and the wind slices into me, starting my teeth chattering.

I feel his arms around me, and then the blindfold lifts away, and it's just the two of us, face-to-face in the blinding winter sunlight.

"Okay," Adam says. "Last question." There's nothing in his expression but regard and tenderness. "Want to go inside and get a goddamned cup of coffee?"

I smile, brushing away the last of my tears. "That sounds really, really good right now."

Chapter 32

Adam

The lodge has a library off the great room that's small and dim, with dark mahogany bookshelves and two stuffed chairs. It's as much privacy as I can get us right now, while still being part of the day's program. I claim it for Team Quick-Wood, taking Ali there as the other teams stake out other spots throughout the house.

We weren't the only team hustling inside for shelter five minutes ago. The weather's taking a turn for the worse, which could be a problem. Jackson airport only has a single runway and a good storm could get us stranded here for a few days—not a good thing with Thanksgiving the day after tomorrow. As much as my employees like me, I'm guessing they'd rather be with their families for the holiday.

"Right here, lovely," I say, sitting Ali down in one of the huge leather chairs in front of the fireplace. If there's one takeaway from this retreat, I think *lovely* is going to be it. Thanks to Jazz, everyone's taken to the word. "I'll get a fire going."

"That'd be great," she says. She's a little shaken up by what she just told me, and she's shivering from cold, but I feel a steadiness in the air between us now, and a keen awareness of the trust she just placed in me.

It feels incredible to have her faith in me. I want to let her know she's safe; I won't let her down. I want to take her hand and tell her she's brave, and that she should forgive herself.

What she told me also gives me plenty to consider where Graham is concerned. I've always been wary of him. But, added to what Ethan told me and to Rhett and Cookie's feelings about him, it's painting a pretty dark portrait of the guy. I can work with assholes, but a person who has major character flaws—who can manipulate his own daughter so cruelly—that's something I need to think about. Not now, though. Later.

Now, warmth. A fire to warm Ali.

Once I get that burning, I stand. Ali has tucked herself into the corner of the huge leather chair, all folded up. Her ski jacket is off, and she's in a white cashmere sweater. Her boots are off too, and her socks are purple with pink polka dots. Her blue eyes are just a little swollen from crying, but she's smiling. She's moving forward. She looks cute and sexy and beautiful the way she is—everything. I wish I could take a picture of her, but that's the last thing she needs right now.

"Stay put," I say. "I'll be right back with our coffees."

"Okay. But don't think for a minute you're escaping this, Adam."

"Didn't forget. Just wanted to take care of you first."

I hesitate before I go. Even though I can hear Paolo and Sadie laughing in the great room just outside, it feels like Ali and I are the only people in the world, and I don't want to let go of that feeling. Then something changes inside me, and fear starts scratching at my chest. Fear that if I walk away she won't be here when I come back, because life can change like that. In a matter of seconds. I know it can.

Alison tilts her head questioningly, responding to my mood.

"I don't like leaving you," I hear myself say.

"The sooner you go," she replies, softly, "the sooner you'll be back."

It's just the motivation I need.

In the kitchen, Mia stands at the espresso machine. She pours steaming milk from a can into a mug. "Hey, Adam. What's your poison?"

"Double espresso, if you're taking orders. And Ali likes—"

"Latte with cinnamon on top. I made one for her yesterday."

Jazz, who's waiting for Mia on a barstool, beams. "This is such a marvel to witness. I truly don't know of any other organization whose employees are so in tune with one another."

"Well, he's not an employee," Mia says. "He's the boss."

"But look at you two lovelies. You're simply beautiful together."

I lean against the counter and cross my arms. Mia and I share a look. We're definitely not beautiful together. But there's something between us that's unique, for sure. We're connected in a strange way, through Ethan and Alison. Through a tumultuous, twisting past that seems to be straightening out and settling.

My eyes pull to the windows. It's snowing again. And even though it's only three in the afternoon, the mountain looks shadowed and dark through the windows, making it feel much later.

"Hey, Galliano. Do me a favor and get an update on Jackson airport? I want to make sure you're back in Ethan's arms for Turkey Day."

"You got it, lovely."

In the library, I hand Ali her coffee. Then I pull the other chair right in front of hers and take a seat.

"You ready, partner?" she asks me. She seems relaxed. Happy again.

"Born ready."

"Here we go," she says, tying the blindfold over my eyes. There are no blue cones to navigate for me. We're going right to the heart of things—to the Trust Layovers, as Jazz called them.

For a few seconds, I check in with the way my other senses sharpen. The crackle of the fire sounds louder. The smooth taste of the espresso on my tongue more pronounced. The scent of Ali's perfume has a lush spiciness I hadn't noticed before. And the sound of her voice when she speaks is even clearer and more musical.

"This is a little disappointing, I have to admit," she says.

"Yeah? How so?"

"I was looking forward to leading you around. I wanted to have control of . . . well. Of you."

"You do, Alison. More than you know."

She's quiet. Without being able to see her, I have no idea how she's reacting to my comment. It's a crazy feeling. Not safe like I expected to feel without having to look into her eyes. I realize I haven't been worrying about that lately. Not nearly as much.

Since we got to Jackson, have I at all?

"This is weird," Ali tells me. "I'm nervous even though I'm asking the questions."

I know exactly what she means. This is intense. I can't see, but I feel very *seen*.

After another moment, she asks, "Your tattoo. What does it mean to you?"

"Someone I loved drew it. She died a few years ago." I'm being vague to protect myself. I've been doing it for four years, with everyone except Grey, who knows the truth. But this exercise is about trust, and Ali just bared her soul to me. I make myself say it because I can trust her and because I want to. I want someone to know.

Maybe even to understand what I've been carrying around all these years. "She was my wife."

I pause. I don't realize I'm making fists until I feel Ali's hands settle on them.

"Adam, we don't have to—"

"No, it's . . . Sorry, this just caught me off guard."

I straighten up and draw my hands away from hers. I don't want to regret what I just said, but regret is waging a war against me. What have I done? I'm now a widower in her eyes, and I'm twenty-three. Too fucking young to wear that shit comfortably, and I don't want her pity, and—*shit*. What did I do?

But then there's this incredible relief sweeping through me, too. I can talk about Chloe. I can finally talk about her. So I do.

"Chloe was . . . She was the first girl I ever loved. We met at school, at Princeton. I was a freshman, a computer nerd. I'd already sold a business by then, but I was still . . . I don't know. I was young. Barely eighteen and unsure what the hell I wanted and who I was. Chloe was the opposite. A year older than me. An art student. Wild and creative. She attacked life. Embraced it. Every single fucking day. She was like a human firework and she . . . she fascinated me." I have to stop for a moment because my voice is hoarse and tight.

"The tattoo on my shoulder is from a sketch she drew. She loved birds. But just the flying kind. Not ostriches or turkeys or . . ." I feel like I'm rambling. I feel like I've been talking for an hour. I feel like I'm saying stupid things that sound so dumb but that mean everything to me, so I wrap it up. "So that's who my wife was. That's what she was like. That's why I got the tattoo. Because I loved her and she loved birds and she drew it and she's gone."

It's as much as I can manage right now. Even if I talked about Chloe for a week, it would never be enough to describe her anyway. You can't bring a human being back to life with words. You just can't.

Ali's fingers have woven through mine. Her grip is fierce, like she's trying to give me her strength. The relief I felt earlier grows more solid inside me, regret seeping away. This is good. It's going to be good. I don't want any secrets between us.

I know what she's going to ask me next. It's the logical question. *How did she die?* I wait for it. Question number two. It's inevitable.

She lets go of my hands. I feel her undo the knot at the back of my head. The blindfold comes away. "Why is it hard for you to look me in the eye?" she asks.

I look away. I look at the fire. "You know why."

"I don't."

"Ali, you do. Don't make me say it."

She falls quiet. Then she scoots closer, her legs between mine, her face inches away. "Adam, it's okay," she whispers.

And I feel like it is, for an instant, and that instant is long enough for me to open the door. "Because it fucking scares me, Ali. You don't know what I lost . . . Jesus, Quick." I glance at her. "What are you trying to do to me?"

She takes my hands again, uncurling my fingers and winding them with hers. For a few seconds, I feel her stroke the pad of my thumb. I don't know how she calms me when calm doesn't seem like it's in the realm of possibility anymore, but my racing heart slows down and I'm breathing again. Didn't even realize I wasn't, but now I am again. In and out. In and out until I don't have to think about it anymore. Until I can answer her.

"Chloe used to tell me . . . she used to say that looking into my eyes, she felt like she could fly. That's why it's hard for me to do that. To go there."

I want to tell Ali that she's changed that. She's changing that for me. But we're talking about Chloe now and I can't, so the thought just balloons into this feeling, like I can't wait for the right time to let it out.

"One more, Adam," she says gently. "Just one more."

"Okay. Just . . . be Quick about it."

Such a dumbass joke, but we laugh. I think we both needed it. A moment of relief.

But then we're right back in when she says, "How did Chloe die?"

I'm ready this time. This is what I thought her second question would be so I'm prepared, and I know I'll tell her everything—not what Rhett knows, that I was married once and my wife died. I'm going to bring her into the very center, with Grey. To the truth only Grey and I know.

"Chloe and I," I hear myself say, needing to give her some background. "We did things a little unconventionally. We got married after we'd only been together half a year, in September, and it was a courtroom wedding for a couple of reasons. I come from money, and she didn't. My parents wouldn't have had a problem with that, but Chloe didn't believe me. She didn't want to face any judgment. She just wanted it to be us at first, and so did I. And we were nineteen and twenty, and you just don't do that. Who gets married at that age nowadays? Anyway, we kept it to ourselves. We decided we'd do it then tell our families over the holidays. That way they wouldn't be able to refuse us or talk us out of it.

"Christmas came around, and we were at my parents' house, and it didn't feel right to me. I don't know why, but I wanted to hold onto her, have her just for myself for a little longer. I felt like we had this amazing secret and I didn't want things to change. I told her we should wait until spring, but Chloe didn't understand, and she could get volatile sometimes. Just really passionate. We'd been drinking because of the holidays, and we ended up fighting.

"I don't yell. If I do, it means something I love is being threatened and that's how I felt. She took me wanting to wait the wrong way. She thought I was ashamed of her. It was the opposite of what I was, but once she got an idea in her mind . . . Anyway, we got to yelling. I couldn't believe she thought those things. We were bringing the house down and that only made it worse. With ice on the ground, it was probably the worst time to get in a car. I knew it wasn't safe, and I didn't want her to drive . . ." I've forgotten how to breathe again and the library feels like it's closing in on me. Like the walls are collapsing. "Give me a minute. I'm going to finish. I just . . . . I need a minute."

Ali leans in, and I feel her head settle on my shoulder. It's a gentle gesture, but I feel like she's holding me up. "Okay," she says. "Take as long as you need."

"Jazz has some answering to do. How exactly is this making my company stronger?"

I sense Ali's smile. "Well, I don't want to speak for you, but I feel like our energetic frequencies are definitely aligning."

I have to finish this. I have to tell her what happened on the road that night, so she'll know I couldn't have stopped it, but she straightens abruptly.

Rhett and Mia stand at the door.

They both look from me to Alison for a moment. Then Mia smiles slightly, and Rhett frowns.

"Sorry, but I've got some bad news, Adam," Mia says. "The storm's picking up. It's supposed to hit tomorrow, but flights are already getting canceled."

"We have to get everybody home," Rhett says. "We have to end this retreat right now."

Chapter 33

Alison

I'm tucked into the bottom bunk, doing my best to stay out of the way as everyone scrambles to pack up before traveling back to LA. Adam's arranged several chartered flights, squeezed in wherever they could fit us. Adam and I are last, and I don't know if that's by luck or by design, but I'm grateful to have just a little more time here. I'm reluctant to get home, to have to face my father and tell him I don't have any more information on Adam.

Even though I do.

Who would have thought that two days of playing around in the snow would leave me feeling so wrung out, so exhilarated, so peaceful, and so anxious at the same time?

I feel lighter today than I have in a long time. And yet I'm also carrying around this deep ache, a feeling of being scooped out in the center. I can't stop thinking about Adam. About the way he looked in the library, shrunken and vulnerable. Maybe a lot like the boy he was when he first met—and lost—Chloe.

I can't help myself. I pull out my phone and do a search on "Chloe Randall." I know I won't find much, but there must be some trace of her. I just want to see her, to have a picture in my mind so that when Adam and I talk about her, I'll know her in some small way—for him.

Nothing comes up at first, but I try "Chloe Randall, Princeton, art," and a link to a PDF appears—a newsletter from the New Jersey Watercolor Society. I click on the link and scroll through a few articles until I find a short piece titled, "Maybe Art Isn't for the Birds." It's about Chloe winning a scholarship to a summer art program.

I scroll further, and there she is. I know it even before I read the photo caption. She's beautiful, with gleaming auburn hair in waves and delicate features.

She stands before a row of paintings—all of birds. I recognize her style immediately, can see the inspiration for Adam's tattoo. But more than that, I see the birds aren't falling, like they do on Adam's tattoo. They're flying.

People talk about feeling someone else's pain, and now I truly do. It feels like someone's tightening a wire around my heart. I want to find him and put my arms around him. I want to love him enough for two people—the girl he lost and the girl I'm trying to become.

"Hey, Ali," Sadie says, coming into the room.

I close out of the browser and put my phone away.

Mia and Pippa come into the room behind her, and they riffle through all the blankets and pick up every pillow. Since Sadie's wearing only one boot, I assume that's the purpose of the search.

"Hey, Sadie. You guys need some help?"

"No, I'm pretty sure it's in here somewhere." She drops down onto the floor and lets out a triumphant, "Aha!" Then she pulls out the twin to her pink Doc Marten and plops onto the bunk to slip it onto her foot.

"Hey," she says. "We're all going to hear Mia's roommate Skyler play at The Echo on Sunday night. Want to come?"

I glance over at Mia, who smiles at me. "Skyler is awesome. Electric cello. You should definitely come."

I'm embarrassed by how moved I am by the invitation. And how much I missed this—just the company of other girls. And with these girls, I feel more a part of things—improbably—than I ever have.

"Will Ethan—"

She shakes her head before I even finish the sentence. "Girls night out. But it would be okay even if he was going to be there, I think. Don't you?"

I nod. It would be, I realize. Completely okay. At least with me—and now, it seems with Mia.

"That would be great. Thanks."

Pippa rises from the bunk and insists on a group hug. "Come on, lovelies," she says. "One for the road."

After I see off the first team—my roommates plus Paolo, I find out that Adam's out taking advantage of one last run on the slopes. I haven't gotten to ski at all, and I'm dying to do it, though I know they're going to close down any second.

I zip into my ski suit and clamp on my boots. I need to get out into the open, to have one last moment with the bracing mountain air, the cottony powdered snow. I need to clear my head and just fire like a rocket down the mountain, leave thoughts and worries behind me. And I need to see Adam.

I say goodbye to Rhett, Cookie, and Philippe before I leave.

"You owe me a major debrief when you get home," my best friend tells me. He waves his hand in front of my face, like he's trying to air-polish me. "Whatever's got you looking so glowy is *definitely* a topic of conversation."

"Definitely," I say and give him a long hug. "I love you."

His eyes widen in surprise, which makes me realize I don't say that often enough. Something I really need to correct.

"Love you too, girl," he says. "Be careful out there." He grins and nods in the direction of Adam's suite. "And in there."

"Haha. Please. We'll be a few hours after you."

"If you say so."

The resort has almost completely emptied, and I'm the only one on the ski lift. The attendant gives me an apologetic smile. "I doubt you'll get in more than an hour before we shut it all down," he says. But I'll take just one run if it's all I can get.

As I crest the top of the mountain, the air is bitterly cold, cutting through my layers of clothes like a knife. It feels bracing and welcome after the drowsy warmth of the lodge.

The ground is powdery and soft as I begin my run, and I take to it, letting myself make wide arcs down the mountain. So many people I know prefer groomed, hard-packed snow, but I love the feeling of sinking in, of challenging my body to keep my skis moving, to position myself just right so the snow doesn't grab me and take me down. It doesn't take long until my thigh muscles burn like crazy, but I love that too—that feeling of having worked for something.

I charge on, looping between pine trees, over shallow moguls. Visibility is a little spotty, with a low freezing mist drifting across my path, and a pale sun almost hidden behind gray clouds. The wind whips the tree branches into a frenzy, dumping clumps of snow down on me as I fly along.

Up ahead, another skier charges along the path in front of me. A guy, from the size of him, slicing through the powder like he owns it. His style is impeccable, and I can tell he takes to it like I do—he's all in, making the mountain his own.

Adam, I realize, and feel a huge grin spread over my face.

He's beautiful, absolutely natural. The way his body moves, sliding almost parallel to the snow. The way he thrusts himself forward, the power of his movements. It's incredible.

"Adam!" I call, and my voice disappears in the wind. I dig my poles in and push harder, trying to get close enough for him to hear me.

I call his name again, and this time, he looks back and starts to slow. I smile, and everything in me lifts. He sees me.

Adam executes an elegant hockey stop, sending out a shallow spray of snow. Then he takes off his goggles, waves at me with a gloved hand. He looks so beautiful standing there, tan skin against the snow. I can see his smile from here, inviting, and so warm. He's all I see as I push in to cover the twenty or so yards between us.

Which is why I completely miss the tree stump.

Chapter 34

Adam

Ali's skis catch on something and I watch her catapult off the snow, then she's twisting sideways in the air. She fights to keep her balance as she lands hard, but she's going too fast and her skis are crossed. I know she's going to tumble before she actually does, then she's sliding and skidding over the snow, her skis popping off, her poles rolling away.

I unsnap my boots and sprint toward her. I'm by her side before she's come to a full stop.

"Oh . . . *wow,*" she says, lying back and lifting her mask. Snow covers her jacket and part of her face, but she's laughing. "That was embarrassing."

I can't laugh with her. I don't like the way she came down.

"Hell of a wipeout, Quick. Are you hurt?"

"Yes." It's only now that she winces and reaches down to her leg. "My right ankle. I think I twisted it."

I kneel by her boot. "Did you feel a snap?"

"No. I don't think so." Her eyes narrow and she smiles. "If I didn't know any better, I'd say you look worried."

The wind is starting to howl around us. Ali and I are the only two people dumb enough to still be out here. She's hurt and we're about to get caught in a blizzard. So, worried? Yes. But panicked? Hell no.

"Just assessing the situation here, Ali. Let me help you sit up." That small movement makes her gasp and grip my arms. "Easy, easy. You, okay?"

"Yes," she nods, but I can tell she's trying to be brave. Alison's starting to shake so I take off my coat and cover her, tucking the edges around her to preserve warmth. Then I pull off my gloves and get my phone from the inside zipper of my shell. "Give me a minute to work my magic."

It's only five minutes before a ski patroller shows up with a snowmobile. He introduces himself as Bob. I help him lift Alison onto the back and briefly consider taking over and making him ski down the hill.

"I'll be right behind you," I tell Ali.

She nods, and I notice her eyes are strained. She's in real pain.

I fly down the mountain and reach the bottom only moments after the snowmobile does.

Ali is taken around the ski school entrance to a medical clinic, where I relieve Bob, the patrol guy, of his duties and pick Ali up, carrying her inside. Bob directs me to a small room with two gurneys, a chair, and an awaiting physician's assistant who introduces herself as Darla Mead.

As soon as Ali's ski boot comes off, I know we're in deep shit. It's swollen badly and as Darla checks mobility and feels around the bones, Alison sucks in a hissing breath and reaches for my arm.

"Is it broken?" she asks.

Darla gives me an apologetic look. "We can't know without an X-ray."

"Let's get an X-ray." I'm trying to stay calm, but it's not easy.

Darla looks at Bob, who answers. "The blizzards closed all the roads around the resort."

"I'll get her there on a snowmobile."

Bob shakes his head. "You don't want to go out there right now. We're looking at up to two feet of snow coming in tonight. In another hour, you won't be able to see your own hands. St. John's is clear across town. That might as well be a state away in these conditions. You're going to have to wait for the storm to blow over."

Unlike Darla, his delivery is cavalier, like he's said this a thousand times and couldn't care less.

"Not an option, Bob. She's hurt."

He shrugs. "She doesn't have a choice."

"Bob, your choice is get her to a hospital or get the shit beaten out of you by me. What's it going to be?"

"Adam." Ali slips her cool hand into mine and squeezes.

Bob's palms come up. "I'm done. I'm out of here."

He's not done. He's just smart enough to know my threat was real. I feel powerless. Not a feeling I wear comfortably.

"I'm sorry," Darla says once he's gone. "Bob doesn't have the best bedside manner in the world, but he is right. It's dangerous out there right now. We can't move her, and we can't bring a doctor here. And, anyway, it's possible that even if you could see a doctor right away, they'd tell you to rest it and let the swelling subside before you could get a diagnosis. In the meantime, I can give you some prescription meds for the pain. They'll take the edge off and make you more comfortable."

Ali gives my hand another squeeze. "Okay," she says to Darla. "That sounds fine."

I'm on the phone as Darla prepares a to-go kit of bandages, ice packs, and pain meds. By the time Ali is ready to leave on crutches, I've checked us into the resort and arranged for our bags to be sent over from the retreat house.

Ali listened as I made it all happen and didn't argue. She still doesn't say anything as we take the elevator to the penthouse suite and meet one of the resort employees, who's there with our bags and key cards.

Inside, I get her settled in the all-white living room. White couch, plush white rug, soft white blankets—and, through the window, white snow. The wood floors and the rustic fireplace look colorful by contrast, adding warmth to the modern space.

I set Ali's crutches inside the door—they've been more of a problem than a solution—and get my arm around her. When she gives me her weight like she can barely hold herself up, I lift her into my arms and step inside. The moment feels strangely matrimonial, but also definitely not.

"You want to go to bed?" I smile as I hear myself. "I've been meaning to ask you that for a long time, but in this case, I mean to prop up your ankle and rest."

Ali's smile is sweet and a little tired. She wraps her arms around my neck and lets her head settle on my shoulder. "Can we just sit out here for a bit?"

"We can do anything you want." I carry her to the couch, but she doesn't let go of me when I set her down. So I sit and keep her on my lap. The feeling of her weight and closeness makes me hungry for her, and suddenly I'm not sure what comes next.

I want to kiss her slowly. For a long time. And everywhere.

I want to tell her I'll do anything to keep her comfortable and safe.

I want to get her a pillow and put her foot up on the coffee table.

"You didn't have to stay, Adam. You probably could've still gotten back to LA."

"No offense, Ali, but that's the dumbest thing I've ever heard you say. Do you really think I'd leave you?"

"No." I can't see her face—her forehead's nestled right under my neck—but I know she's smiling. "I'm okay," she says after a moment. "I know you're worried, but I'm okay. I'm actually . . . good."

"Vicodin kicking in?"

"No. I haven't taken it yet." She snuggles closer, her hand coming up to my chest, her finger slowly twisting around the zipper of my ski shell. "If only Jasmine could see us now."

"Personally, I'm glad Jazz isn't here." The sight of her draped over me, all long limbs and silky blond hair, is making me rock hard. I'm straining against my pants, and since she's sitting on me, against her too. "That'd be awkward for me, especially if you moved from my lap. But you bring up a good point. As your trust partner, it's my job to make you comfortable. What do you say, Quick. How about we get you set up for the night?"

She looks up at me, her blue eyes so open and trusting. "That sounds great."

I help her onto the bed. It's not even fifteen steps away and I'm carrying most of her weight, but her eyes are glazed and her face is pale as I get her perched at the edge of the mattress.

She slides onto it, and her face goes pale.

"You're hurting," I say. Seeing her in pain brings back the same tunnel vision I felt earlier at the clinic, like I can't focus on anything except making it go away. "Wait here. I'll get the pain meds."

"Not yet, Adam. Maybe after some food? I'm really sensitive to medication."

"All right. I'll order something." I'm so locked into tasks right now, into easing her pain that, mentally, I'm already offering the hotel kitchen a two hundred dollar tip if they can get my order up in twenty minutes.

"Wait," she says, catching me by the hand. "Thank you." Her face lights up with a smile so raw with kindness, it guts me.

It's only now that I remember the things we told each other yesterday about Ethan and Chloe. How she'd looked at me the same way then. I didn't get a chance to finish telling her about Chloe. We were interrupted by news of the storm before I could, but when it's the right time, I will.

I lean down and kiss her lips lightly, once and then again, hovering over them a second, and then another second, relishing the taste and feel of her. Kissing her feels like the most natural—but incredible—thing in the world. I have to tear myself away.

"Whatever you need, Quick. I'm right here. Rest."

In the living room, I get on the phone with room service and order soup, salad, and white wine pasta—which I'm ensured will be here in twenty minutes. I grab a quick shower, pull on jeans and a long-sleeved shirt. Then I get Ali's suitcase open, find pajama pants and a soft shirt, and I lay those out for her.

I start a fire, then text Grey to let him know I might not make it back for a few days. Finally, when there's nothing left to do, I watch waves of snow coat the world outside—until I hear Ali calling to me.

"Adam? Can you come here?"

Chapter 35

Alison

He's at my side in a second, his eyes sweeping over me, worried. "Everything all right?"

"Yes. I just wondered if you'd help me change into something else." I'm warm in my ski pants, and the slippery fabric's making it difficult to get comfortable on the bed.

"Already ahead of you," he says and heads off to the living room, returning before I know it with my pajama pants and a cotton shirt.

"Those will be so much better," I tell him.

Gently, Adam helps me sit on the bed, straightening my injured foot carefully, his touch so gentle.

"Pants first?" he asks.

I smile. "That's probably best."

He leans close to me, and again his leather and spice scent washes over me. His hair's still wet from the shower, and he gives off a delicious warmth that makes me want to lean against him, breathe him into me.

"Can you ease up a bit?" he asks, getting his hands under my body to pull down the pants.

We work together to get my pants off, and he doesn't hide his interest in taking in the length of me. When he lifts me against him to help pull my shirt off over my head, I feel every bit of that interest, hard and firm along my thigh.

"Bra on or off?" he asks.

"Off, please."

He leans against me to unclasp it, his hands heating my skin, then pulls the filmy material over my arms. Again, his gaze sweeps over me, and his eyes grow serious, their gray turning smoky and full of depth. "You're beautiful, Ali."

"So are you."

And he truly is. I want to drink in every bit of him—his elegant, aristocratic features, strong square jaw, his bright, intelligent eyes. And his beautiful hands—artist's hands, I think—with their long tapered fingers and neatly squared nails. They have a roughness to them and a polish—so perfectly him.

We decide it's too much work to put on my pants and shirt, so he helps me into a plush white robe and settles me gently back down against the pillows. I can feel the warmth of the now-roaring fire across the room. It's warm and delicious, and I want to sink into the pillows and pull him down with me.

"Do you want to put your foot up?" he asks, sitting down beside me.

"No, I'm fine, really," I say. The ankle is still sore, throbbing a little, but it's the last part of my body that needs attention right now.

He takes my hand and brings my palm to his lips. He plants a kiss there, trails his lips over my wrist. I wonder if he can feel how wildly my pulse is pounding. "What can I do for you?" he asks. "Tell me what you want."

"I really want your hands on me," I say, surprising myself again. I could get used to saying it, to asking for what I want. Something about Adam makes me feel safe to do that. And here, in this lush room, with the fireplace, and snow sealing us in, it seems right to express any desire, to claim every need.

Adam makes a sound like a groan, and his arms come around me. "I want you so fucking much, Alison," he says. "It's killing me."

He buries his hands in my hair and moves his mouth down to capture mine. His kiss is fierce, and I fall into it, clutching onto his broad shoulders. My robe falls open, and the buttons of his shirt chafe against my bare skin, his jeans rough against the inside of my thighs. I pull him tighter to me, my tongue seeking his, needing the taste of him, the softness of his lips, the taut strength of his body.

His lips trace a path down my throat. I sink back against the bed, all of me open to him, wanting him everywhere. He stretches out beside me, the bed sinking beneath his weight. I want to wrap my legs around him, pull him against me to feel again how hard he is, how much he wants this too, but the pain in my ankle makes that impossible. So I clutch onto him, running my hands through his soft hair, feeling his lips and tongue move over me, down to my breasts, circling them with his tongue, bathing me in a warm, perfect pressure.

His thumb spirals over my nipple, his tongue teasing the hollow of my throat now. He feels so good. Every part of him feels like perfection, and I want so much more of it.

Someone knocks at the door, and we freeze.

"That would be dinner," Adam says and offers me a sexy, devilish smirk.

"But I don't want dinner," I say, holding his face in my hands and rising up to tease his earlobe with my teeth. "I want you."

They knock again, and Adam buries his face in my shoulder. We're laughing. And everything feels so slow and sexy and right.

"You'll have to get rid of them," I tell Adam.

He takes my hand and presses himself against me. The feeling of him, the weight of his need, fills me with warmth, starts an insistent, throbbing ache that pulses from the center of me. "And you'll have to get rid of those panties," he says.

Another knock, this one more urgent. With a sigh, Adam pulls away. "I should get that, or they'll just keep knocking."

"I suppose."

He kisses me and then does his best to tuck himself back into his pants and leaves his shirt untucked.

"Stay where you are," he tells me.

"I wouldn't leave this spot."

He goes to answer the door. My cell phone vibrates on the nightstand—Adam must have put it close by for me—and I look at it.

My father. Of course.

I fire off a text to let him know about my ankle and that I'm stuck here for another couple of days because of the storm. He texts back something about being in the perfect position now.

Dad: Hope you're getting the goods on Blackwood.

I smile at his phrasing and answer back.

Ali: Definitely getting everything I need.

He doesn't have to know that I mean Adam—his strength and intelligence and goodness. Or that what I need, I've decided, is to forge my own path. That will be a discussion for my return.

"What's funny?" Adam asks.

I turn to him. "Just life."

He sits and runs his fingers over my skin. Again, that heat, that feeling of being lit from within by another person's touch.

"You know what I think?" he asks.

"No. What?"

Adam leans down, his lips against mine. "I think the hell with dinner. We can eat later."

He traces my lips with his tongue, and I capture it between my teeth, draw it into my mouth. I can't get enough of the taste of him, the feel of his tongue darting between my lips. His kisses are perfection. The weight of him against me the best thing I've ever felt.

I know we should be making promises. I should tell him I'll quit working for my father. Or he should tell me he doesn't need my father's money. We should say that we'll carry this moment back out into the real world with us, that it means something, that it's more than the magic of being contained together, our two bodies drawn to each other in a way that feels inevitable. Eternal.

But I don't speak, and neither does he. If he's like me, he doesn't want to be reminded of all that. He just wants to be here, in this moment. The two of us and the storm and no tomorrow. Not yet.

I reach up and unbutton the first few buttons of his shirt, rising up to kiss the tan flesh exposed there. I'm dying to feel more of him, to be skin to skin with him, to take possession of his beautiful, solid body.

"Can you take this off?" I ask. "Or like, maybe everything?"

He laughs and peels off his shirt, tossing it onto the floor beside us. Once again, I can't get over the sight of him. His broad swimmer's shoulders, lean tapered torso. The shadow and light of his muscled abdomen, and the beautiful artistry of his tattoo, the birds falling—no, flying, becoming clouds.

I run my fingers over the marks and think about Chloe and what he's lost. It makes me feel close to her, the way I did when I saw her picture, charged with carrying her love forward into the future I share with Adam. It feels like an honor.

"Better?" he asks.

"Much."

Adam kisses me again, his warm muscled chest grazing my nipples, carving my insides. His touch is electric. It's heaven. And I never want tonight to end.

His fingers leave a searing path on my skin. They brush over my breasts, my belly. He helps me take off my panties. Everything feels seamless, predestined. His tongue trails against my throat, my mouth, my collarbone, as he parts my thighs and touches me, gently at first, and then more insistently. His fingers move against me, and I'm open to him, so ready for the touch I've been craving for months. Wanting it more than I've ever wanted anything in my life.

"I want to make you feel good, Ali."

"You . . . are . . ." I tell him, but my words are air.

His hands move over me, firm then light, flicking then circling. My body arches up to him, and I capture his hand in mine, pressing him to me, moving up against him, reaching for that place of burning light that I can feel tingling at the edges.

He rises up, our hands locked, bodies moving together, and he looks down at me. The firelight gives his skin an even more golden hue, turns his brown hair to shades of gold and amber. And then I realize that he's *truly* looking at me. His gray eyes lock onto mine, his expression more tender and more searching than anything I've ever seen. It feels like coming upon something wild and rare, something you don't want to frighten away with sudden movement.

The sight undoes me, and the burning spreads through me like a forest fire, hard and lashing, seizing me, searing everything away. I have to close my eyes, to give myself over to the devastating, insistent pull. My body trembles fiercely, and all I can see in my mind is his expression, his gray eyes locked onto my own. Wave after wave sweeps through me until I'm emptied of everything but a floating lightness—joy.

Finally, I open my eyes again, and he's still looking at me. Beau-

tiful. Strong. And now, it seems to me, more boyish somehow. Un-
burdened.

"Alison," he breathes, and he doesn't have to say anything else.

I put my hand against his face and cradle it for a moment, taking
in his direct, beautiful gaze. Without saying a word, I try to tell him
everything I feel. We lie together like that for a long time, and then
we break the moment with a slow, deep kiss, the kind that makes me
forget who I am, who he is, where either begins or ends.

Chapter 36

Adam

*W*hen I wake up, Ali is sprawled across the bed beside me. I have to smile at how much real estate her legs take up.

"Look who's a little bed hog."

My lowered voice sounds louder than it should. The quiet and stillness in here is the kind that's only possible in the middle of a blizzard in the mountains. Through the window, I see snow coming down heavily, but it's not a whiteout like last night.

I take a minute to appreciate the long, graceful groove of Ali's spine. All that smooth, flawless skin sweeping down and then back up to the curve of the one round cheek not covered by blankets. Toned legs that go on forever—one of which ends with a thick bandage.

That ankle's putting a definite damper on my sexual prospects for the foreseeable future. She's a temptation. I've never wanted anyone this much, and I'm aching for her. But I won't do anything that could worsen her injury.

I'm glad she seems comfortable asleep.

Climbing out of bed, I pull on sweatpants and find the bag of supplies from the clinic in the living room. Laying a pillow under Ali's leg, I break open the activator in an icepack and drape it over her foot. Then, reluctantly, I pull the blankets over her. It's a crime to cover her body, but the room has a chill this morning.

She stirs a little, sweeping her blond hair away from her face. "Adam?" she says, sleepy blue eyes fluttering open.

"Right here." I sit next to her and smile, loving that she asked for me before she was fully awake. I reach under the blankets and rub my hand over her warm back, then brush her hair away from her shoulder. "Hey, beautiful. Go back to sleep. It's early."

"Why aren't you in here?"

"I will be in a minute." I'd join her right now, but I hear my phone buzzing in the other room, and part of me never fully relaxes when I leave Grey alone for a few days.

"Good." Her eyes close again. "We have unfinished business."

"Is that right?" Just like that, my body's responding. "What about your ankle?"

"You can't keep using that as an excuse, Blackwood."

I laugh. "Okay. You've talked me into it."

Smiling, she peers at me through her lashes, sleepy and seductive, and I find myself wanting to frame her face and stare into her blue eyes, because anything less than that feels like not enough now. Amazing how that happened. She flipped a switch inside me with that sweet smile, and I want her. Body. Mind. All of her.

"Sleep a little more, Ali. We have time. We'll get to everything."

"Everything? That sounds good."

"Aim higher than good, Quick. We're going for mind-blowing."

"You mean again?"

"I mean always. Every single time."

She laughs. I kiss her bare shoulder then give her perfect ass a little pat on my way into the living room.

"Hurry back, lovely," she says, already sounding sleepy.

"Will do, you exquisite creature of beauty and light."

In the living room, I throw a few logs on the fire to get it burning again, then I grab my phone from the coffee table, and set it down when I realize that Ali and I have the same model, and hers is the one I heard buzzing.

I find mine in the inside zipper of my ski jacket. There's a message from Rhett—nothing from Grey—but what grabs me is the time. I'm shocked to see that it's ten o'clock in the morning. I can't remember the last time I slept this late. And I can't remember the last time I felt this good, either, and then I'm just a complete idiot blinking back tears in my sweatpants, staring at my phone, because *holy shit*. It feels so good to feel this way and I never thought I'd have it again. I never thought I'd have anything even close to this again, like I want to do everything for a girl. *Everything*, just like I told her.

It's real, and I feel different inside, like I'm vibrating with this insane power. This *need* to protect her. To hold her. Make her happy. And then I'm fighting off a laugh, because Jazz had it right.

I *am* made up of millions of energetic molecules—and each and every one of them feels charged and sure and just—fucking—*awesome* because of Ali.

I want to head back to her side but instead I summon a huge amount of willpower and check Rhett's message. He wouldn't call unless something legitimate was up.

When I play it, the quality of the recording is poor, like the storm's affecting service.

"Adam, hey. It's Rhett. You're not going to like this but, remember I told you I was looking into things? Well, I just heard from my contact at Quick Enterprises. Graham Quick's been digging around.

He's doing deep background checks on you, man. He's spending a mint on them. And he's been in contact with the Board, too. He's met with Inoue and Sladek in private. This looks like mighty shady shit, Adam. He's pulling out all the stops trying to get some dirt on you. I wanted to tell you as soon as I heard. Call me back."

I'm hitting the call back icon before the message has fully played, pacing up to the window. There's nothing outside but snow. No one and nothing. Just the white, rounded shapes of the lodge, the restaurants below. The trees and mountains in the distance.

The call doesn't go through. I try again, and get nothing again. And then I turn, because Ali's phone is buzzing on the coffee table.

I grab it to turn the ringer off so she can sleep. When I pick it up, I see a string of messages lit up on the main screen. It's an exchange between her and her father, and how can I not read them when my name jumps out at me? When they're communicating about me?

> **Dad:** Text when you arrive, and let's make a plan of attack.
> **Ali:** I'm here. Let me do things my way. Trust me.

A heavy weight settles in my gut.

> **Dad:** Any progress?
> **Ali:** Just getting started. But I told you, I've got it. Will fill you in tonight.

Text after text like this. I scroll through dozens of them until I get to the end of their exchanges.

> **Dad:** Really hope you're getting the goods on Blackwood.
> **Ali:** Definitely getting everything I need.

And then Graham's reply, which came through just now.

Dad: Good girl. Call me ASAP. I need to know what you
        got on him.

I go so still I'm pretty sure I'm not even breathing. I can't make
sense of it. Nothing adds up in my mind.

I flip the silence button on the side of the phone and set it down.

Chloe.

My deceased wife is the "goods."

That's what Ali has wanted this whole time.

Information for her father. Dirt, as Rhett called it.

Leverage.

Blackmail.

Two days ago, in the partner trust exercise, I told her my wife
died in a drunk driving accident—something I've been covering up
for years.

But now that they know, if they dig enough, they'll find the
police report.

Could I have possibly given her a better weapon?

Graham has everything he needs to publicly humiliate me and
rock the company I've built to its foundations. To drag Chloe's
memory down and—

Alison.

Who I thought was . . .

How?

How could she do this? How the fuck could I have missed it?
Did she know who I was all along on Halloween? Did she come
after me?

I move back to the bedroom and stare at her sleeping form. I
want to rip the blankets off her. Let out the rage that's ripping around
inside me, tearing me up.

I talked to you.

I fucking *trusted* you.

I was ready to give you my goddamn *heart.*

But I don't say a word.

It takes me less than two minutes to pack up the few things I'd taken out of my bag. I do it without making a sound. Without looking at her again. Then I grab my ski jacket, even though there's nowhere to go in this storm.

I'm not trying to go anywhere.

All I know is that I can't be here with her.

Chapter 37

Alison

I wake, smiling, to a knock on the door.

"God, those room service people are persistent." I turn, expecting to find Adam there, but his side of the bed is empty.

"Adam?" I call. No answer.

I hear the electronic beep of a key card in the door, and struggle to sit up, pain slicing through my ankle. Adam must have gone for some breakfast—or lunch, I think, noting the high slant of a pale sun through the suite's picture windows. Outside, the snow's still falling, but the sky is blue beyond, and the fierce winds seem to have tapered off a bit.

The door swings open, and Darla, from the clinic, comes into the room.

"Good afternoon," she says cheerily, but even from across the suite, I can see that her mouth is set in a grim line.

"Hi," I say, drawing the blanket hastily around me. "What—"

"Mr. Blackwood asked me to stop by and look in on you."

"He did?" My brain is awash in static. I look at the window again, look around the room. Something's wrong. "Where is he?"

She comes to the side of the bed and sets down a navy blue medical bag. Her broad, friendly face looks troubled. "Can I look at your ankle?"

"Of course." I gather up the blankets, pulling them off my feet. "But what did Adam say?"

Darla focuses on unwrapping the bandage on my ankle. I can feel her weighing her words, and my heart starts a wild crashing in my chest.

"He left," she says, finally. "He asked me to look in on you. And I know he made arrangements with the hotel. Paid for the room and all incidental charges."

"Was there an emergency? Is everything okay?"

I pick up my phone from the nightstand and don't see anything from Adam. No calls. No texts. Only one from Philippe, saying everyone got back safe and sound, and one from my father, nagging me for details.

Darla peels off the last of the gauze covering my foot. The bruise looks worse—mottled purple and yellow—but my ankle's less swollen. "I'm pretty sure this is just a bad sprain," she says. "But the roads are better. We can get you to the hospital for an X-ray if you want."

What I want is to know where Adam is. I think back to last night, to his eyes on mine, to our connection, which felt truer than anything I've ever felt in my life. What happened between then and now? Where is he?

"Darla," I press. "How did he look when he talked to you? Did he say anything else? I'm worried."

She shakes her head. "He just looked . . . in a hurry. Distracted.

He came by and gave us a ton of cash and asked us to make a house call up at the resort. Gave us his key card and your room number."

"That's it? Nothing else?" I brush my hair back from my face and try to map it in my mind. I half-remember a drowsy, affectionate conversation in the morning. He pulled the blankets over me, touched me sweetly. Smiled. Everything was fine. Or seemed fine, at least.

"He just said he'd cover any other expenses but that he had to go," Darla tells me. She finishes rewrapping the bandage. "Why don't you talk to the hotel? I know he talked to the manager and the concierge. Maybe they can tell you more."

I nod, but in my mind, I keep reliving the steady, serious gravity of his eyes staring into mine.

"*Do* you want to go to the hospital?" Darla asks again.

I shake my head. "You're pretty sure it's a sprain?"

"Ninety percent."

"I'll take my chances then." I want to be left alone. I need to get Adam on the phone, to find out what's happened.

Darla offers me a painkiller, and my ankle hurts enough that I take it.

"All right," Darla says. "We're in good shape here."

You might be, I think.

She props my crutches next to the bed and brings over a robe and a change of clothes. "The concierge is standing by to assist you," she tells me. "Anything you need. Help with anything. Just ask. Can I help you change before I go? Take you to the bathroom?"

As if I don't feel humiliated enough. "No, I'll be okay. Thanks for your help."

She goes, and I pick up the phone to call Adam. My pulse spikes, and I feel like I can't swallow.

My call goes straight to voicemail.

I pick up the phone to text him, but I can't find the words. *Where are you? Why did you leave? Did I imagine everything about last night—about us?*

I'm scared of what he'll say. Scared that I've been so wrong about him—about everything.

Where is he?

A powerful desire pulses in me. A need to dull things, to blunt the ragged fear coursing through my body. I can't sit with it. I'm scared to feel what it will mean if he's left me here. If he never really cared about me.

I struggle up with the help of my crutches and hobble across the room. Everything feels strange, vertiginous, like I'm going to plummet through the floor or fly off into the atmosphere. My ankle lashes me with pain, and it seems to take me forever to cross the few yards to the mini bar.

There I unscrew a small bottle of Absolut and gulp it down straight. Then I do the same with a bottle of Tanqueray, chased with a slightly larger bottle of white wine. So thoughtful of the Four Seasons to keep so much in stock.

For a second, I think I'm going to be sick, but I breathe, get ahold of myself, feel the warmth of the alcohol spread through me. With the painkillers, it's a different kind of buzz, like having my brain encased in plastic. The room is a boat, and I'm riding wave after wave. I can't feel my face or my hands. Or much of anything. Which is what I wanted.

I make it, barely, back to the bed and sink onto it, throwing my crutches onto the floor, the whole bed swaying. The pain in my ankle's remote now. The room stretches around me, growing cavernous, white and sterile like a mausoleum.

My phone buzzes in my hand, startling me. I drop it and search through the folds of the heavy comforter for it. Finding it, I see that it's Philippe.

I'm almost crying as I answer. My lips feel numb. I can't feel the phone when I lift it to my ear.

"Jesus in a hand basket," Philippe says over the line. "It's Armageddon around here. What happened?"

For a second, I can't speak. I don't *know* what's happened, and it's like I've been turned inside out and emptied of everything.

"What's going on?" I manage, and my tongue feels thick in my mouth. "Are you okay?"

"I'm fine," he says, sharply. "But are *you*? You sound weird, Ali."

"I'm . . . fine. What's going on?"

"Rhett just kicked us out of the offices. The whole team."

"What?" This would be the part where I jump out of bed and start putting on clothes, go into emergency coping mode. But I'm too busy drifting on my mattress—so much white everywhere. It feels like the absence of everything—not just color but life.

I make myself focus, try to home in on Philippe's words.

"He didn't look happy about it, but yes. He came in about fifteen minutes ago and told us we had to go."

"Had he talked to Adam? Did he say?"

"No, but I assume the order came from on high. Isn't he there with you? How's your ankle?"

"It sucks," I say. "All of this sucks."

"Ali-girl, what's going on? You don't sound right." The concern in his voice makes the tears come for real, and then I start to sob. My body's wracked with it. I can't breathe for a long moment. I can't make sense of anything.

"I don't know. Adam just left. He threw a bunch of money at people to look in on me and disappeared."

I hear Philippe's intake of breath and then a long moment of quiet as he tries to process. "That doesn't sound good."

"No," I say, shakily. "It doesn't."

"What can I do?"

"I don't know yet," I tell him. "I guess just clear out and—"

"Already done."

"Okay. Tell the team I'm sorry."

"There's no reason for *you* to be sorry. Something's fishy here. I'll dig around, try to find out what's up. And I'm going to call your dad."

"No, wait—" I start to say. If my father gets involved, he'll want information from me. Want me to tell him everything I know. But I need him to help me get out of here. And I *need* to get out of here.

"Go ahead," I tell Philippe, and we end the call.

Family's everything, I hear his voice say. *We need to choose each other every time.*

But I haven't chosen family. I've chosen Adam.

And look where that's gotten you, the voice in my head tells me.

My phone buzzes in my hand again, and I know without looking that it's my father. I put it on speaker. I'm too tired to hold the phone anymore.

Vaguely, I hear him speaking to me. His tone is soothing, solicitous.

" . . . can't believe that jackass left you there . . ." I hear, and I want to argue, but I can't believe it either.

"Alison, honey," he says. And his voice is quiet, confidential. "I'm getting on Thad Weaver's private jet, and we're coming to get you. Give us a few hours, and we'll come take you home. Okay, sweetheart?"

I nod, though I know he can't hear that. I want so badly to be at home, curled in a ball in my bedroom. I want my mom and dad. I want not to hurt anymore, not to feel the grief and anger carving into my high.

"Tell me what's going on," my father says, in that same gentle tone. "What did you find out?"

Collapsing back against the pillows, I look around the suite. The snow's died down. The room is quiet, filled with Adam's absence. Not a trace of him. Like none of it happened. Anger sweeps through me, searing away everything else.

"Nothing, Dad," I say, but I start to cry again, and I know he knows I'm lying.

"Alison," my father repeats, and his tone is so gentle, so whee-dling. "I'll be there in no time, but you have to tell me. What did you get on Blackwood?"

I'm tired. So tired. And I can't think of a reason to protect Adam. He's not here. He's not the one who's going to bring me home. I look down at the phone for a long, long time.

And then I tell my father everything.

Chapter 38

Adam

Thirty hours after leaving the resort in Jackson, I'm finally getting to my house in Malibu. There were no flights, so I rented a car and drove. Stopped at a roadside motel to grab a couple hours of sleep when my eyes wouldn't stay open. Hit five different states trying to avoid road closures. Barely remember any of it.

As I step into the kitchen, rich, fragrant smells flood my nose. Grey's standing at the stove, stirring something in a small saucepan. He's set the table, and on the island, I see a carved turkey, mashed potatoes, string beans, and rolls.

My brother's pretty much a screw-up, but he's a decent cook. Bizarre for a nineteen-year-old kid, but something just translates when he touches food.

He turns and spreads his hands. "Happy Turkey Day, bro."

I drop my weekend bag and stare at him.

For an instant, I'm tempted to tell him about everything that happened in Wyoming. But that urge is gone pretty fast, leaving no trace behind.

"What's going on, Adam?" Grey says.

I look at the food he's obviously spent all day preparing. "This is cool of you, but . . ."

I can't finish. I can't say the words *I can't*. They go against my moral code.

I move to the bar and grab a lowball glass, a bottle of Dewar's, and head for my room. My favorite leather chair sits in front of a floor-to-ceiling window to the Pacific. I sit and pour and take a long pull. The sun is just setting over the ocean. The moon is rising. Such a solid, eternal thing, planets and continents and oceans.

The surf pounds against the sand. The gulls circle and dive.

Clouds float and night falls.

Nothing is steady.

Friday.

At some point, in the morning I'm almost sure, Grey comes in and asks me to surf. We argue. About surfing or something, and I tell him to fuck off.

I watch the beach and I try to forget.

I try to stop replaying every moment with Ali.

When it works, it's because I'm thinking of Chloe, or the mistake I've made that could affect my company like a cancer.

At some point Grey comes back and tells me I need to talk to him. Rhett's worried and he's been calling Grey to check in on me. Mom—"your mother"—called him directly since I didn't check in with her on Thanksgiving, which Grey's especially pissed about. Not that he ever answered the call. He let it go to voicemail.

I let him finish then I tell him to fuck off again.

Saturday is more of the same except I switch my brand to Maker's Mark for a little variety, and my scruff is starting to itch.

Sunday, I feel better. Well enough to leave my room and take the bottle out to the back deck for some fresh air.

"What the fuck, Adam?" Grey says, when I sit at the table and refill my glass.

"Grey, come here."

He comes over, and stands over me. His eyes are drawn and he looks tired, like he hasn't been sleeping, which is weird because insomnia is my job, but I also see a flicker of desperate hope in them.

"Check it out." I point to the beach. "Lucky's figured out his timing. He can launch *over* waves for the tennis ball now."

"Fuck you, Adam. You're not allowed to fucking fail," he says as he walks away.

I spend the rest of the day trying to figure out how he could possibly say that to me when he knows about Chloe.

Monday morning brings a surprise.

Someone pounds on the door. Since it doesn't stop, that means Grey's out somewhere. I get up from my spot on the deck and answer it.

Graham Quick pushes past me and looks around my living room like a repossession agent, measuring my worth by my furniture and the prints on my wall. Seeing everything he's going to take from me.

"You screwed up, Blackwood," he says, his back turned to me. "And by the smell of you, you know it."

"I just want to be clear about something, Graham. You're trespassing right now."

"Are you going to call the police?" He turns, regarding me with Alison's intelligent eyes. There's no gentleness in Graham's though. But maybe there never was in Ali's either.

Adrenaline makes me feel weightless. "No. I was thinking I'd take care of it myself."

"Relax, I'm not going to keep you long," he says, his eyes darting to the patio outside. Through the open glass door, the bottle of whisky and my glass shine on the table, gold and amber in the sunlight. "You look like you're busy with important matters. I've come here with a proposal."

"Is that right? Let's hear it."

"I'm willing to increase my investment in your company to thirty million. That's a lot of money, Adam. I think even a spoiled little shit like you can recognize that. But in exchange, I want majority share. Fifty-one percent. And I want the chairman position on the board. You agree, and I don't say a word to anyone. No one needs to know you're a pathetic drunk who wrapped your wife around a tree four years ago." He smiles. "That would be bad, wouldn't it? For Boomerang's bottom line? For the studio venture with Brooks Wright?"

My head feels scattered with all the whisky, without any sleep, and it takes a minute for the words to hit. When they do, I'm transported back to that night with Chloe. I'm seeing the car spin out, and the tree move at us so fast, like it's flying over the icy road instead of the other way around.

I feel a shaking inside me, deep in my chest. This was my grief and I kept it safe. I kept her safe and now she's not. Her life is cheapened by Graham Quick's words. She's a bartering tool now. A weapon.

Chloe would have hated this.

But not as much as I do. As much as I hate that I let this happen.

"You've built a good foundation, Adam," Graham continues. "Blackwood Enterprises is healthy, I'll give you that much. You seem to have enough balls to get things started. A business. A marriage. But you're a real fuck-up on follow-through. At some point, you'll see that I'm helping you. You need me. But for now, it's time to step aside and let a real businessman take over."

"If you mention my wife to me again, I will beat the living shit out of you."

Graham's thick eyebrows climb. "Such violence. That's it, son. Throw a punch so I can get you on assault, too."

Something snaps inside me and I'm striding to Graham. He flinches and steps back. "You're a fucking killer, Blackwood," he says, moving to the front door. "But I've got you cornered. I think you know it already." He reaches for the door handle. "Oh, there's one other condition I forgot to mention if you're interested in retaining your reputation and your company. Keep your hands off my daughter or I will destroy you."

When he's gone I head back outside, but I can't sit down. I pace like a wild animal trapped in a cage. I can't bring the glass up to my lips, either. Sky and ocean are everywhere around me, but all I see is twisted metal and blood. Then everything changes, and all I see is white snow. Ali's long legs, stretched out all over the bed.

I grab the edge of the patio table and lift. The sound of glass shattering sounds wrong and right and perfect with the cry of seagulls and the crash of waves behind it.

I go to the key hook by the garage but I stop myself. I know better. I know not to get shitfaced and get behind the wheel of a car. I've learned at least that much in my life and her house is only a mile up the road. I pull on my Nikes and take off at a run.

Chapter 39

Alison

I trundle around the stable on my knee scooter, feeling perfectly useless and like I'm suffering the world's first weeklong hangover. Luckily, my ankle's only sprained and, now that it's encased in a proper bandage and an orthopedic boot, it's feeling better. But all of the rest of me feels bruised. No, broken.

The scooter and the bandages upset Persephone and Suede. I'm foreign to them. I must smell different, and I'm sure it's like I'm a different creature—half girl, half machine. Suede backs up in her stall when I come over. She paws at her mat, kicking up shavings. Her ears twitch like she's on high alert.

"Come on, lovely," I say. "It's just me."

I hold a palm full of oatmeal and raisins out to her, but she clomps around in her stall, turning her back to me.

"Great." I'll have to have Joaquin come in later and take care of them. Heat rises in my throat, and my eyes prickle. It's ridiculous to feel personally rejected, but I do.

I start to wheel my scooter around to head back out of the stable when the door swings open, crashing into a wall full of tack and making a heavy iron rake drop to the ground.

It's Adam. But not. He's unshaven, disheveled. He's wearing gym shorts and a band t-shirt. His brown hair flies everywhere, and his face is red with exertion. I've never seen him this way.

He stalks up to me, and I start to back away, but he seizes the handles of the scooter, anchoring me in place. The odors of alcohol and sweat waft toward me, and I can't reconcile them with the person I know.

I feel suddenly, unaccountably frightened, and on this scooter, there's not much I can do to protect myself.

"I will never give you and your father what you want, you hear me?" His gray eyes look darker, almost black, and they drill into me now with so much anger, it's hard to believe I ever found tenderness there.

Calm down, I tell myself. *Don't let him rattle you.* "I don't know what you're talking about," I tell him. "But thanks for dumping me in the middle of a blizzard."

"Come on, Alison," he says, and every word comes out sharp and derisive. "I took you for a lot of things but never for a liar."

"And I took you for a lot of things, too," I say. "I guess we were both wrong."

It hurts to see him like this. In some private agony I don't understand. Part of me wants to rush in to try to make it better, but he doesn't deserve that. He isn't what I thought. He left me like I meant nothing.

Adam releases the scooter and steps back. Scrubbing at his scalp, he says, "I need to know whose idea it was. Yours or your father's."

"What idea? What are you talking about?"

"Please," he says, and his jaw clenches. "Just answer me. I need to know what was real. If this was just some plan you had all along or if it happened later. You need to tell me. Now."

"What plan? Adam, I swear to God I don't know what you're talking about! All I know is that we spent a night together that I thought—" I can't say it. Can't give it to him. I can't tell him that I thought that night meant something. Meant everything. I can't be vulnerable with him. Never again. He doesn't deserve it.

"Thought what, Alison?" He comes back up to me again, and I see he's unsteady, swaying. His eyes look glassier, and it's like his body is draining of energy right in front of me. "That you'd make me feel like a complete asshole? Like the world's biggest sucker? Is that what you thought?"

"No! Of course not. I don't—"

"Really hope you're getting the goods on Blackwood," Adam says in a mocking tone. "Does that sound familiar? *I'm getting everything I need.*"

It does sound familiar, but for a second I don't know why. Then it dawns on me. My cell phone. He read my texts. He thought . . .

"Adam, I didn't . . . That's not what I meant."

My ankle throbs violently, and I'm having a hard time staying upright on the scooter. I need to sit down. I need him to hold me and to believe what I'm saying. But his expression, his rigid posture, tells me how impossible that is.

"Really? Because it's pretty obvious what you meant. And it's pretty obvious you went right to Daddy and gave up *my life* and *my pain,* so you could both get what you want."

"No, I didn't."

But I did. I did exactly that. Only it wasn't planned. It wasn't a scheme I'd been concocting all along. "You have to believe me. It wasn't like that."

"Did it make you feel good to run her through the mud? That's what you Quicks do, isn't it?"

"Adam, that's not fair. I didn't mean—"

"I loved her, and you fucking used her. I just don't understand why," he says. "Don't you get that Boomerang is the one thing I do right? That it's the one thing in my life that's not fucked up? Why would you want to take that away from me? Those people. The work. I created all of that. Maybe that feels like trivial bullshit to you and your father, but it's everything to me. Everything."

"No one wants to take it away from you," I say.

He arches an eyebrow. "Right. No one except your father."

"We're just trying to invest, not control it."

His laugh is an ugly bark, but understanding brightens his clouded gaze. "Jesus Christ, Alison. You really don't know, do you?"

"That's what I've been trying to tell you." Reaching out a hand to seize his, I say, "Please, just explain it."

But he pulls away from me and backs off a few steps. "Ask your father to explain it," he says. "Ask him about how he just came over to my house to blackmail me. And call me a killer." He puts his hands over his face, and his shoulders shudder. Muffled sounds fill the silence between us, sounds of raw agony that rake through me. "You gave him everything he needs to ruin me."

I can't stand to see him like this and know I'm the cause of it.

"I never said anything like that," I tell him finally. "I never called you a killer. I'd never do that. I just said you drove drunk and had an accident. I know I shouldn't have said even that, but I was so hurt. I didn't know why you left me there. I felt like you used me and threw me out. Those texts. I was just giving him an answer so he'd leave me alone. I never planned to hurt you. I'm so sorry I did."

I try to get off my scooter, to go over to him. I want to put my arms around him and help in some way, but I can't. I know I can't.

He sees my intention and backs closer to the door. "No, leave it alone," he says.

"Adam, you're not a killer. You're good. You're so—" There aren't words for everything he is. Everything he means to me. "It was just a mistake."

"You're right," he tells me. "It was a huge mistake. It *should* have been me. *I* should have been the one driving the car. But it was Chloe who drove."

And then he disappears through the stable door, and I hear his footsteps, slower now, receding into the quiet night.

Chapter 40

Adam

After seeing Alison, I regress and end up back in the chair in my room. I want night. Darkness. The sunshine offends me. But the day seems to want to continue, despite what I want.

My phone rings on the table beside me. Linda and Lucky throw the tennis ball for an hour and go home. A family I don't know has a picnic and rides boogie boards and builds a sandcastle. Don't understand that, building sandcastles. Why build something if it's only going to get washed away? All of this as the sun drops lower and lower.

At six at night, my phone is still ringing and buzzing every ten minutes.

Texts come from Rhett. Cookie. Brooks.

My mother. My father.

Rhett again. Brooks again. Mom again. And so on.

Even Jazz calls. Sweet of her.

But no Alison.

And I hate that that's the one call I'd take. The one person I wouldn't be able to resist right now.

She didn't *know*? Is that true? Am I supposed to believe that?

The problem is I want to. I think I need to believe her.

Yeah. I do.

I tell myself I'll go to work tomorrow—Tuesday. Tuesday I tell myself Wednesday, and the whole week disappears that way.

It's a shitty mindset, but I didn't build a company from nothing to end up having a minority stake in it. But I can't think of a way to get it back without dragging Chloe's memory through even thicker, shittier mud.

Finally, on Friday, Grey barrels into my room. It's maybe noon. Midday, I think, and I've gotten too tired to sit and drink. I can't keep up with the waves and the sun, and Lucky's gone and sandcastles depress me so sleep has become my new thing.

"You know what?" Grey announces. "I changed my mind. You can fail, Adam. Actually? I think you *need* to fail. I think you need to fucking fail, and I'm here to help you." He claps his hands together. "Let's do this. Right now."

I lift my arm and peer at him. Jesus. He almost fills the doorway. And when did he get so ripped? With his shaved head and his tattooed sleeves, he strikes me as the kind of guy you don't mess with. Unless he's your little brother.

"Shut the door on your way out, will you?"

"Get up, Adam. Get your sorry drunk ass up."

"Okay. Fine. I'm going." I roll myself up and wait for the room to stop spinning. Then I walk past him, downstairs, into the kitchen. To the bar. "Good call," I say, reaching into the liquor cabinet. "It was about that time."

Grey pins me so fast, I never even see him coming.

I'm reaching up one instant, the next I'm hitting the wall and staring right at my brother's eyes.

"I need you to fucking *listen,*" he says, jamming his forearm into my neck. "Can you do that, big brother?"

I've seen this side of him, but it's never been directed at me. Never, because I know the last person Grey would ever want to hurt is me. Which means he's scared. Scared enough to go completely against his nature. That's a wake-up call.

I nod. "I can listen."

"Good. Sit down." He shoves me toward the breakfast table. Then he pours a huge glass of water and sets it down in front of me.

For a few seconds, we're quiet, and I can almost feel us both adjusting to this new order. To the Grey who challenges me as an equal. To the fact that maybe, for once, he's the one with the right idea.

"Here's what I think," he says, crossing his arms. "You did this big cover-up about Chloe, right? About what happened to her. You spend almost four years hiding it, telling a lie. Telling our family and her parents that you did it. That you were driving because you think . . ." Grey lifts his shoulders. "Shit, I don't know. Because you're trying to *exalt* her memory, or honor her life by keeping her rep clean or some shit. But you know what? You didn't just do it to protect her. You did it to punish yourself. You did it because you, Adam Blackwood, can't fucking stand that it *wasn't* your fault, because you're a goddamn control freak, Adam. You're so—"

"You don't know what you're—"

Grey uncrosses his arms and points at me. "You said you were going to listen so let me fucking finish, okay? Jesus. Thank you." He drops his elbows on the table. "So you cover for Chloe, then you add another layer in the bullshit cake by covering up *that* lie from the public because you've got this fancy company, and no one can know the truth—which actually isn't the truth, it's your cover-up—about that night. So now you're controlling Chloe's past by rewriting history. And you're controlling your company's future by hiding your own lies. Are you seeing a pattern here, Adam? Mr. Puppetmaster? You're fucking doing it with me by playing the go-between with Mom. Letting me live here and putting up with all my shit."

Grey shakes his head and falls quiet for a moment. "You can't make all our lives perfect. You can't fix everything. You can't take everyone's bullets. You've got to let go, Adam. You're going to kill yourself this way if you don't. And if that happens . . . shit. I'm as good as dead too."

I have to fight back tears for a few seconds. I think Grey does too. I can't lose someone else I love.

We're quiet for a long, long time. Just sitting. Just breathing. And when my thoughts turn to that night on Christmas Eve, I let it come. I let the images streak before my eyes in high definition, without pushing them back.

And I see Chloe, and how we fought because I just wanted a few more weeks of having her all to me.

"What does that even mean, Adam? Are you regretting this? Me?"

We were in the basement game room at home. Upstairs, the festivities continued without us, Christmas carols and eggnog and the sound of my dad's laugh, followed by Grey's.

"Chloe. That's not what I said at all."

I couldn't find a way to explain. My parents' marriage was so public. My mother and father had always moved in social circles. Their time together was restaurant openings and galas. Write-ups in the society pages. I was fine with that, someday. If Chloe and I both wanted it. But not yet. I wanted what we had for a while longer. The feeling of the two of us discovering the world together like we were tourists in a foreign country. Untouchable. Invisible.

I didn't want to share her yet. I just wanted a few more months.

But no matter how much I tried to explain, she seemed to hear, "I don't want anyone to know about you."

"You're embarrassed about me because I'm not rich, like you are. I don't have a big house like this. I don't have a goddamn pool table in a game room. I don't have a perfect family like yours. Why can't you just admit it, Adam? You made a mistake. You shouldn't have married me."

"Chloe, please listen to me. Come here." But she wouldn't come near me. We'd been drinking, and she was crying. She couldn't keep still.

"You're afraid of my moods, Adam," she continued. "I'm not always calm and rational like you. Well, this is me! You're stuck with this now!"

I'd seen her mood swings before. I wasn't afraid of them. I loved everything about her. "The only thing I'm afraid of is losing you."

"How is it so easy for you?"

"Because I love you, Chloe."

She whirled and ran, snatching the keys off the hook.

My family went quiet as we tore through the kitchen and headed out the front door. Chloe jumped into the driver's seat of my car and I didn't want to tell her no. She was so upset. So mad at me. I just wanted her to be happy. So I took the passenger seat. As she gunned it out of the driveway, I saw Grey. Grey at just fifteen, skinny as a flagpole, standing in the driveway.

And it was too fast. Everything was. Our words. Her tears. The car. We'd only gone a few miles when she lost control and the tree came flying. And everything went black. And then after—on the bloody ice, where I found her, where she was thrown from the crushed convertible. In the ambulance, at the hospital and the morgue and the church and the cemetery, how all I could think was that I could've stopped it. I made her cry, and I made her run, and I made her lose control on the ice. I made that tree fly.

I should have been driving. I deserved to take the blame.

So I took it.

I made Grey swear he'd never tell the truth, that he saw Chloe drive away. Then I lied to my parents and hers. To the lawyers, who blamed the icy roads over the alcohol level in my blood—which wasn't all that high. Not nearly as high as Chloe's.

No one asked questions.

They grieved for Chloe. They grieved with me, for my beautiful wife.

We packed her death away in the lies I created for four years.

And it has been destroying me.

Grey scratches his jaw, pulling me back to the present. "You've got to let the bad shit be what it is sometimes, Adam."

I hear myself laugh. "Wow. That should be cross-stitched on a pillow."

Grey smiles. "Damn right, brother."

"You were saying I shouldn't be the rescuer, the middle man. So what you're telling me, Grey, is that I should kick you out?"

His eyebrows rise. "Oh, hell no. I'm not going anywhere. It was just an example." He pushes up from the table. "Come on," he says.

"Where to now, Buddha?"

"The water. I'm tired as shit of surfing alone."

Chapter 41

Alison

My father's asleep in the study, *Forbes* magazine draped across a knee, and his reading glasses sliding off the bridge of his nose. I listen to his guttural breathing, watch his chest rise and fall. He seems so different to me now. His face—chapped from so much time in the sun and wind, with circles of white around his eyes from always keeping his sunglasses on—looks like a stranger's face. His jaw looks more slack. His hands, clasped over his stomach, look like an old man's hands.

For three days he kept himself away. On "business," though the only business he seems to have lately is ruining people's lives. And when he returned, he made sure to do it on an evening when we have company—my mother's book group. Which makes me realize, as though I needed more proof, that I've been totally played.

A feeling washes over me—a strange, acute kind of buoyancy that makes me feel like a balloon, filling up, up, up, about to float into the stratosphere. It's the sensation I have when the *Ali Cat* powers away from the dock or when Zenith used to break into a gallop, the two of us in perfect sync. I feel exultant and filled with possibilities.

I go and sit down next to my father, remove the glasses from his face, close the magazine and tuck it away beside me. And then I shake him awake. Not gently.

He starts and blinks at me, slowly bringing me into focus. "Jesus Christ. You could have given me a heart attack."

"Don't do this to Adam."

He sighs. "Alison, please."

"I mean it, Dad. It's not right to blackmail your way into owning a company. You *have* to know that."

He sits up then, fixing me with a glare that once would have withered me on the spot. Instead, a glassy calm settles over me. I'm here with him, but I'm also gone. Some part of me has broken free for the first time, truly free, and I know he can't sway or scare me anymore.

"Did Blackwood come to see you?" He pounds the couch between us with his fist, but it's like the gesture of a little kid. "Damn it, I told him to keep away."

"Of course he came to see me. He was angry, and he had every right to be. What you did was wrong."

"It's business."

"It's still wrong. To him and to me. If I'd known what you had planned I never would have gone in there."

He chuckles, and the sound stiffens my spine like a fork scratching against china. "Which is why I didn't tell you what I had planned."

I know this. Of course I know this. But hearing the words, put so bluntly, still comes as a shock.

"So you used me."

He shakes his head. "Stop being so dramatic. I *employed* you. A smart employer understands the assets at hand and makes the best use of them."

"You're talking about me like I'm no one! I'm your daughter!"

"*I'm* well aware of that," he says. "Are *you*?"

"What does that mean?"

"It means you need to get your priorities straight. It's our family business. You should be happy we'll get to guide the future of Black-wood Entertainment. I'll put you in charge of Boomerang. That's what family does. We help each other succeed."

Using my crutch, I rise shakily from the sofa. I can't stand to be close to him anymore. "I don't want to succeed on those terms."

"Stop being so goddamned high and mighty. You'll have your own company to run. At twenty-two years old. Think about it. You can fire that Mia girl if you want. It'll be up to you. Because I want that for you. Because I *got it* for *you*."

A feeling blasts through me—sharp and gutting. It's like my chest is suddenly home to a million prickling icicles.

"You have got to be fucking kidding me," I say.

My father's eyes widen, and his tone is quiet and cold. *"What did you just say?"*

"This is for me? Taking over a business that someone else spent his life—"

"His life? He's twenty-three goddamned years old. What life?"

"How does that matter?" I cry. "It's *his*. It's not yours. You don't get to just have everything you want all the time. You don't get to gobble people up and spit them out. You don't get to lie to me. You don't get to cheat on—"

"Stop it, Alison," my father interrupts, eyes cutting to the doorway. He gets to his feet and starts to push past me, but I grab his arm. I'm aware of how big I've always thought him to be. How he towered in my imagination. And now I see he's not that giant. He's not very big at all.

"You're always talking about family. But we don't matter at all, do we? We're just . . . We're like your accessories."

"I'm done with this conversation," he says, and pulls away from me. I stagger back, hurting my ankle and struggling for balance on my crutch. I know it's pointless. I know we're done.

"Fine," I say. "Just one last thing."

"What?"

"I quit."

My father stalks out of the room, and I stand there, suddenly weak-limbed and trembling. A voice inside me asks, *now what*? Now I need to do what I can for Adam.

I limp out of the study and head for the kitchen, where I find my mother sitting in the dining nook by the window, staring out at the scrub-covered foothills and, beyond those, at the far off sliver of surf as it pounds against the shore.

"Mom?"

She looks up and gives me a faint smile. "Want some tea, sweetheart?" she asks. Even in the dim glow of the under-cabinet lights, I can see her eyes are glossy, her posture sunken.

Sitting down beside her, I rest my crutch against the table and look at her. "Did you . . . Did you hear us?"

She gives me a faint smile. "Yes, but it wasn't anything I didn't already know. Except that he'd involved you too."

"You knew?" I ask. "About dad and—"

"I'm not a fool, darling."

I'm floored and sink back in the upholstered chair, bumping my head on the frame of the picture hanging behind me. A painting my mother had done of Zenith. I don't remember thanking her for it.

"But Mom, I don't understand. How could you stay with him? How could you be all right with it?"

"Of course I'm not all right with it. But you and your sister were so young the first time. And I didn't know a thing about being on my own. It sounds ridiculous, I know." She shrugs. "But I couldn't imagine life without your father. Even if it's meant this . . . *this* life. And this life affords me opportunities that I'd never have otherwise. All of those charities. I can do so much good."

I can't believe what I'm hearing. My mind carries me back through my whole life, to every missed birthday party, recital, and horse show, to every holiday filled with extravagant gifts for my mother. Furs she never wore. Bold, expensive jewelry that never seemed to come out of the boxes. My mother's small protest, I realize, and my fingers drift up to touch the earrings I have worn every day for months.

I did what she resisted: I let him bribe me.

"He told me it didn't matter," my mother says, circling a burgundy-polished nail on the glossy kitchen table. "He said these were just . . . moments outside of our life together. What matters is—"

"Family," I finish.

I wonder if somewhere along the line he and Catherine had that same conversation. If that's why she's so distant from all of us, because she's been carrying around this secret, too. All of us, played against one another for my father's convenience.

We're both quiet. Only the sound of the dishwasher clicking off interrupts the silence. Sitting here, I feel like it's not just the rug that's been pulled out from under me but the entire house.

Finally, I ask, "What now, Mom? We can't just . . . keep going like this, can we? It's so wrong. And it's not just us."

She takes my hand and squeezes it. "I know."

"So is there any way to stop him? What do we do?"

My mother pushes her chair back and stands. "We go to bed, darling," she says. "And we get up in the morning."

I groan and put my face in my hands. "That's it? We just keep going like this? No one ever stops him? He just steamrolls over everything?"

"I'm not saying that," she tells me and pulls my hands away from my face. "I'm saying we get some rest so we can get up and fight again."

"There has to be something we can do," I insist.

"If there is," she says, "we'll figure it out tomorrow."

Chapter 42

Adam

The office is quiet as a church as I hit send on an email to Brooks, locking in the screenwriter for our first feature, and sit back. I wait, but I don't feel the stir of excitement I'd always imagined this moment would bring.

Blackwood Films is happening.

I just took another huge step forward in realizing my dream.

Of owning forty-nine percent of a film studio.

I shake my head at myself and glance at the empty hallway outside my office. I let everyone go at noon today, the Friday before New Year's Eve, but now I wish someone were here. Maybe this would feel better.

As I shut down my computer and pack up to leave, I can't help but think about the past month. I spent December trying to find a way to keep my company *mine,* but Graham was right. There was no way. He had me cornered. If I refused his offer, he'd have broken the Chloe news to the press. And even if I'd stepped up and told the truth, admitted it wasn't me who drove that night, I know how the media works.

Tabloids. Newspapers. Investors and business analysts. They see scandals from ten thousand feet up. The details don't matter. If you're anywhere close, there's stink on you.

A young, reckless CEO who killed his wife in a drunk-driving accident is just the kind of scandal that can sink a company—even a healthy one. I couldn't get rid of Graham without exposing myself and my company to a huge amount of bad press so I had to accept his offer.

As soon as the lawyers organize the contracts, Graham and I will be business partners.

It'll feel like signing a deal with the devil, I'm sure, but I'm trying to keep Grey's words in my mind. *You've got to let the bad shit happen sometimes.*

No matter how I look at it, though, locking into a relationship with the guy who's blackmailing me seems like the kind of bad shit I *shouldn't* let happen.

Grey's advice has helped in other arenas, though. I've talked to both Chloe's parents and mine and told them the truth about that night, and while it wasn't easy, it was easier than I thought it would be.

Christmas, too. The four-year anniversary of the night I lost her.

Grey cooked lasagna and Brooks came over. It was a decent night. The best Christmas I've had in four years. Granted, the look on Grey's face when he unwrapped the karaoke machine I bought him played a big part in that.

I've let go of the lie I'd been keeping for Chloe—which should've made me feel incredible—but Graham nailed me to a wall at pretty much the same time. With everything with Alison, it's been a better-but-worse kind of feeling.

As I lock my office, I stop and stare at the keys in my hand, fighting off the feeling for this place. There's nothing I can do.

Another week or so and it'll be Graham's too.

Rhett catches me as I'm getting in the elevator.

"Hey," he says, darting inside as the doors close.

"I didn't realize you were still here, Rhett."

"Just wrapping up some last-minute stuff. I saw that you were here and had a question—about the party tomorrow at the Quicks?"

Graham decided to throw the company's holiday office party at his home. *As a gesture of goodwill* was how he put it on the phone. *The night's on me.*

But it feels more like he's making a statement. That statement being *your kingdom is now in my full control.*

"What about it?" I say.

Rhett's smile is lopsided. "We were all just wondering if you want us to meet at your house first, so we could go over together? You're right down the street, right? We won't cause you any work. We just thought it'd be cool if we met at your place and went together."

"Who's we?"

"Well . . . everyone."

"The whole company."

Rhett lifts one shoulder, to match his crooked smile. "Yeah."

The elevator opens and we step out of the elevator into the garage. "Sure, Rhett," I say, smiling. "I'll see you then."

The drive home to Malibu is all Alison, just like it's been for the past month.

It's Ali as Catwoman. Ali in her scuba gear, puffing her cheeks out like a grouper. Ali in snow gear. Ali in the stables, looking crushed as I yelled at her.

I'm totally zoned out on the drive. I don't even realize I'm pulling up to her house until I'm there, idling in front of the Quicks' wrought-iron gate.

I think about punching in the code, driving in, but Graham lives here and this isn't about him. What I have to say is only for her, so I text her instead.

Adam: I'm out front. Can we talk?

I stare at the phone, not sure what happens next. Maybe she tells me to fuck off?

I know I'm going to see her tomorrow at the party—and maybe that's why I'm here now—because seeing her and not being able to talk to her . . . that's going to kill me. I need to talk to her, and I don't want to do it tomorrow in front of other people.

A full minute passes. I'm just accepting the fact that she's not going to respond to my text when the gate opens and she comes running out, a flash of wavy blond hair and a flowing red dress.

She jumps into the passenger seat, pulling the hem of her dress up so she can shut the door, and then she's right next to me and there's not a single thought in my head anymore, only relief. Only a massive dose of relief that knocks the wind out of me like I've just been punched in the solar plexus.

I back out of her driveway and head to my house.

The drive is short. The only sound is the rev of the Bugatti's engine as I accelerate onto the freeway, but I'm hyper aware of her. Of the way she smells and the way her fingers drum nervously on her leg. Her ankle seems fine, and it's one thing. Just one of the millions of things I want to ask her about, and say to her, but I don't want to rush. I was such an asshole to her the last two times we were together. I want to treat her right. If there's any chance at all, I have to treat her the way she deserves to be treated—and she deserves the best. She deserves everything.

We get to my house, both of us still quiet, careful.

Alison steps into my living room like her father did a month ago, except different. She's calm and steady, nothing like Graham's aggressive presence, and she doesn't observe the *things* in my house either. She moves to the glass doors and stares at the ocean. She stands there and drinks in the view like I would. Like I do.

It takes me ten seconds to realize I could watch her this way forever. Every second with her is a rush and it feels right to have her here. With me.

"I've wondered what your view was," she says, breaking our silence. "I've been trying to picture what it is you see from your house."

"I look exactly where you're looking, Ali. But I see you."

Ali glances at me and I see a flash of surprise, then pain, before she looks away. She walks over to the kitchen and picks up the basketball Grey left on the counter. Naturally. Because that's where basketballs go.

"Is this your brother's?" she says.

I nod. "Grey."

"Is he here?" she asks.

I hear the slightest tremble in her voice.

"He's in San Diego for the weekend."

Grey's there for a New Year's Eve gig. His second time singing on stage. I hate that I can't be there, but I can't miss my company party.

Ali's not looking at me. Now she's the one, I think. She's the one who won't look at my eyes. But I can't go there again. I'm done hiding. Done with lies and silence and distance. Done with everything that keeps me away from her.

I walk over and take the basketball from her, setting it back on the counter. Then I take her face in my hands and look into her blue eyes.

They're teary, and the pain I see in them slays me. I put it there by leaving her in Jackson. By yelling at her. I will never do that again.

"I'm sorry, Alison. Forgive me."

Her words come fast. "It was my fault too. I didn't know, Adam. I had no idea what my father was doing. I thought he was trying to protect the company. My family. And I told him—"

I bend and catch her words with my mouth, kissing her. "I know," I say. "It's okay." I kiss away the tear on her cheek, and come back to her lips, tasting them over and over. She's so sweet and soft. I can't get enough of her. "We're okay now. It's over."

"You're not mad at me?"

"Mad?" I lean back. "No way. I'm so happy. I'm so fucking happy right now, Ali. You have no idea."

She smiles and her arms circle around my waist. "I think I do."

"God, Alison. I've missed you." The words tumble out easily. I bury my fingers into her long silky waves and let them go. "It killed me when I thought I lost you. I haven't stopped thinking about you. I couldn't get you out of my mind. Not for a minute. Not for a god-damned second."

Ali lifts up onto her toes so our eyes are even as she listens. She looks into my soul, and I let her. I know that right now, she's giving herself to me. That I'm doing the same. She's mine and I'm hers, and I trail off because nothing else matters anymore. Nothing except her.

She feels it, too. She smiles, and then we're just smiling at each other, a pair of fools, until she laughs.

"Hi, lovely," she says, and then she kisses me.

I turn into raw need. I pull her into my arms and kiss her back. Her mouth opens to mine, so willing and hungry. She presses her breasts against me and my hands are all over her.

"Yes," she breathes.

My desire shifts into high gear and I'm blinded to everything that's not her. The need to be buried deep between her legs is the only thing. I've wanted this so long. "Alison, I want to do this slowly, but—"

"Let's do slowly later," she says.

Chapter 43

Alison

*A*dam smiles, and every last bit of me melts. He firms his hands under me and pulls me even tighter against him. He's so hard it makes me gasp, my body instantly reduced to one pulse point, a sharp ache where our bodies join.

"I don't know if I can make it to the bedroom," he says.

"I'm not picky."

He laughs, but still he carries me through the living room, down a short hallway to a master suite with glossy cocoa-colored walls, slate-blue accents, and a modern leather chair by a wall of floor-to-ceiling windows looking out over the ocean. The space is sleek and luxurious—so perfectly Adam that it's like I've been here already. Like it's home.

His tongue teases my mouth, and I squeeze his waist with my thighs, grip his hair to pull him closer, as close as I can get him. We tumble onto the bed together, still kissing but laughing too, trying to find our way up the bed without breaking our kiss, without our hands having to do anything but touch each other's bodies.

He pushes my skirt up my thighs, presses himself against me, coarse twill against silk. I arch up to him, and we rock there, mouths crashing together, and already I feel that dizzying, cresting feeling. My body wants to climb toward that place, toward that bright undoing, and I want it but I also want to ride this, to make it last forever.

Easing off me, he slides off the end of the bed and stands there, facing me.

"Come here." His eyes shine. His mouth looks moist and bruised from our kissing. Leaning forward, he slips his hands beneath me and tugs me toward the edge of the bed, until I'm at the very end, legs dangling off so my toes scrape the wood floor.

"I'm glad you're not in your Catwoman costume," he says, grinning. "Or in scuba gear. Or a snow suit." Reaching beneath my skirt, he pulls down my panties, his fingers skimming over me, heat against heat.

"I'm . . . glad . . . too."

He parts my thighs, looking at me with so much desire, such intense focus that my body starts to tremble.

"I thought you didn't want to go slow," I protest.

His hands brush over my breasts, squeezing them, tempting the nipples with his firm agile fingers, then trail over my belly, down along my legs. And then he moves to kneel at the edge of the bed.

"Adam—"

"I have to taste you."

Just the words make me moan. I don't know if I can take more than that. Take his mouth on me, his fingers. I want him against me. In me. Waiting, even for this, feels like torture.

I start to protest, but I feel the heat of his breath against me, feel him move my legs up to cross against his back. His head dips down, and I miss his face, miss looking into his beautiful raincloud-gray eyes. I haven't had my fill of that yet. I know I never will.

He presses his mouth against me, his hands moving over me, fingers and darting tongue and heat like I've never felt, like I'm burning from the inside, my entire body a scalding fever. I give myself to it, arching up to him, body rocking like a wave, like the ocean flowing and receding. It's never been like this. I've never felt like this, pulled to this aching, yearning center. Never felt like a prism, sparking light in all directions.

I'm close . . . so close, but I want more. I want him. I breathe his name, and somehow he knows. Or he wants it for himself. He rises and strips off his shirt, and I've never seen anything more beautiful than the sight of him, standing there. I start to rise, hungry to touch him, to feel the amazing strength of his muscles, to trail my hands, my tongue over the channels of his tapered abs.

But he pushes me gently back onto the bed and unbuckles his belt, eyes fixed on mine, pinning me in place. He sheds his pants and briefs, and stands there with that smile that undoes me—with his incredible body on display.

"You're amazing," I tell him, and he is. He's more than I could have imagined, and I've imagined him many times.

"That's you," he says. He gets a condom from the nightstand and hands it to me to slip onto him. I do, looking up into his eyes, and then he slides over me, pressing against me, warm and hard and so perfect. All of me opens to him. Every part of me wants to enfold every part of him.

Adam slips himself into me slowly and then with a final motion that makes us both gasp. I close my eyes, giving myself over to the feeling of it, to the ebb and flow of our bodies, his hands brushing my hair back from my face, the feeling of his mouth closing over my nipples, sucking one then the other between his teeth.

Fierce darts of pleasure shoot through me. My breath comes in shallow gasps, and I cross my legs around his back again, pulling him to me, needing him to be closer than my own skin. He moves up, intensifying his movements, looking down at me, at the place where our bodies intersect.

I slip my hand there, to the place where we join, and the feeling breaks me. It's not a climb this time, but a sudden, shocking pulse that ripples through me, growing deeper and deeper, consuming me until it's everything, until I'm crying out from the pleasure of it, wave after wave pouring through me, deeper than anything I've ever felt. It takes me, sweeping me along, and I hear myself say Adam's name over and over, hear Adam's panting breathing until it's everything, until his voice is the air I breathe.

His strong hands brace my hips, holding on, moving intensely now, with a purpose that drives me, that makes me shudder. We rock together, on and on, until his breaths become groans, until his body trembles wildly against mine, fierce and insistent, until he shudders hard against me.

We still, and I lie there, letting my heart rate slow, letting myself come fully back to my body.

I rise up to kiss him, to run my lips over the sheen of perspiration on his chest, to breathe him in, feel the life of him still pulsing within me. He kisses me back hard, and then we move up to stretch out on the bed.

He lies there, a wide grin on his face. And then he laughs.

I nip his shoulder. "What's so funny?" I ask.

"When you take over Boomerang," he says. "You're definitely going to have to kill that no-dating policy."

"That's not going to happen, Adam. I promise."

"It doesn't matter," he says and pulls me into his arms. "Only this does. Only you."

Chapter 44

Adam

I lean up on my arm and stare at Ali who's, unsurprisingly, monopolizing the bed, and brush the back of my fingers along her shoulder.

She stirs awake. "Hi," she says, smiling.

"Hey, beautiful."

Her eyes darken—reflecting the need she must see on my face. I run my hands down her body and love the way she watches me, surrenders to me. I could explore her forever, and I tell her that between kisses. How I can't get enough of her. It's been a night of this, our bodies always connected. Over and over, we've driven each other over the edge, but we're both still starving. We can't get enough of each other.

"Adam, please," she says, taking me into her hand and guiding me home. She's ready for me, warm silk, and as I sink deep inside her, as she arches her back like even this closeness, us joined to-gether, isn't enough, I don't see how that could ever change. When she shudders in my arms, my name on her lips, nothing else com-pares. Nothing in the world has ever felt this good or this right.

Eventually, we make it into the shower together. I notice she's not wearing her "A" earrings.

"Ali," I say, rubbing my thumb over her earlobe. I can't stop looking deep into her eyes now. They're so pretty. They're so gentle and intelligent and . . . *good*. "Did you lose them?"

"No." She shakes her head and her smile fades. "They were a gift from my father." The finger that's been tracing the lines of my tattoo stills. "He gave them to me after . . . after I caught him. And I just can't wear them anymore."

I'm already thinking about buying her new ones. Better ones. More carats. Maybe spell her entire name out in fat diamonds. Or maybe a horse, because I know that would make her happier. Yeah, I'm buying her a horse. The best one I can find.

"About today, Adam," she says. "There's something I wanted to talk to you about before the party."

That reminds me. It was close to one in the afternoon when we got in the shower and the party starts at two—which means my em-ployees will probably be knocking on my door any minute.

"Can it wait? Because we only have a little while, and there are other issues I'd like to attend to first."

Ali smiles. "Ah, yes. Pressing issues." She wraps her arms around my neck, bringing her sleek, perfect body to mine. "Okay. Let's address those first."

Ali takes my car to drive home. Her hair is tied in a damp knot on top of her head, in her red dress, and I don't think I've ever seen anything hotter than that—then her smiling at me from inside my Bugatti as she carefully backs out of my driveway.

"Come on, Quick!" I shout. "Let's see what you got!"

She laughs and rolls her eyes at me, and makes the most adorably slow trip up my street, using the turn signal and everything as she disappears around the corner.

Jesus. I've got it bad.

I shave and pull on some sand-colored jeans and a button-down. I find myself rushing, and I realize it's because I want to get back to her.

The doorbell rings. When I answer, my quiet street resembles a busy parking lot. Rhett smiles at me. Pippa, Paolo, Sadie. Mia and Ethan. Brooks and Cookie. The guys from accounting. My entire IT department. Everyone's congregating on my driveway.

My eyes travel to my brother, who's next to Brooks. Grey was supposed to be in San Diego for his gig.

"Brooks texted me this morning," Grey says, shrugging, like it's no big deal that he's missing something I know he was excited about. "I wanted to see this."

This—which is the crystal-clear message my team is sending me by being here.

Quick might have my company, but their loyalty is still with me.

We arrive in a caravan at the Quicks' estate. Graham has spared no expense, and the lavish grounds are perfect for a party. Fresh flowers are planted everywhere and fill huge vases on every table. There are string lights on every tree and servers in tuxedos carrying trays of wine, champagne, and hors d'oeuvres wander around.

My employees and I wind up by the pool, where a live band plays on the expansive courtyard to the right. The day is bright and sunny, unseasonably warm for this time of year. We get drinks, and settle into the party, which is a mixture of my people and Quick's.

I haven't seen Graham yet or his wife, but I'm not anxious. I'm ready to see him. I'll learn to work with him, for my employees and for Alison. There's no anger inside me now, even though he's taken so much from me. I have no room for it.

How can I be angry, when Sadie and Pippa are freaking with Grey—who looks way too comfortable with the situation? How can I be angry, when I see Raylene and Rhett curled against each other on a lounge chair? Mia and Ethan laughing, in their own little world. Philippe and Paolo talking like they've been friends for a decade. Brooks and Cookie in a deep conversation, which . . . is a surprising mismatch, to say the least.

As I look around me, anger is not a possibility. It just isn't. I'm lighter now that Chloe's parents and mine know the truth. And I have Ali in my life now.

Once again, I scan the party for her. Where is she?

Arms wrap around me from behind and squeeze. "Found you," she says.

I pull her close, wrapping my around her. "What took you so long?" I see what she's wearing—a black miniskirt and a tight tank top—and bend by her ear. "How about you show me your bedroom?"

She smiles and brushes a kiss on my lips. "Later." Her gentle blue eyes are surprisingly serious and focused. "First, there's something we need to do."

Chapter 45

Alison

*W*hat's that?" Adam asks, giving me a warm, inviting look. It makes me smile to see him relaxed and joking with the Boomerang staff—who remain nearby, having fun but with the vigilance of bodyguards. They've rallied around him.

"Come with me," I tell him, and take his hand.

"So, you *are* going to give me the bedroom tour?"

I grin back at him. "I'm going to give you something even better."

He lets go of my hand and seizes me around the waist, pressing in close. His fingers skim the band of skin between my tank top and the waist of my skirt, and I shiver. "I'm pretty sure there's nothing better than last night."

"And this morning," I remind him.

"And tonight."

"Come on," I say, and tug him along. We wind through pockets of partygoers, and I grab a dodge around a caterer carrying a tray of mimosas, running into another with a tray of Bloody Marys.

"Take one," I tell Adam. "You'll need it."

"What about you?"

I shake my head. "I'm giving it a rest for a bit. But you go ahead."

"You know what? I'm fine. I've made peace with all this." And I can see he has, that he's made peace with so many things. He still has the bright intense energy of the boy I faced off with in the offices of Boomerang, but without the sharp edge to it. I realize we've become the people we pretended to be on Halloween night, and I stop and give him a kiss to celebrate.

"We do have a destination, right? Because at this rate we'll be old before we leave your patio."

I laugh and pull him over the threshold into the house. People have gathered in the kitchen and in the family room. I say my hellos, anxiety swelling in me. This has to go just right.

Before we enter my dad's study, I turn to Adam and kiss him one last time.

"What's up, Ali?" he asks, his gray eyes searching mine.

"Do you trust me?"

Without hesitation, he nods. "With everything."

"All right, then. Come on."

I push open the door. Inside, my mother and father sit on opposite ends of the sofa. My father, who should be basking in his victory, looks edgy, uptight. And my mother, who is about to do the bravest thing of her life, looks twenty years younger—almost glowing in a trim navy sundress with dangling silver earrings.

My father glances up, and his gaze levels at our joined hands, at what must be the unmistakable energy between Adam and me. His expression darkens, but it doesn't reach me. It's like one of those days on the water, when the sky is overcast and foreboding but the rain never comes. And even if it does, I won't mind, and I won't be afraid.

"Now do you want to tell me what's going on, Vivian?" my father asks. "Are we putting on some kind of show here?"

Adam looks at me, equally confused.

"Sit down," I tell him, and lead him over to the leather wingback chair by the fire—my favorite.

"We need to get back outside," my father says, eyes darting between us. He's calculating, I think, working on damage control, though he doesn't know yet what form the damage will take. "We have eighty guests here."

"Oh, they'll be fine," my mother says. "This won't take a moment." She looks at me and gives me a subtle nod.

"So, here's the thing, Dad." I take Adam's hand. "You're not going to take ownership of Adam's company."

My father crosses his over his chest and regards me with a raised eyebrow. "Oh, I'm not?"

"No. Because you know those partnership papers you signed?" He and Adam both nod. "Well, your shares are about to be cut in half," I tell him. "Which means you'll only own twenty-five percent of the company."

"And how the hell do you plan to pull that off? Some kind of magic trick?"

"No," my mother says and reaches beside her for a fat package of documents. "More of a *legal* trick."

She pulls the papers from the envelope and lays them on my father's lap. He glances and then looks more closely. His mouth gapes.

Plain for all of us to see are the words "Dissolution of Marriage."

"A divorce?" my father says, tossing the papers onto the coffee table before him. "Don't be ridiculous."

"I've never felt less ridiculous in my life," my mother says, and I know the feeling. To Adam she adds, "This legal trick being what it is, I'll own half of my husband's—my *ex*-husband's—shares in your company. And I'd be willing to sell them back to you at cost."

Adam shakes his head. "I've got a better idea," he tells us, and it's clear he's already taken in the situation, weighed his options, and settled on a plan. "Keep the shares. They're going to be worth a fortune. I have a feeling we'll work well together and that you'll help me keep my *other* partner in line."

"I'll tie you up for years in litigation," my father says. "This little exercise of yours is pointless." He leans forward in his chair, face almost purple with rage. "And you," he says to Adam. "I can still ruin you. I still know all your secrets. Nothing's changed there."

My mom chuckles. "Honestly, Graham. You sound ridiculous," she says. "For one thing, you still own a substantial stake in his company, which makes it against your best interests to give this boy any more grief."

"Also," I say. "We know *your* secrets, Dad."

My father shrugs, but he looks trapped and indecisive, some-thing I never thought I'd see. "So what?" he says. "A few indiscre-tions. Big deal."

"More than a few," my mother says.

Adam glances at me, measuring my response. But I know it all now. And none of it matters. What matters is making things right with him. What matters is pulling free of my father and making my own way.

"And some of them, my dear, show *extremely* poor judgment." She picks up the envelope again and riffles through it for a moment. Then she shows my father something, another sheet of paper that she keeps carefully turned away from me.

His face grows ashen. "How?"

"I just had to follow the trail of jewelry, Graham," she says. "One peek at your credit card statements gave me so much to work with. And over the years, it's given a number of private investigators a lot to work with too. You'd certainly better hope a judge is more generous about your past mistakes than you've been with your daughters. And to Adam here."

She rises. "I'll leave this with you," she says, tapping a nail against the envelope filled with documents. "It was more satisfying to present everything in hard copy, but I'm not so old-fashioned. There's plenty more where that comes from, in digital form."

I know a good exit line when I hear one, so I rise too. "You shouldn't have been such a jerk, Dad," I tell him. "You don't have to be, you know. You can be in charge without making everyone else feel small." I take Adam's hand again and hold it with both of my own. "I learned that from our new partner."

Back out in the sunshine, Adam catches me in his arms and swings me off my feet. "Holy shit," he says. "That was amazing."

He laughs, and it's boyish and charming, and he's so clear in his happiness—like sunshine streaming through spotless glass—that it makes tears spring to my eyes. I don't bother wiping them away. I've got nothing to hide.

"You're amazing," I tell him. "I love you, you know." I didn't expect to say it, but it's another thing I refuse to hide. No more masks. Just me, whatever that means. Whoever I become.

He sets me down slowly, and the feeling of his body against mine still thrills me every bit as much as it did that night in the Gallianos' car. "Love you too," he says lightly, but his eyes tell me even more. We gaze at each other for a long, long moment, the party fading to white noise around us. "Jesus," he says, as though struck by everything all over again. "We have to tell everyone."

"That we love each other?"

"About Boomerang."

He drags me over to a group that includes Philippe, Paolo, Mia, and Ethan. Philippe gives me a hilarious, smarmy look and I punch him in the arm.

"Shut up," I say, but I can't stop smiling back.

Ethan takes in Adam and me, standing side by side, Adam's arm curled around my waist. I catch his eye, and he gives me a subtle nod and tips his beer bottle in my direction.

Adam gives the abbreviated version of the story, and in no time, the news travels around the party. Somehow, magically, the volume on the music cranks, and my father's associates seem to fade away, though my mother comes out and holds court under the shade of a covered chaise.

"Dance with me," I say to Adam and hold out my hand.

His eyes light with memory, and he crosses his arms over his chest. "Is that a question?"

"No," I say. "Come on."

He grabs me and pulls me up tight against him. "I've got a better idea," he says.

"Oh, you do?"

"Yes," he tells me, and his grin broadens. "Let's swim instead."

"Really? I—" But before I know it, Adam's hauled me off my feet to swing me over the pool. I shriek, and the two of us plunge into the water. I surface, laughing, and splash him.

With an ecstatic whoop, Brooks plunges in beside us, followed by Paolo, Sadie and Pippa, Mia, Ethan, and others I don't know yet—but will. I don't think I'll be working at Boomerang after all. I want to talk with Missy about a partnership with Horse Rescue, to help her expand the facility and rehabilitate the broken horses that come into her care. It feels exactly right, and I can't wait to get started. Still, I know all of these people who've come into my life will remain there.

Adam's brother Grey hollers and does a colossal cannonball, drenching half the people on the deck with half of the pool's contents.

"Sorry, bro," he calls, and he has Adam's same devilish grin, though in a rougher form.

And then it's a mayhem of splashing and shrieking, laughter and a game of Marco Polo that seems mostly like an excuse for people to grope each other with their eyes closed.

I glide over to a corner of the shallow end, and Adam follows. I wind my arms around his neck and draw him down to me, kissing him, out in the brightness of day, with the cool water lapping around us. I shiver because the water is chilly, but mostly because of everything I feel, which is now, finally, *everything*. I've let go of the guilt that's been dogging me for a year and made room for this. For everything I've ever dreamed of and didn't know I deserved.

"Alison," he says. His hands travel over my back, and I think how in his element he looks, with water soaking through his shirt, his eyes the same bright almost silvery-gray as the bubbles rising to the surface around us. "You gave me back so much. Not just the company. My life. I don't know how I'll ever thank you."

I rise on my tiptoes, clinging to his strong shoulders, fitting myself to him—perfect.

"We'll think of something," I say.

Acknowledgments

*A*s always, I want to acknowledge the support and love of my awesome family. First, the "London 2014 Crew"—Lisa, Mustafa, Alex, Elizabeth, Andrew, Dina, Samantha, and Abbey. You make second degree sunburn so worth it. *¡El próximo año en Israel!* And then my Florida family of Brenda and Anna—brilliant, hilarious, resilient women who inspire me all the time. Love you all.

Big thanks, too, to our editor Tessa Woodward for her insights; to Gabrielle Keck for picking up the reins; to Megan Schumann, publicist extraordinaire; and to Molly Birckhead for all she does.

Lastly, shout-outs to all the supportive bloggers and reviewers; to everyone who made such an effort to come out for the *Boomerang* book launch in Tampa (also to Stephanie and Inkwood Books); and to the BONI Lasses, with special props to Jo Cooper for her generosity in all things and Sylvia Musgrove for her stories—written and told.

—LO

We're so fortunate to have an amazing publishing team behind us. My deepest gratitude goes to Tessa Woodward and Gabrielle Keck for the editorial wisdom and behind-the-scenes guidance that brought this story to life. Thanks also to Julia Gang and Georgia Maas for making us look great and read well; and to our own Team M&M, Megan Schumann and Molly Birckhead, for their marketing and publicity efforts. We appreciate you all very much.

Thanks to Adams Lit for top-notch agenting, and to my incredibly talented coauthor, Lorin. You're a treasure, Lolo.

To my family: You're my heart, soul, and world. Thank you for your love and support. And finally, to readers and bloggers, thank you for taking another journey with us. It's an honor to write for you.

—VR

About the Author

What do you get when friends pen a story with heart, plenty of laughs, and toe-curling kissing scenes? Noelle August, the pseudonym for renowned editor and award-winning writer Lorin Oberweger and *New York Times* bestselling YA author Veronica Rossi, the masterminds behind *Boomerang*.